ALSO BY JARRETT MAZZA

<u>The Doormen Series</u>

Dawn of the Trade

Revenge of the Fallen Sons

Overtaker Territory

PRAISE FOR ERADICATE (THE CUSTODIAN 1)

"With a brass-knuckled, blood-dusted prose style that picks up where brutal icon Mickey Spillane left off, author Jarrett Mazza pushes men's adventure fiction into darker territory. *Eradicate* pits mercenary Kyle Quinn against a sinister cult lodged in the bowels of the Louisiana bayou, and with no limits on his methods, bodies start hitting the floor at a rapid clip. Don a crash helmet and mouthguard, because Quinn's termination list is long and full of wrenching twists and turns. Mazza doesn't skimp on violence and thrills, and doesn't shy away from challenging the protagonist's—and the reader's—sense of right and wrong in a dangerous, grey world overrun by monsters."

—Jarret Keene, author of the *Kid Crimson* series

"Jarrett Mazza's novel, *Eradicate*, thunders ahead, gaining speed like a locomotive as protagonist and black ops assassin Kyle Quinn strikes a secret sect that harms children. Quinn also seeks to understand the demons driving him to kill. This intense tale entices readers to dive into scene after scene late into the night and even until dawn."

—John G. Bluck, author of the *Luke Ryder* series

"This book is a masterful, truly original work of suspense that has strong characterizations and clever twists. Eradicate is a quick, smart, engrossing read featuring a character in Kyle Quinn who readers will wish had their backs in any situation."

—Eliot Parker, award-winning author of *Double-Crossed*

EXTRICATE

EXTRICATE

EXTRICATE

THE CUSTODIAN
BOOK 3

JARRETT MAZZA

ROUGH EDGES PRESS

Extricate
Paperback Edition
Copyright © 2025 Jarrett Mazza

Rough Edges Press
An Imprint of Wolfpack Publishing
1707 E. Diana Street
Tampa, FL 33610

roughedgespress.com

Paperback ISBN 978-1-68549-546-6
eBook ISBN 978-1-68549-545-9
LCCN 2025930821

For Mom.
Always there, always prepared.

EXTRICATE

EXTRICATE

PROLOGUE

The meeting was held by invitation only.

Five tests. No way out. Certain to die. *If you succeed, then...*

The order was provided by the classic man in a classic suit. But should Kyle Quinn—or any of the other *candidates* earn their right—then they would be given their *rings*. Once they had their rings, then they would be told about the rules—the rules of the *game*.

This was the brotherhood all of them would forever be part of. It was the elite of the elite—a constant guardian and an undeniable killer.

A Custodian.

"Number?"

Quinn was asked this by a man hidden behind a galvanized door. Quinn heard the twisting of a heavy lock and after, saw only a pair of eyes.

"Quinn, Kyle. Designate number 11315."

A series of beeps followed. On the other side of the door was a stark setting. The first sight Quinn saw was a man standing among a group of inglorious-looking grunts. Each one stopped and stared at the new arrival.

Quinn was the last to join the meeting.

"Welcome, Kyle. Thank you for joining us. Please, sit. We were just about to begin."

Priest, inviting and cordial, was also effusive and interesting.

He glowed with delight seeing Kyle Quinn standing in his doorway. The rest of those present were mostly men: same age and same type. Brooding, alert, and dressed in rugose garbs, no one there quite cared for their appearance. Everyone was a stranger, and yet, Quinn felt like he had seen them all before. Every face was imbued with a sorrow Quinn instantly recognized. Proceeding to enter, the door slammed shut behind him.

Maintaining distance, Quinn was silent as he crept.

"Okay," Priest said. "Let's begin." Priest glided across an empty screen, which Quinn thought was a projector. What followed later was an image on a screen that everyone in the room knew quite well.

More than this, they were all a part of it.

It was a map of America in all her beautiful glory. Yet, the one here was divided into sections. This was but another point of speculation for Quinn. One region was marked by his number and it was carmine—the same shade as blood. It covered Wyoming, Idaho, and Montana. It was not far from where he lived.

"First, I'd like to thank everyone for being here."

Quinn's first impression of Priest? He was entranced by this vigor, which was only a ploy to distract everyone from seeing what lay beneath.

"And I would like to commend all of you for your talent and your skills, which is why you have all been asked to come here tonight."

It was another cordial greeting Quinn chose to ignore. He had another look at the other recruits. The first to catch his eye was an Asian man slouched in a fitted suit.

There was a noticeable scar along his neck. Likely cut by a blade at some point in his life. Everyone seemed comfortable, they were not as much as this one man in particular.

Ronin.

"Now, if you're waiting for a scene whereby a man in a black suit suddenly comes out and tells everyone that they should all be afraid of him, well...then you're all looking in the wrong place." There was a clear change in Priest's tone. The once suave man had been replaced by a drill instructor addressing his troops. Quinn's senses instantly sharpened. The thought of his father had emerged in his bustling mind.

"See, I'm not into this whole mystery men, ghosts in the dark, black ops nonsense that everyone spews like they're actually familiar with the real shit that goes down in this world," Priest said. "And, though it's not untrue to say that some of that will be going on here, in the end, I don't employ spies, hotshots, and goons for some off-the-book bogus jargon like you see in movies."

Quinn was still at the back of the room listening. Few could see him, but there was another man Quinn spotted in the crowd; a man with broad shoulders and bad posture. Almost slovenly, this man's back was wide as a refrigerator and his forearms were the size of pipes. It wasn't until years later Quinn would discover his name was as terrifying as how he looked.

Briggs.

"I manage talent," Priest continued, "and I manage prestige. I like people who are passionate about what they do because, see here, gentlemen, I'm all about precision, performance, and power." Priest described his preferences and his hands moved like he was conducting a symphony. Everyone was listening now more than ever before. "And above all else," Priest said, "I'm all about efficiency."

Quinn had encountered Priest once before the meeting.

At this moment, Priest mimicked the personality of a sophisticated CEO. Priest was engaging with his employees while also assigning them their tasks and duties. Recognizing this tenor, Quinn did not know Priest. He also did not know anyone else who was here in this unforgettable room.

"We are not some run-of-the-mill, work for hire group of ex-military grunts," Priest continued his exposition. "No, see, what this unit is—or what it will be—is a more refined group of professionals that spend a lot of time assessing, planning, and checking. Every outcome must be carefully considered and every fraction of the scene must be left totally spotless, as in no target ever gets to live. You are major players operating in the shadows, see? You will rely on anonymity, subterfuge, and whatever else you might bring to the table. All of you possess a wide range of gifts, and because of this, not only will you be compensated, but you will also receive the highest protection from the highest levels of government. I promise little interference if you choose to stay within your mission's parameters. Now you can yourselves assassins or mercenaries, but I prefer the term that describes us best. *Custodians.*"

Everyone in the room acquired the same look of pure satisfaction and delight. The title sounded elusive and cool.

"Operating solely within the jurisdiction of this country, together we will ensure our homeland's integrity, principles, and values are upheld. And if necessary, we will remove and destroy any and all who seek to threaten it."

"Correct me if I'm wrong, but aren't there already a number of agencies that fit that description?"

It was a snarky comment, but Quinn asked himself the same question.

The NSA, DEA, and FBI were organizations that specialized in what Priest described. Nonetheless, those here weren't assembled to abide by the rules that other organizations had to follow. Black ops was a secret. This did not mean it was unsupervised or unseen. There would be rules—limits they would have to adhere to, or so Quinn had assumed. As of now, Quinn was unaware of what these rules would be or how they might be explained to him. Yet, the comment was made by a man sitting in a chair near the front. He wore a two-piece navy suit and was not as fashionable as Priest. Still, it was nice and the man who wore it looked good too.

Years after this day, Quinn would learn differently.

The man was a chameleon. He was whatever he needed to be to win.

Onix.

"Yes," Priest said, an endearing look occupied his once determined visage. "But as you can probably already guess, we'll be operating in a much more fluid manner."

"I should assume so."

Priest went on to explain the rest of their expectations. Quinn adhered to all the Custodial Commandments. This was another term coined by Priest. Should anyone break these commandments, then they would become *marked*. This was a classification not invented by Quinn. No, it was one owned and distributed by Priest.

"One: no one is to ever know who we are or what we do. You're ghosts, phantoms. You're there in an instant and then gone just as quickly. You are required to execute not only high-value targets who are a danger to our country, but you are to erase any and all potential threats that may be linked to certain assets."

"Erasers," Onix said.

"Clean and remove," Priest confirmed. "Stainless and polished, like you were never there at all. Sanctioned, of course, with a certain domestic intention, but that's just the first rule. The second rule is, should any Custodian require assistance," Priest continued, "then any and all Custodians are to respond right away. If one of our own is killed...then we are to answer and react by, how you say... over-answering and overreacting?"

Quinn said nothing. His ring was given to him shortly after.

It was housed inside a decorative box. The ring was black and included a crisscrossed symbol of a sword penetrating a swirling flame.

"And the third and final rule," Priest continued, "this is an order, and it is a brotherhood. Therefore, it is not a sanctioned organization, not exactly. Once you are welcomed here, then here you have to stay. And should you not abide by our exit rules, for whatever reason, should you seek to extricate, then you could be deemed as a hostile and a mutinous entity." Priest's hands slid to his hips. "However, this only happens if—and only if—you alter your plan, if you disavow or refuse to keep your word. In this business, your word truly is your bond."

Quinn listened to his boss's exposition. However, he was also distracted by his colleagues' appearances. All of them seemed so familiar to Quinn, like he could see himself inside each one. Priest made the decision to elaborate on his expectations. He explained the functionality of the rings and said the bands contained a universal tracking chip. Anyone wearing it could be located anywhere in the world. The rings were also embedded with the user's DNA.

This allowed for a beacon to be sent out to everyone else who had one.

In the end, there was only one conclusion Quinn could draw from this briefing:

Once a Custodian, always a Custodian.

"Now is there any part of this that you do not understand?"

"So you're saying?" Onix said, "If anything happens to us, like we're compromised or we go down, someone will initiate a search and rescue. There might even be a sweeper team to come and get us?"

"No," Priest said. "*We* will come. *We* will find you."

"Any situation?" another Custodian asked. "No matter what?"

Priest's answer, given with a gleeful grin, he leered as he spoke. "No matter what."

Quinn rotated his ring and considered this promise and also weighed the logistics of such a guarantee. What Priest offered was something so deep it was profound.

"Real courage depends on real men, real people," Priest continued. He turned to the others. "We do what no one else does. We kill the ones who can't be killed. We fight the big fights, and we never lose. Ever."

"Everyone loses." Quinn's words came unexpectedly, but still, they were enough to garner everyone's attention. He had the audacity to question someone who sought loyalty above all else. "We are not invincible," Quinn said. Onix and Briggs looked in Quinn's direction. "You also said we can't leave. Once someone is in, they're in for life. No escape. No way out. *Ever.*"

Few had the courage to dispute a man like Priest. Quinn noted how even the most capable person was still human. Doing this at the first meeting with all the Custodians sealed Quinn's reputation. He wasn't afraid to speak or challenge, no matter who he was serving or why.

Remembering it all as if it were a dream, in some ways, it was.

As Quinn recalled the day when his life as the world's most elite killer would finally begin, he blinked once and then suddenly he was back. He was back to today, to what lay ahead of him now. He knew what would happen, because he was no longer Kyle Quinn, the Custodian.

Instead, he was Kyle Quinn, *wanted*. Kyle Quinn, *traitor*.

Kyle Quinn, *the soon-to-be dead man*.

CHAPTER 1
NOT SHAKEN, NOT RUNNIN'

IN THE END, ALL HE COULD DO WAS BREATHE.

Although Quinn was still in possession of the same weapons and gear, today he was harnessing more of his body than he was any of his other more profound tools for extermination. Tonight, he was less Old Testament and more New Age-ghost-in-the-dark-gangster-shit featured in the pages of pulp fiction. Emerging from the shadows, Quinn was hooded and wielding his tonfa. Like a cobra, Quinn knew how to hold his position before pouncing on his prey. However, tonight, Quinn *was* the prey. And so, when Quinn removed his tonfa, it was not the exact weapon that it used to be.

Much had changed since his extrication. The tonfa was once a bludgeoning and fencing weapon. Yet, this was not the only characteristic acquired by this multi-purpose, multi-dimensional instrument.

There was now a *new* addition.

It was something Quinn had been customizing for some time. The baton was still crafted from titanium. Within it now lay two blades that could be ejected via a switch built into the *handle*. This extended the weapon by four inches. Quinn could wield it with one blade, two, or maybe both at the same time.

Now that Quinn was exiled, he was also hunted.

There was no place he could go. Wherever he went, they would find him.

And so, given his status, Quinn's hands were tied. At this level, the game was always kill or be killed. However, now it was kill or become horribly mangled, mutilated, or worse. Killing a Custodian was more than suicide, it was a one-way ticket straight to Hell. But tonight, Quinn was not here to think about the consequences.

That part was over.

Tonight, Quinn was here for one purpose only: survival, war, and death. While most insisted on finding a place to mount a defense, Quinn refused to stand by and wait for the hunters to come to him. After he left Wyoming, it was the last time he would likely ever see it. Quinn entered his AMX. He glanced back at the house he had practically built with his own hands.

What lay ahead would not be easy. The true game of hunter versus prey and villain versus monster, in many ways, had only just begun.

———

In Washington, a nameless man in fancy shoes scampered down the White House's infamous West Wing. This man was neither a soldier nor a spy. While most would travel to the Oval Office to speak to the commander-in-chief, this man had come to see Vice President Howard Lament. Howard was known to handle particular strains within the country's defense. The man passed the secretary and moved in through the double-doors, and there, Mr. Lament sat behind a fashionable desk.

Looking through his bifocals at the one who barged in unannounced, Lament sneered.

"Sir, we have a problem." The man who informed Mr. Lament was complacent. He did not move. The man's lips coiled, and his posture was prim, almost soldierly. He stood this way despite not having served a day in his life.

Mr. Lament removed his glasses and rose. He was working on important material and rarely were problems reported to him directly. Even more rarely were they phrased in such a way.

"Explain." At Lament's request, the man unloaded a long and detailed explanation. He outlined the problem and mentioned only the points that pertained to the following topics: black ops assassin, rogue program disrupted, and many secrets about to be exposed. Most importantly, the man spoke of the impending possibility of lots and lots of dead men.

"Jesus." Turning red, Lament looked like he was having acid reflux as every part of his face flexed simultaneously.

Kyle Quinn.

Once this was explained, Lament responded with a demand.

"Where's Priest? Tell him I need to speak with him now."

He provided this order while the man standing before Mr. Lament accepted his superior's demand and abruptly left the room.

The messenger worked in this cabinet for some time.

Therefore, the name Priest was one passed around and one that, while spoken infrequently, was uttered in times of great duress. Raymond Priestly, a.k.a. Priest, was appointed as the unofficial head of this deadly outfit that employed the country's best operatives. All were tasked with removing high-value targets and operated only within America. Advertised as *one-man units*, each one could rival an entire strike team.

They could eliminate all enemies single-handedly.

At least, this was Priest's promise when assembling the group.

———

When Priest arrived at the White House, he was known as a nomadic individual with a clouded and dark past. As he came in, it was not in a timely manner, for Priest was never one for haste or disruption. He strolled into the office and was ready to meet with the country's second-in-command.

"Raymond."

When Howard referred to Priest by his first name, the Lock Smith cringed. To everyone else, he was Priest. Even to himself, Priest was fucking Priest.

"Mr. Vice President." Priest slipped into one of the chairs. "To what do I owe this very abrupt meeting, sir?"

"Don't be cute," Lament said. "This is a serious matter and something I know you are aware of."

"Well, you know me," Priest said. "Everything is serious when I get a call."

"That it is," Lament snapped. "So, am I to assume you have an idea as to what it's about then?"

Priest shrugged. He had his ideas, sure. However, to properly assess which one was the most accurate would take some time as well as more information. He waited to hear both.

"It would seem your rogue killer was just spotted in New York City. I thought you said he was being handled. So far, he hasn't been."

Priest stared past the vice president and looked at a heap of eight-by-ten photographs. Seeing these pictures,

Priest couldn't help but leer. Kyle Quinn was present in all of them. He was without his mask and was wielding either his tonfa or his carbine. Sometimes, Quinn was killing one man or two or more.

"I take it you were...expecting him to be where he should be?" the vice president asked.

"I was," Priest said. He touched one of the photos.

Custodians were not supposed to operate outside their own territory. New York did not belong to Quinn. So, he wasn't allowed to be in any city without Priest's permission, but Quinn had gone rogue, and right now, he was fighting anyone who came looking for him. In essence, he was fighting back. He was *winning*.

"In the entire time to which you have employed your *erasers*, not one of them has ever gone rogue, is that true? Could it be a result of your phase, the one that you had spoken to me about?"

"*New phase?*" Priest flinched when he said these words. His fingers rolled into his hand. His knuckles cracked. Priest glowered at the VP. Saying these things out loud was not appreciated.

New phase was a secret. No one was to speak of it *ever*.

"No."

"Are you sure?" Now being grilled by Lament, Priest's hand detached from the photo. He leaned back and sat in the VP's comfy sofa.

"Yes."

"Either way," said Lament. He joined Priest on the couch. "You have a very big problem that needs to be fixed."

"I am aware," Priest said.

"And by aware," Lament added, "you mean you have a plan to make sure he's taken care of, before he continues to go even more outside the lines?"

Priest glimpsed at the photograph. "Yes," he said quietly. "I do."

"Good." Lament's response was a vengeful snap. "Then you will handle this soon, yes?"

Priest's lips had puckered. He moved side to side. "It's already being handled as we speak."

"I hope that it is," encouraged Lament, "because while your Custodians might be a part of the past, the future is happening right now, and we can't have any loose ends going forward. I hope you understand that."

"Like I said," Priest replied, glaring at the man who was supposedly in charge. "It's being *handled*."

Priest looked again at the photos.

When Vice President Howard Lament stood, such was an indication that the meeting was over. Priest's exit cue was now presented, and yet, he chose to stay. He wanted one final look before moving along. If Priest didn't have Quinn killed soon, it would only be a matter of time before more became aware of the growing situation. NSA, CIA, FBI, even local Law enforcement would start to see a mass pile-up of bodies. And should this happen, than the phase referenced by Lament would not only cease to exist, but Priest would too.

Priest had skin in the game. He was as much a wanted man as Kyle Quinn was in some ways. While the bell was rung in a manner of speaking, Priest understood now was time to initiate the greatest manhunt among the greatest man-hunters in the country.

Custodians, it's time to work for a living!

———

If Quinn wanted to stay alive, he needed to keep moving. His plan was to journey to public places—spaces where he could hide and cover.

At the start of his plan, Quinn tossed his Custodian ring so he could not be traced. He stayed at the cheapest, sleaziest motels he could find and still had everything he used back from the job in Austin: same weapons, same gear.

But now Quinn decided to bring his AMX 3 American muscle car.

There were specific details Quinn could recall from his latest mission. He remembered Hyper-X, the chemical agent now coursing through his bloodstream. He remembered it was what Priest was using to build his army of upgraded, more efficient, more programmable Custodians.

Quinn recalled KEYS. *Kinetic Enhanced Youth Supplementation Program.*

Yet, the most important piece of information Quinn uncovered was how Priest was behind everything. He was linked to Quinn's past as much as his father. Quinn also lost his brother, Cane. When Quinn refused to join Priest on his new endeavor, he betrayed the Custodial brotherhood and violated the code he once swore to defend.

He did not finish what he started. This thereby ended the agreement shared among himself and the Custodians. Extricated from the order, Quinn was keeping himself open and letting his enemies come to him. He was doing all of this here, in New York fucking New York.

Quinn walked through the bustling metropolis and proceeded down to the subway station. It was a gloomy, rainy September day in Manhattan. How Quinn dressed was determined only by how fast he was able to pack back in Wyoming. Now, Quinn was wearing sweatpants, a sleeveless shirt, and his classic Viper boxing shoes. Quinn trotted through the musky underground and heard the humming of a train echoing through a dark tunnel.

There, a man followed closely behind Quinn.

He was spotted earlier. Quinn saw him first when he

turned the corner and when he moved to the subway station. Despite being in public, it was still possible Quinn's stalker would draw a gun and shoot him in the back of the head. This would be the most dishonorable method of execution. If this person was a Custodian, honor was the basis for recruitment and entry.

Quinn was uncertain if that's who or what was following him.

It was more than likely another Custodian. It could also be someone else Priest hired to track and kill Quinn but who could kill Quinn besides a Custodian? So far, all of this was unclear. Quinn knew he was being followed. He boarded a train, and not to his surprise, the man did the same.

"Please stand clear of the doors."

Quinn listened to the automated voice talking from a speaker in the train.

Those in the way abruptly moved. Among civilians, Quinn slipped past a woman carrying a bag of groceries and covertly motioned toward the first seat he could find.

When he heard a whistle, Quinn leaned back and turned. He could see a group of bystanders loitering about the transport. Quinn looked up. The one who followed him was still. His hands were in his pockets. Quinn could see this. When he did, he stood up. Giving his right side, Quinn stared at the man now approaching.

He knew he had a tracker.

The man's hands slid along the hood covering his face and, with a dramatic push, revealed himself as the first hunter as well as the very first Custodian.

"Hiya, Quinn."

Quinn's confusion was eliminated by a sudden surge of déjà vu. "*Suloco.*"

The man in the hood had a name. He had a name *and* he had a past.

Like Kyle Quinn, Deante Suloco was a Custodian. He was no level 5, but he did have some solid kills. Also, Suloco had less of a reputation than Quinn did. He was still undeniably skilled and undeniably willing, hence he was here now.

"I see you've come to answer *the call*," Quinn said. His head dipped forward and he gave his fellow Custodian the respect he deserved.

"The code is the code," Suloco said. "And you *broke* it."

"Is that what Priest told you?"

"Not about him or me," Suloco replied. "No, it's about what needs to be done, same as always. A scene needs to be left spotless, Quinn. No marks. *You know how it goes.*"

When Quinn heard Suloco's answer, he remembered it wasn't long ago he provided a similar statement. The black Custodian then eased into a Wing Chun Kung Fu basic stance, Suloco's main fighting style. Quinn was relying on aikido so he was set in kamae. Quinn lifted his right arm, straightened his right hand, and placed his left down near his waist. He was never the one to attack first. Often, Quinn shifted this onus to his opponents.

All that was about to change.

Now the one doing the waiting, Suloco was quite the formidable fighter.

Then again, so were the other Custodians. Soon, Quinn's memory would be refreshed on just how lethal and deadly they were. Suloco smirked and Quinn paused. With no time wasted, he stepped forward and entered the fight.

"*Ayah!*" First attack out, Quinn understood this battle was not at the level previously experienced. He assessed Suloco's strength. The amount of power placed into his straight kick was not only hard, it was damn accurate too.

Quinn swiped his hand down like the tip of a sword and cut Suloco's hard-ass kick.

"Fah!" Suloco exclaimed, while Quinn backstepped and raised his hands.

Soon as Suloco had finished one round of kicks, he hit back with three more. Suloco torqued his body. With a swift rotation, he swung his leg. Delivering a clean hook kick, Quinn ducked. Falling to one knee, Quinn watched his opponent's leg circle above his head. From here, Quinn fastened his grip. He pulled Suloco's shoulder and locked him spread-eagle to the point where he actually looked like a birthing woman. The rival Custodian swung his free leg to do another sweeping kick. Quinn stood poised and continued to rely on his Aikido.

Seeing the next kick, Quinn opened his hand, snatched Suloco's ankle, and slipped underneath. He held Suloco's leg and Quinn used his downward momentum to produce the perfect throwaway. In this case, it was a heaving toss. It sent Quinn's attacker all the way down the subway. After Quinn tossed Suloco like a sandbag, some people ran and some others stayed. And, while still on one knee, Quinn was done with his defense.

Now, Quinn summoned his offense and sent the fight into overdrive.

Quinn slipped into Shotokan and initiated two front snap kicks. Quinn struck Suloco like he was holding two strips of hardwood. None of his blows were obvious or subtle. No, each kick was prompt and resolute. Quinn's legs blurred and each kick was delivered in immediate succession. He struck one and then another, and Quinn knew exactly when Suloco was set to block. After the second one was delivered, Quinn turned and hit back.

Now with a reverse hook, Quinn struck Suloco's face. If Suloco was a scarecrow, this kick would have surely taken off his fucking head. Suloco was down but far from out. And, if Suloco was the typical opponent, he would have been sent to his grave.

But again, this Suloco was *not* a typical opponent and this was not a typical fight.

Suloco summoned his own kick. Facing a roundhouse, Quinn blocked and hammer-fisted Suloco's joint, snapping the bone. He wrapped his hand around Suloco's ankle, pulled the leg, and pivoted.

"Ah!" Suloco's screams were sharp and pitchy.

Quinn snatched Suloco's swinging arm and then, using his hip, completed a Judo Hane-goshi that took down the frustrated animal of a fighter. Quinn hunkered. Channeling the glorious surge of adrenaline-fueled rage, he bombarded Suloco with hammer punches. Once Quinn had his man buried, he pressed his knee into Suloco's neck and then clamped his hand over Suloco's mouth to cut off circulation. Once this was done, Quinn chopped Suloco's throat in a brutal attempt to collapse his windpipe.

Now, Quinn wanted to take Suloco out of the fight for good.

Suloco opted to slug Quinn's arm with his knee. When he couldn't finish this, Suloco flipped like a contortionist. Miraculously, he managed to get back onto his feet.

"Mother fu—" Suloco spat, frustrated and fuming.

He reached down to his belt and drew a Benchmade Arvensis 119 knife. The weapon was curved and sleek. It was a clip-point model and embodied lots of cutting edge real estate.

Quinn recognized the blade. He knew it and he liked it.

Suloco waved his knife and Quinn withdrew his tonfa. Flipping the baton, Quinn held it special. He squeezed the handle and ejected a six-inch blade.

"Wow," Suloco said, admiring the added feature. "That's a neat trick."

"What till you see the finale." Quinn loathed frivolity.

And yet, Suloco charged like a bat flapping from a crusty cave. He stormed with his knife inverted, contorted his wrist, and cut in all directions. Now with several stabs conjured, there was much strength in each attack. Quinn blocked with his tonfa—its blade was still visible and thereby still usable.

Quinn cut Suloco's chest. He opened his flesh and Suloco bled. Falling back, Quinn looked at his wound.

"*Muh-ha.*" Suloco was speechless as Quinn twirled the weapon.

Seeing what he had inflicted, Quinn squeezed the handle. He returned the blade to the inside of the tonfa. Blood filled Quinn's tight hand. Suloco gasped and ran. Quinn slid the tonfa back into its case. He shook his head to regather himself. He knew where he must go from here. He also had a plan to bring his fight to his enemies. He refused to give them the privilege of getting to him first.

It was Quinn's hunt now.

Everyone who accepted Priest's offer to eliminate him would be marked just the same. This was Quinn's game. He was the one in control.

Most importantly, he would decide how it would end.

———

When Quinn exited the subway, he had the appearance of a cage fighter. His face was peppered with bruises, and his cheeks and chin bled like packets of ketchup smeared along his skin. After he crept out of the station, Quinn found himself in the middle of bustling New York City.

"Shit."

In Times Square, Quinn was startled by the lights

shining from all the signs, posters, and flashing icons. So bright, Quinn had to cover his face. He had a simple strategy for how to find Suloco. Follow the trail of blood.

Quinn knew he wouldn't get far in his state. And so, he marched. With his 34 concealed, Quinn made the mistake of thinking a slice to Suloco's chest would be enough to bring him down.

Now he knew otherwise.

Quinn scurried after the trail like a kid following candy. When he came to its end, Quinn saw a new set of lights shining against him. Quinn squinted to see through the brightness as best he could. There, he heard the sound of a V-8 belonging to an energized sports car flying down the road.

"No."

Suloco's choice of vehicle was a Ferrari Spider, a glorious transport and the envy of near every teenage boy. Quinn heard its engine but also heard the chattering of a full auto-gun pattering the concrete. Suloco's rage had converted into gunfire.

Among the fleeing civilians, Quinn jumped and rolled. He pulled his Glock.

On his back, Quinn spat several shots into the flying car. He aimed for the tires, but Suloco's Ferrari could accelerate to top speeds in a matter of seconds. And so, once Quinn's gun was out, Suloco raced down the street.

"Fuck." Now up, Quinn clenched his 34. He wielded the weapon with two hands and sent two clean rounds straight into the rear of the Spider. Blowing out the windows, Quinn was attempting to target Suloco's seat. He knew he wouldn't succeed.

Quinn holstered his weapon. He took a second to take a look around.

"Jesus Christ, man...who...who the hell are you?"

Quinn was with a civilian who gawked at the enigmatic man.

Who was he?

This guy didn't want to know.

Suloco's Ferrari fled from the glowing city of Manhattan. Quinn, while watching, felt limber, and thankfully, he was absent of any significant injuries. He couldn't get anywhere on foot, and so, Quinn hurried into an alley not far from the subway.

Approaching his own car, it was parked exactly where he left it.

Quinn didn't drive from Wyoming. He flew in his Cirrus Vision jet but arranged for his car to be transported after he touched down. To do this, Quinn contacted Ally right before arriving here, in this city. She assisted with the vehicle's transportation while Quinn took care of the cost.

"New York first," Quinn said. *"It's where it all began and a possible location for Priest. Just make sure my car gets there at the same time I do."*

Ally offered to help despite knowing she was putting herself in danger. And for Quinn, this was his most notable asset. He had Ally. No matter what, she would always be there for him.

"Is that it?"

"For now," he said. *"For now."*

Unlike the imported Ferrari, Quinn's choice of transport was something ingrained in his country's profound ingenuity. American Muscle cars were one of the few joyous staples of Quinn's complicated yet instrumental childhood. The 1970 AMC/AMX 3 was Quinn's most secret tool as well as his most applicable. It was like a life-size version of the Hot Wheel toys Quinn and his brother collected long ago. It was a two-seater with a leather interior and a secret compartment between the seats for additional weaponry. With a maroon exterior, there were also two black racing stripes drawn along its center. The hood was long and thick and could barrel through walls as if made out of cake. Quinn slipped in through the window and squeezed the steering wheel.

Turning on the headlights, Quinn fired up the engine.

By now, Suloco had gotten far, but not far enough.

His taste in vehicles would expose him. This made him easier for Quinn to find.

No one drove a Ferrari, and no one drove in New York fucking City. There was only one way out of this place. Quinn was sure to corner Suloco before he got there. Vehicular warfare was not quite Quinn's game. The car he was driving was built mostly for hard terrain.

And there was nothing harder than this.

The AMX blitzed out of the alley and exploded into the street. Inciting honks and dirty looks from other drivers, Quinn drifted the backside of the AMX. He squeezed the wheel and pulled hard on the clutch. He accelerated, but the AMX was a bloody beast. It was a metal predator roaring to life. Designed also for convenience, this was not Quinn's intention when constructing this hulk of a machine. For him, convenience meant that every quadrant had something extra. In this case, the passenger's seat could be lifted. Beneath was a vast assortment of guns usable should the situation call for them.

It most certainly did now. Quinn pulled the gun closest to him.

The model selected was a Heckler & Koch MP5A2. It was standard SMG. It used a box magazine and fired straight. It was built with a hammer-firing mechanism, and as far as portable machine guns went, HKs were the way to go. Tonight, Quinn was glad he had this bad boy handy.

Quinn raced along the road and seized the wheel. He pressed his foot hard onto the pedal and hit almost eighty mph. The streetlights and the nearby buildings provided additional light. This enabled Quinn to see a great deal of the other cars currently occupying the road.

None were Suloco's Ferrari.

Nevertheless, Quinn stayed focused and ready. He pushed harder and drove faster. Veering in and out, the AMX's tires were secured around a set of polished, top-notch rims. It gave him suitable traction. Quinn listened to the rumbling from his beast, and while he was fast, he was still in Manhattan.

Quinn held his gaze as he rapidly switched lanes. There was a short amount of road still left, so Quinn pushed on. Approaching the intersection, Quinn spotted a pair of rectangular taillights that could only belong to one vehicle. In a flagrant show of epic fearlessness, the AMX flew off the fucking road and Quinn rammed the Ferrari's shoulder.

"Ah!" With his MP5 still on his lap, Quinn stopped.

Body turned; Quinn looked out the window. He could see Suloco, bloodied and shaking and using only one arm to drive his luxury car. Suloco glowered. Now at the end of his rope, Quinn scowled back. Refusing to hide his emotions, Quinn showed no empathy toward his opponent. No, Quinn was here to finish what Suloco could not. Quinn pulled his MP5 and took one hand off the wheel. The stock of the machine gun pushed into Quinn's shoulder. And, grazing the trigger, Quinn waited for a split second to line up his shots.

There was nothing more difficult to shoot than a moving target.

Suloco flinched and Quinn rained fire. He peppered the Ferrari, and with no shortage of ammunition, gazed at the cascade of spitting sparks. Suloco showered his car too, and the two vehicles continued to bump before swerving into civilian territory.

Quinn shifted his hand from wheel to trigger. He

punctured the Ferrari in a continuous assault that would have made a car collector cringe. The entire Ferrari was savagely ruined by Quinn's unrelenting gunfire. He poked the nose of his AMX into the sports car and knocked it aside as both vehicles raced. Now jammed in the metropolis, they could run for miles and miles and still encounter more vehicles.

None of this mattered.

What did matter was whether Quinn could erase Suloco before the entire scene was swarmed by NYPD. They were two men in a death match while in the subway. Here, they were participating in a massive shootout right in the middle of the explosive city that was New York.

Quinn would say this justified immediate action.

In fact, Quinn was surprised the cops hadn't made an appearance.

New York City was a metropolis crawling with police.

Running low on ammo, the MP5 had lightened significantly, but Quinn's grip was tight. It was difficult to reload under these circumstances. Yet, with Quinn's ammo starting to dwindle, Suloco pulled a new weapon.

Holding a Beretta full auto, Suloco fired back.

He smoked Quinn's vehicle and the AMX retained no serious indentations amid the heavy assault. Quinn outfitted the car so it was completely bulletproof. The AMX was galvanized and was capable of withstanding nearly anything a car could endure.

Having driven it to the max, Quinn's MP5 was empty.

He dropped the weapon and looked for another.

With the light about to change from green to yellow, there was not enough road to accelerate and pass through. Quinn maneuvered and slugged the ass of this Italian luxury. Pushing the Ferrari into a concrete divider, the car was totaled, wrecked. The speed, combined with the disruption, had forced the vehicle to flip and then roll.

Then, in a series of epic tumbles, the endless rolling cratered all of Suloco's transport.

Quinn watched from the shoulder as the Ferrari was reduced to scrap metal.

When it finally became free from the storm of collisions, what was left behind was a smoking mess. Quinn watched fine tendrils dance from the car's thrashed engine. He vacated his AMX and unholstered his Glock. Stepping closer, Quinn gazed just as Suloco slipped out from the shattered window.

The rival Custodian slid along the wet road.

"Gah!" Bloodied up, Suloco could keep up with Quinn in almost any capacity, but not here, not now. Quinn was steady as he moved toward his fallen adversary. Suloco glared as Quinn crept.

"You...you...lucky son of a..." Suloco chuckled. He rolled on his back like a subservient dog. Quinn could see he was unable to move. Quinn also understood that only one of them was armed. Therefore, Quinn waited for Suloco to embrace the cold and certain reality.

"Oh, Quinn," said Suloco. He grinned madly as he rested. "You truly have no idea what's coming, do you?"

"Yes," Quinn replied while inches from Suloco's stagnant body. "I do."

Quinn pointed his Glock and his heart sank. It was only a few sharp decisions that left Quinn standing but left Suloco lying in a pool of his own blood. Now grateful the fight with Suloco was done, Quinn refused to think about the outcome more than he had.

"And I don't care." The last words spoken, Quinn's hand was up.

His gun stayed on Suloco. With no time to waste, Quinn sought to execute his enemy with honor and precision. He shot Suloco in the head. The shot was clean. It sent Suloco to his death just as the police sirens emerged.

At last, Quinn's first hunt had come to an end. Quinn examined the wreckage. If this was a preview of what was to come, then perhaps Quinn's cool, carefree response was inappropriate.

Did he understand what was coming? Was he prepared for it?

When Quinn finished Suloco, he proceeded back to his AMX. Though not an inconspicuous car, Quinn's next move was to get the hell out of New York while he still could. His name was fucking mud here, so his priorities had shifted. Quinn had to kill the Custodians because every last one of them was coming for him.

Rolling across Brooklyn Bridge, what Quinn needed was time to rest and recuperate. And, who better to assist him with this than the man known as the "Toy Maker"? The approaching meeting had been arranged by Quinn and Ally. The man was as much Quinn's contact as he was Ally's, and it was his next stop.

He drove there like his life depended on it, because it did.

In the Bronx, Quinn found himself among vagabonds and rapscallions.

Toy Maker's location was set in an impoverished neighborhood and was not easily accessible. Last Quinn heard, the man was the proprietor of a seedy nightclub called the Fade. Quinn pulled his AMX curbside and found a snug space twenty feet from the glowing doorway. Although his car was not completely destroyed, it did garner a few stares from a few people waiting in line. Keeping his head down, Quinn sought to avoid any attention cast in his direction. But again, he didn't know who was in the crowd and whether or not they wanted him dead. Quinn stoically approached the door but before heading in, he was stopped by a bouncer a whole foot taller than himself.

"Hold up there, pal. Where you think you're going?" This bouncer was bald. He wore a tight shirt with the word security written across the chest. In the company of another bouncer, it was a scene that couldn't be more cliché if Quinn was the star of his own action movie.

"I'm here to see *him*," Quinn spoke clearly as his busted-up face would allow. His words came out hoarse and broken.

"Him?" the bouncer barked, arms crossed.

Both were two three-hundred-pound beasts who shared the same scowl.

"Him who?" Chuckling with closed mouths, they looked at Quinn like he was nothing.

"You know who."

The bouncers grinned. One lowered his arms and inched closer. "Well, anyone who wants to get inside needs to be on the list, so unless your name is here..." The bouncer playfully tapped his clipboard and played along. "Then you ain't goin' nowhere, son. Best to leave now so actual customers can come inside. After all, they've been waiting here a lot longer than you."

A fiery gawk overcame Quinn's once-tepid demeanor. "No, they haven't."

"Hmm," added the bouncer. "Well, what is your name?"

"My name is..." Quinn began. "Let me in or I'm gonna knock the teeth out of your head."

"What the hell did you just say to me?"

Quinn couldn't make the threat any clearer. He also understood that saying what he had would only escalate the situation. Since being marked, Quinn was becoming less tolerant. And what Quinn was facing down now was a fight of brutal, epic proportions.

He looked up and knew exactly what to do.

"I won't ask again." This was the last warning given. Quinn did it only as a courtesy. He had no intention of playing this easy or fair.

"That's it, Hugo, let's show this asshole what we can —" Before the call was made to the other bouncer, Quinn spared no time.

Usually, he was not one for striking first. He did exactly as a good attacker should. In a sudden act, Quinn's hand shot forward and he delivered a solid jab smack into the bouncer's fat nose.

"Aw!"

This hit was only done as a distraction. The next one after was more complex. Quinn slipped behind the first bouncer and pounded his kidney with a perfectly placed, well-timed fistful of pain. First bouncer down, Quinn moved onto the second.

Quinn, feeling light on his feet for reasons he could not explain, jumped with more panache and flare than he had intended. He sprang to deliver a brutal yet stunning 540 spinning hook kick. A sweeping course of action, something like this kick needed to be watched in slow motion in order to be seen and appreciated.

"Ha!"

How Quinn was able to perform such a difficult move was attributed to his lack of patience. It was this, as well as the fact that he needed to put both bouncers down quickly. Fighting them was not at all part of Quinn's plan, but plans change depending on how many variables are added to the equation. And these men were not only variables, they were goddamn liabilities. They were standing in Quinn's path, and so, they stood directly in the way of his mission.

In the club, Quinn was assaulted by a cascade of flashing lights and incessant, ear-rattling music.

Inside, Quinn passed a swarm of gyrating bodies and he scoured the floor. Wherever Toy Maker was now, he needed to be somewhere close. Quinn searched this level and saw two more guards approaching. Quinn's adrenaline surged and gifted him with a burst of undeniable power. When he felt a hand on his shoulder, Quinn snapped. He was prepared to do whatever needed to be done to protect himself and that was not required now.

The person who stood behind him was, fortunately, someone he knew.

"Take it easy there, Quinn. Just take it easy."

Full of vigor, Quinn gazed at the face of the man who had spoken so calmly.

The man stood in a silk magenta smoking jacket. Moonfaced and with sunken eyes, he was older than Quinn and spoke with a tamed Irish accent. His hair was slick and his cheeks were puffy, like he was holding marbles in his mouth. Although this man was an ally, Quinn would never refer to him as a friend. There were no friends in this game and definitely none now.

Ally was right.

"Jesus," Toy Maker said. "You really are on edge, ain't ya?"

Quinn's harsh stare was not meant for Toy Maker. Given the circumstances, what he had just done and endured. It was difficult for Quinn to change his persona. And yet, he still backed down.

"Welcome, Quinn. It's very nice to see you again."

————

Away from the bustling section of Toy Maker's decadent nightclub, Quinn was escorted to a private room that overlooked the brimming setting below. This new room was dim. Quinn felt as though he was in a porn studio, which was another hobby practiced by Toy Maker.

"Drink?" Toy Maker stood by a bar among a fine selection of alcoholic beverages.

Quinn was thirsty, but damn well he didn't want anyone else pouring him a drink. He would stick it out, for now.

"No, thank you."

"Suit yourself." Toy Maker poured himself a glass, stepped back, and unbuttoned his coat. "So, I take it from you being here, and abruptly making your way into my club, that you have come for protection or advice, or was it both?"

Quinn checked the windows. He was still not safe. He didn't reply to Toy Maker's question.

"But seeing as how you just laid waste to some of my security," Toy Maker said, "protection is not something you seek, but upholding your reputation, now...that is something you do care about."

"Ally told you about my extrication," Quinn said.

"Of course she told me," Toy Maker said. "Right now, my skills of deduction are telling me that the reason you're here is because you need my help."

"I need what anyone is willing to give to me," Quinn said.

"I see." Toy Maker leaned over the suede sofa in his office and smiled. Until now, Quinn hadn't noticed the couch. Until now, he wished he had. Toy Maker sloshed the booze in his fat mouth and swallowed what was there. Then, he slammed the glass and pulled on the lapels of his coat.

"Well, then, let's get started, shall we?" Toy Maker clapped and the shelves behind him rotated to reveal an entirely new arrangement right there, in this space. In this next set of shelves, was a cache of assorted and modified firearms; all appealing to Quinn in ways he shared with only a few.

"Say hello to my little friends."

Quinn nodded to accept Toy Maker's offer and then he had a look around.

"Hello."

Toy Maker turned. On one shelf were a vast assortment of carbines, rifles, full autos, and shotguns arranged in a spectacular formation and shined like presents under a Christmas tree. On the other were pistols, like Glocks, SIGs, and Smith & Wessons. Each one fit in their own section. Everything was tight and organized, but all were identifiable. They were also accompanied with all the bells and whistles, and so when Quinn saw all of this, his fingers began to tingle.

"Now I am familiar with your affinity for the Benellis, but for what lies ahead, I suggest the Beretta 1301 tactical with a pistol grip," Toy Maker said, "and Magpul parts."

Quinn was familiar with said gun. When Toy Maker handed it to Quinn, the Custodian raised the weapon. Quinn had played with the sleek, black semi-automatic work of fucking art before. The rifle was textured. It was fashioned with a three-inch chamber and was a model 12 gauge.

"Big and brutal," added Toy Maker. "This weapon fires six plus one, and if you buy now, you get eighteen on the house, from me."

"Right." Quinn continued to squeeze the gun.

Toy Maker presented Quinn with an ammo belt to go along with the rest of the prize. Quinn completed the first stage of his selection, but often, choosing weapons was done in four stages: shotguns, rifles, pistols, and blades.

"Next?" said Quinn. He pivoted back to the shelf and Toy Maker pulled a rifle from the center.

"May I present to you the HK416D carbine."

Quinn checked this new weapon. It was light and comfortable. He stared through the sight and Quinn was already imagining what it would be like to fire.

"Fitted with 10.4-inch barrels, PMags, and BCM stocks, that's a holographic sight you're looking through now. They are Vortex AMG, and the last piece you see there is a SOCOM 556 sound suppressor. No one will hear a goddamn thing. In fact, even you won't hear a goddamn thing."

Quinn nodded and placed the weapon in a stack along with the others. Not bad advice. Quinn leered. "Ammo?"

Toy Maker removed three magazines. They were curved and carried twenty rounds each.

"Happy to start you off with three."

"Better make it four," Quinn said. "Keep going."

Toy Maker's smile spread across his plump face. A happy little elf.

"Here is the Triumph Master Alpha Glock 34."

"Hmm." Quinn lifted this new pistol up to his face, which was still dominated by an intense captivation. He liked his old Glock, sure, but this new one was something more unique, if not also...far more compelling.

"*Triumph*," Quinn said. "Like the name."

Narrow and light, everything about this pistol was custom. And, while Quinn wasn't much of an import car aficionado, this firearm made him feel like he was holding a fucking McLaren Senna in his fucking hand.

"Specially designed five-inch barrel," Toy Maker said, "it's Grade Bull and is equipped with slide cuts, an extended slide, and mag release. There's a dual port compensator and a mounted frame optic too."

"Shit," marveled Quinn.

"Shit is right. Super custom, as you can super see," added Toy Maker. "And I know you clearly see that. With this bad boy, you'll be shootin' bad guys like fish in a barrel. Reloads easy, shoots even easier."

Quinn gazed at this Triumph Master Glock. It was more than just a straight shooter, it was a fast-draw, highly responsive weapon. Through the scope, he envisioned all the Custodians staring back at him.

They would be ready, but then so would he.

"I can give you *one*."

"Perfect."

"Good," Toy Maker said.

"No," Quinn said. "Not finished yet. I need something for...*close encounters*."

Quinn mentioned this last classification while Toy Maker's ear pricked up. His brows furrowed. Quinn's request was very intriguing.

"Indeed," Toy Maker said. He stood before the elite merc, and in his hand was a decorative box with gold trimmings. Toy Maker held this ornamental casket with a secret, but then Quinn knew what was inside. Toy Maker carefully lifted this lid and it was precisely what Quinn had thought.

Knives. *Special* knives.

"You will find that these new OTFs have a little, how you say, *added feature?*"

Quinn pulled one knife from the box and ejected its blade. He stared at the shimmering knife and could see its sharp sides, its sleek edges as the lights gleamed against its fine edge and showed Quinn just how ready to cut it was. Quinn was thinking about the damage it could do with a single swipe from an even simpler hand.

"Looks *longer*," Quinn said.

"That's because it is," Toy Maker said. "See, each knife here is fitted with a seven-inch blade that folds up into the handle. Then, using a small magnet, it reconnects said blade once ejected."

Quinn tested this to see if what Toy Maker said was true. Quinn's thumb pressed the button at the side of the knife. The handle gobbled the blade as it folded back up. Quinn flicked the same switch again. The knife popped and was suddenly twice the size of a standard OTF. Like Toy Maker described, it was separated into two separate quadrants and connected by a magnet.

"With this," Toy Maker said, "you'll have double the length of your blade, and while you might think it's only for slicing throats, the titanium makes the knife able to withstand immense pressure. The magnetization holding the blade together is so strong not even a fucking sledge will tear it apart. Not your average switchblade by any means," added Toy Maker. "No, with these bad boys, you'll be begging for a close encounter. My advice? Take two."

"I agree," Quinn said.

"So..." said Toy Maker, "I suppose that marks the end of our transaction??

"Just one more thing," Quinn stared Toy Maker up and down. "I'm in the market for a *shell*."

"A *shell*?"

"You know what I mean," Quinn said.

"I do," Toy Maker said. He blushed. His admiration for Quinn had now deepened. "Follow me." He and Quinn walked through another door and entered yet another room. Shell was code for armor, as in *body armor*.

What Quinn was seeing now fit this description.

"May I present to you..." began Toy Maker, now in a separate area. Next to him was a black two-piece suit comprised of textured, glossy material. Quinn had no idea what this was, but he liked how it looked. He liked it so much his eyes burned from being opened too long. "The Phalanx Scale, Model 1, elite armor unit."

"Phalanx?" Quinn asked. The name sounded impressive. Right now, it made little sense to Quinn, but again, he was intrigued.

"Name coined," Toy Maker said, "because once you put this shit on, you'll have the support of a full-on Spartan Phalanx, you feel?"

"Yeah," Quinn said, infatuated. Eager. "I feel." Hypnotized by the exotic material, Quinn didn't know what this armor was capable of yet, but he was excited. He was doing his best to imagine. It was crafted with a visible chest plate and included elbow padding and forearm guards. There was a codpiece and a flexible material aligned between the joints. How it managed to disassemble, as of now, was unclear.

"With Phalanx armor, the wearer is accommodated by all the usual protection tech: ceramic matrices, polymer alloy, silicon carbide. All the rest," Toy Maker said, "but *this*...this is divided into four separate parts: legs, chest, back, and arms. Here, you'll be faster, lighter, and the suit itself can accommodate a variety of ammunition. Even its connecting layers offer some solid protection. In addition, there's holsters and several slots designated for extra clips, and other weapons, not to mention a very *prominent* add-on feature."

Toy Maker circled around the armor he called Phalanx and proceeded toward its back. When Quinn saw him move, his head tilted with a pronounced sense of curiosity. He followed him. He could see two slots, crossed and reserved for melee-attack weapons. In this case, that weapon was Quinn's tonfa.

He grinned with unbridled delight.

"But, of course, that's not all," Toy Maker said. Quinn's neck cracked as he gazed.

"You mean there's more?"

"One last thing."

Quinn watched the jolly man walk to a new section of the armory.

"You couldn't go into battle with your head all exposed, now could ya?"

Quinn said nothing. No, he would never enter a war without the right protection. So far, he had not received anything to cover his head and then he saw what Toy Maker was packing.

"May I present to you...the *Corinthian*."

"The what?"

From what Quinn could gather, what Toy Maker had was a helmet or what appeared to be a helmet. Circular and smooth, it looked light and was fitted with the usual tools—night vision and a thin red line that looked like some kind of breathing apparatus. Its exterior was highlighted by an array of pigmented, shifting glows that made Quinn remember where military ingenuity was now, and most of it was right here, in his fucking hand.

"Your *mask*," Toy Maker said, "if that's more helpful. Its name comes from the helmets worn by the famous Spartans of old. But, this puppy here has it all..." Toy Maker reached into the mask and pressed a switch along the jaw. A series of graceful-sounding slides emerged and the helmet began to open like a flower in reverse-bloom.

"Customized to fit any user and removable in an instant."

Quinn inspected. He looked twice at the lenses. Each one was distinct and shining a bright red so intense it was stinging Quinn's retina. The display showed what Toy Maker had mentioned. It included a series of sequences and features that gave Quinn the tingles. It was more palpable than how Quinn felt when holding any of the guns.

"Go ahead," Toy Maker said. "Try it on. Give it a go."

Quinn placed the mask over his stunned face and felt

the edges close around his cheeks, forehead, and chin. It fit like a glove and automatically enhanced Quinn's vision. He could see Toy Maker standing before him with a long grin.

"Oh boy," Toy Marker said. "Shit shines like a new penny. So, whatta ya think?"

Corinthian on, Quinn was next to a mirror. He inspected his reflection. There were grooves and angular designs sketched along Quinn's face. The Corinthian's lenses were shaped like sunglasses turned upside down and the mouth was a rectangular strip of pure silver. It was shaped almost identically to the masks once used by old hockey goalies and was even accompanied by swooshes grooved along the margins. Quinn looked like a modernist's painting of a tiger and was now the living embodiment of a predator scouring the night.

And, given the circumstances, this could not be a better comparison. It was perfectly sensible. Quinn remained poised next to the man who had given him so much so soon.

"So...am I to assume that...you'll be taking this as well?" asked Toy Maker.

Quinn's hands were on the Corinthian and he clicked a switch and removed the mask. Now off, Quinn turned to give his final word.

"This?" said Quinn. His chin shifted up and down. "This I want. Actually, I want it all."

Quinn smiled. He assumed Toy Maker wasn't surprised by the request. After all Quinn had inspected and seen, how could he possibly deny the appeal of every single item?

"Excellent. Let us work out the details first and then we can arrange a way for you to get all of this out as soon as possible."

Toy Maker was now back at the table. And standing

before Quinn's impressive array of arsenal. Quinn held the Corinthian by his waist. He stepped to Toy Maker and proceeded to place the mask down. Soon as Quinn did this, the faint whistle of a clean gunshot echoed throughout the room.

Quinn flinched but Toy Maker fell. "Ah!" Quinn dropped.

Assessing caliber and model, Quinn faced his fallen friend. Body bent back, Quinn gazed at the hole he could see in his ally's chest. Although he tumbled, Toy Maker did land on the leather couch just as Quinn had tried to catch him.

"Shit. Are you..." Quinn clutched Toy Maker and tried to restrict blood flow and keep him steady. It was a straight shot and terribly accurate. Toy Maker gasped and blood gushed past his elongated tongue. Cradling his friend, Quinn peered over his shoulder, and tried to see what he could see. Quinn inspected the dance floor and then glanced at the ceiling. There was a beam with strobe lights and wires stretched from one side to the other. There, a man armed with an MK 12 SPR/Special Purpose Rifle appeared among the flashing lights.

The gun was full auto, and while the first shot was subtle, what came later was not.

Armed with a sound suppressor, the gunshots rained down on Quinn as he covered behind the sofa. The rounds ripped through the furniture. Quinn's surroundings were struck by a storm of bullets and smoke. It tore up the floors and blew out all the windows. The shooter was either merciless or just having a good time. No apologies, the shooter's intention was to mop up the entire office.

Quinn scurried toward the couch and continued his evasion.

"Son of..." Quinn mouthed these words to himself. He knew to watch for snipers.

He didn't think he had to watch out for Toy Maker though. In a more closed area of the club, Quinn stayed hidden. He looked to where he was once standing. Armed with everything he needed, all Quinn desired were his guns. He also wanted his new armor so he could suit up for the inevitable fight. Whether or not this was Quinn's *only* attacker remained to be seen. All of this was irrelevant to the completely on-edge Custodian. Right now, he was primed for anything.

Quinn waited until the shooter was done. Then he chased after the many crackling bursts. Quinn slipped on his Corinthian and the mask gripped his face tight. Eyes glowing an ominous white, the Corinthian was on and it sent Quinn a quick message.

Ready to begin?

Fully suited, Quinn held the Triumph Master Glock he swiped from the counter. He didn't need to say anything, but he did anyway. Doing so would make the next act all the more admirable and fun.

"Let's go."

CHAPTER 2
IT BEGINS

THERE WAS LITTLE KNOWN ABOUT QUINN'S PAST. He never spoke of it, not to anyone.

In Quinn's mind, it was best not to discuss the things that happened before he left home.

He was eighteen then, and upon leaving, he had willed himself into a ghost. He simply went from place to place devoting his life to his art with little interaction or engagement with people or places except for the dojo, the range, the road, and the sky so he could fly his prized jet. So long as Quinn had his mission and his guns, then in his mind he had purpose.

And, if Quinn had purpose, then he didn't need to remember anything else.

So, Quinn never did. But, despite trying to forget, every person still has a past. In Quinn's case, all of this began when he was born on July 1st in one of the greatest countries in the world.

Canada.

Of course, this was only his mother's opinion. She was the one born there. She, like Quinn's father, was also a soldier. Her mentality about Canada drew Broder's attention. Broder Quinn was born in Montana. Quinn's mom was told to cross the border and meet with a colonel there to discuss a new training program designed for covert operations, their agents and soldiers.

This was how Quinn's mother and father met.

"You think Canada is the greatest country in the world, do you?"

Their banter started out as playful flirts. It also marked the first part of a story that Quinn's mother had shared with her children. She spoke of the circumstances that led to her marriage. She said it began with a friendly exchange with Quinn's dad about which was the better country to serve.

Now, Quinn's father had a very different answer to the very same question.

America.

Both of them still had so much in common.

Broder Quinn was a Green Beret, while Kyle Quinn's mother served in the cadets since age eleven. Eventually, she enrolled in Canada's Secret Intelligence Service known as CSIS. There, she developed a reputation for being a swift and cunning field agent.

"Pretty tough for a Canadian." Broder Quinn always joked with the only person in his life that really mattered to him. Unimpressed by the comment, Maria Quinn kneed Broder in the gut and then proceeded to flip him onto the floor.

"What, you think all Canadians are pussies, is that it?"

Broder didn't say a word. After he was hit, it was clear that Broder had found his soulmate. He knew exactly who he wanted to spend the rest of his life with. And while it was both Quinn's parents' story, it was also the story about how he came to be too.

Quinn was raised in Saskatchewan.

His father moved to the province when offered a job

as a training officer. He was assigned to work in a joint-effort between the two countries to train soldiers for new combat missions. According to Quinn's mother, it was her initiative to combine American force tactics into the Canadian military.

Broder Quinn would develop a system that was approved and overseen by his wife.

In its earliest stages, it was instilled and practiced in their very own home. This was where Quinn trained as a child.

Killer Quinn.

This was the first nickname given to Quinn. He stunned and shocked his fellow Canadians and was awarded for his efforts.

In JTF 2, Quinn was gifted with two Victorian crosses and three Crosses of Valour. He was the best damn soldier in Canada before eventually going to America to serve in yet another Special Operations unit. Returning the home where he was raised, Quinn was looking forward to seeing his mother.

Yet, what he saw instead was her bedridden. What he saw was her...dying.

Struck by a severe case of breast cancer, Maria Quinn was diagnosed just weeks before her son was deployed. Quinn enlisted in Delta Force on the auspices he would be given more opportunity as well as more advancement. Upon completing his three years of service, Quinn landed in Wyoming. This was where he would make his new home. It's also here where Quinn would be staying, given that his old home didn't feel quite the same anymore.

Quinn purchased a farm for pennies on the dollar and moved into what was described as a *fixer-upper*. Quinn liked the space, and even more, he liked the solitude. It was an impressive multi-bedroom home with two garages.

Quinn sought to improve his newfound residence and all of this began after he received the first phone call.

It was from his father.

Even now, Quinn can still hear his dad's voice and remembers exactly as he felt at the time. It was quick news but stung so bad. He can't think of another pain capable of producing the same kind of ferocity.

"Your mother's dead, son. She's gone." Cold, Quinn's father refused to say anything else. "She's in the ground. It's done."

Quinn exploded.

His father had robbed him of something he felt he was owed. Quinn never had the chance to say goodbye. His dad's character and his utter lack of empathy drove Quinn into a terrible fit. When he returned to his parents' old house, Quinn unleashed every facet of his fury. He lashed out soon as he was told by his father to stop being such a pussy and accept what is.

"People die, even the people who are the closest to us. Sometimes, we have to put them out of their misery, so you can just accept the loss and go home."

The words putting someone *out of their misery* was what enraged Quinn most of all.

Back when he was younger, Broder Quinn would force his children to kill animals, including Quinn's own dog, Brucie. After it was injured by a coyote, Quinn was told he had to *take care of it*. Quinn's Beagle was found squealing in the middle of the woods. Quinn didn't want to kill it, but his father insisted he do. He didn't even give Quinn a rifle so the death could be quick and painless. All he said was, "Just get it done."

Broder Quinn handed his son a knife so he could stab the helpless animal to death. When Quinn stuck his dog Brucie, all he could remember was the sheer look of betrayal and sadness gleaming in his dying pet's eyes.

His father was an inhuman monster, so when Quinn broke, he broke hard.

Once he learned of his mother's death, Quinn lunged at his dad, and a fight unfolded so volatile it involved all three Quinns at the same time. All were thrust into an epic showdown that left the entire family injured and tore apart nearly the entire house.

This marked the last time the family would ever meet.

Quinn was twenty-nine when he became estranged from his father and family. He abandoned his brother. He told him that should he ever see him again, then Quinn would finish what he started.

He would end his dad's life the same as he ended his mother's.

This was Quinn's vow. This was his life's new mission.

Broder Quinn said nothing to Quinn when he told him his life would someday end.

And then, one day, Quinn simply rose up, stepped into his car, and drove off into the sunset. Quinn decided to go back to Wyoming, where he worked in the private sector as a full-on, ready-to-go mercenary. One day, his dad did call, and he did leave a message for Quinn. He would have hung up the phone, but he couldn't find it in himself to do it.

His dad spoke so fast that Quinn didn't have the chance to interrupt.

"Go to your bank now."

With little explanation given after, Quinn traveled to his local branch. He walked straight to a teller and gave his name. He did this and Quinn also wanted to ask the woman why she was looking so flabbergasted and shaken.

Shaking her head, the female teller looked at Quinn, stunned and beguiled by his request.

"It would seem that someone made quite the deposit

into your account recently. I am not sure why we didn't notify you, but we should have. It came via wire transfer, but Mr. Quinn, you're...you're..."

Quinn had no time for this...whatever it was. He asked himself: what the hell was going on? "What?"

"Well, it would seem, you're...you're...*rich*."

At last, the teller revealed what was troubling her. Quinn was bombarded with a life-altering truth. His heart thumped hard in his chest and he hadn't felt a thrill like this in a really long time.

"Is that..."

"Yes," the teller immediately replied. "It is."

The *it* she was referring to was the same one Quinn was referring to.

The *it* was the amount of money that had been added to Quinn's account. The Custodian's wealth didn't just double or triple. No, it was well beyond anything he had conceived in reality or imagination.

It was ten million dollars.

"Holy shit."

In that moment Quinn became what so many wanted to be.

He was rich. Well, he was rich enough.

The inheritance Quinn's father was granted was split among the other children. How much anyone got was Quinn's guess, but he didn't care to know. When he walked out of the bank, Quinn remembered being in a daze. He was semi-deluded yet also completely exhilarated at the same time. He thought about all the ways in which he could spend his newfound wealth. And the more Quinn thought this, the less interested he became.

Money could change many things for a person, except what's in their hearts.

For Quinn, it was once a soldier, always a soldier.

And neither wealth nor status would change that.

This is what Quinn learned after receiving his money. It was also something he knew to be true all his life. With all the money deposited and ready to be spent, Quinn pulled up to his modest farmhouse. He examined the setting with a keen, now imaginative eye.

What could he use the money for? Was there room to improve?

Always.

With more to fill his life now, Quinn decided to invest in his home first. He transformed his residence into something so cutting edge it would impress any modern designer. Besides, Quinn loved working with his hands. This entire venture had provided him with different ways of putting them to good use.

Using his new money, Quinn added new flooring and finished off his basement.

In fact, he converted the entire downstairs into a tier-one mission control center. Equipped with all the best toys, Quinn had the same tech as the CIA. He also contacted an old military pal who installed a top-of-the-line security system, which allowed Quinn to see his property from multiple angles and all points of view. There was also a new weapon vault, a panic room, and Quinn opted to mount solar panels on his roof for green energy efficiency. He built a dojo to practice in and converted the barn into an elite airplane hangar; Quinn's most ambitious goal to date.

Quinn was recommended flying by soldiers who were battling PTSD. Quinn's outlet for alleviating his own struggle with his own pain needed to be more than just shooting guns at moving targets. Three months in, Quinn was between rescue missions and kill orders. He worked part-time as a bouncer and a protection specialist too. When he wasn't busy with these jobs, Quinn traveled to an airport only thirty minutes from his home. There, he took to the skies.

Soon after he earned his pilot certification, Quinn was in the shop for a plane of his own.

He knew the exact model that fit his liking.

The one chosen met all of Quinn's needs and the merc landed on the Cirrus Vision SF50 jet. He bought it for a flat two mil, with digits shaved off because he managed to pinch out a solid deal. And, while Quinn had spent much of his inheritance, he hadn't even scratched the surface of what else he could afford.

When Quinn bought the plane, he also purchased a prized American Muscle sports vehicle. For Quinn, the car selected was a much-desired—and very difficult to find —AMC AMX/3.

A sleek supercar, Quinn spent nearly two hundred grand customizing it. He added new rims, bulletproof windows, and slots for his guns. Quinn fortified the entire transport to the point where it rivaled a tank. Although it stayed mostly in Quinn's garage, he didn't know when it would be of use.

He knew one day that it would be.

And when he turned thirty, this was how Quinn spent his life.

He trained every morning and accepted other menial jobs. He flew wherever he wanted and his life became much more structured, much more efficient. Quinn's time in the military came to an end, all of this changed. Quinn found himself entering a new phase of search and destroy. He was contacted via phone. At the time, this man didn't introduce himself, not right away.

"Is this Kyle Quinn I'm speaking to?"

Not sure who was asking, Quinn had just returned from a hard workout when he answered. "It is."

Quinn listened. He tried to determine whether he had heard this voice before.

But Quinn didn't recognize the speaker. If he knew him, or if he had somehow managed to cross paths with him, Quinn was drawing a blank. Yet, when the man gave these introductions, another phrase quickly followed.

"My name is unimportant, but I work for the SAC, as I'm sure you might've already guessed. What I do, however, isn't as important as what you do, Mr. Quinn. And I heard what you do is...*you paint houses.*"

Quinn grunted before a hiss of mild laughter squeaked out of him. He recognized the line. It was one supposedly said by Jimmy Hoffa to Frank Sheeran. He was a hitman for the mob, and the saying, *I heard you fucking kill people.*

A popular axiom, Quinn did more than paint houses. No, he fucking varnished them too. "I do."

This marked the first interaction between Quinn and Priest. It was a casual engagement. What followed later was nothing more than a quick back and forth.

"I go by many names, but for now, why don't you just call me...*Priest?*"

The name sounded cliché and mundane. Quinn thought it had come from a Clancy novel.

"I absolve people of their sins, see?" said this man. "And I grant them a new purpose by putting them on a new path. And that's why I'm calling you now, see? Mr. Quinn, a terrible darkness is trying to take over our great nation. New and powerful forces are emerging each and every day and I'm looking for the best people in the world who can fight to stop it. I'm looking for people who aren't afraid to go up against the worst of the worst, like those who know how to resist and rise up, see? I want people who fight till the fucking end and show no mercy. Do you understand me, Mr. Quinn? I want the best."

Priest's speech was similar to the god-awful military speakers Quinn heard back in the day. Whoever this Priest was, he did have an intriguing sales pitch.

"Now I want to know if you're willing to join me on this epic quest, Quinn. Are you ready to do what needs to be done for greater glory? Are you ready to make sure that the country you hold near and dear remains protected and honored?"

Quinn recalled every second he shared with Priest those many years ago. When Quinn reflected on it now, it seemed all the more vivid. Like it happened yesterday, Quinn recalled exactly how to respond to the question that would change his life forever.

"Yes, I'm ready."

There was a pause on the other line, as well as a hint of a giggle. Quinn had to wait for Priest to say more.

"Excellent, my son. Absolutely excellent."

A fog of snapshots went on to plague Quinn's mind. They emerged in deep, palpable waves. Some nights, Quinn would wake up, and all he could think about was the past. Fighting, shooting, and now flying were all outlets that provided Quinn with only a temporary solution to alleviate his complex, deep-rooted psychological issues. But, so long as he stayed in these categories and completed the assigned tasks, Quinn could reduce the impact of his trauma. He could *contain* his pain. He liked to think he was a man with a higher purpose by doing this. His life had become about survival and the desire to prove to himself so that he could convince himself that all his personal hardships and terror had all happened for a reason. And, so long as Quinn continued to use what he learned, how to fight and how to keep winning, then he was stronger than his father.

He was better.

Trauma lingers like a terrible smell.

Once you catch a hint of it, the stench takes you back to the time when it was first conceived. When Quinn smelled these smells, he'd close his eyes and count down from ten. This was Quinn's practice done to regain control. It was also a test of his strength. Quinn would never be rid of his pain, not completely. What Quinn believed now was he needed to find the person who made him and make him suffer.

Therefore, Quinn once sought only his father. Quinn didn't know where his old man had gone. After the fight, he disappeared and Broder Quinn's whereabouts eventually became a mystery that Priest promised to solve. Before, when Quinn agreed to join Priest's new initiative, Quinn was said to operate solely within the United States, where he would infiltrate and eliminate various targets that were a threat to his country's integrity and safety. He would map out all potential points of access, kill, and disappear. The duty of all Custodians is to clean the slate. They safeguard and protect and they fight to ensure that everything important is upheld and maintained against any and all threats.

A Custodian is, by definition, a person tasked with care and courtesy.

And, after Quinn enlisted in the Custodian program, murder and total devastation became his chief skills. They were also the very things that ensured his own survival. But, as he would come to learn, they did not have to be the things that defined him. The demons of his past and the ghosts Quinn saw at night might still be haunting him, but he did not have to serve or listen to them.

As a result, the cure Quinn desperately craved was still not his to hold.

Quinn's new code of righteousness was supposed to be something real. It was not all there was or all there needed to be, but after Quinn escaped from Priest, he thought he was escaping the nightmarish outcome that would be his life, so he lived a life absent of any friends and family. Often, all Quinn had to keep him company was the men he killed and his reputation as a chief murderer feared by many.

None of this enticed Quinn, not anymore.

The phrase *turn over a new leaf* could not be applied to a person like himself.

He left too much in a state of chaos and disrepair. For so long, Quinn couldn't embrace his calling of greater purpose or the path to redemption he might one day find. He was more than a killer. No, Quinn was someone who resisted and endured. He pushed and he did so without being afraid. When Quinn made the choice to betray Priest, he decided to lead a new, better life.

But this was his decision because it was Quinn's life to own now.

And Quinn did this because finally he understood.

Fear is not greater than honor, and no good ever comes from lies. Heroes are not conceived without first accepting the worst parts of themselves and then vowing to be more, to *be* better. Becoming a man with a cause and a creed...so long as Quinn had this, then a path to salvation would one day present itself.

All Quinn had to do was believe that it would come, and then he'd wait, and he'd hope.

No matter what...he'd fight to have hope.

Quinn hunkered in Toy Maker's lair and held the hand of the man he once believed to be a friend. He watched as the light in his eyes began to fade and squeezed Maker's trembling fingers and leaned in closer. "Hold on."

Quinn had done his best to stay covered. Unfortunately, Maker was not granted the same opportunity. No, Toy Maker died right there, in Quinn's arms.

Now secured behind a couch, the Custodian was not wounded but was also not close to an exit. Stocked up with everything he needed, as soon as the firing stopped, Quinn blitzed to the window. The Beretta shotgun was behind Quinn's back and both Glocks were loaded into his thigh rigs. These compartments were actually built into Quinn's Phalanx armor. The Corinthian was activated and Quinn's HK416D was locked and loaded. Quinn could endure more gunfire in this armor. Actually, he could fucking survive a goddamn grenade to the chest if necessary.

This was how confident Quinn was in his new tactical gear.

Quinn raced to the window and leaped through the glass. He descended to the dance floor and never felt so light and protected.

After making a hot entrance, Quinn smacked the floor and watched as several patrons scurried like rats. Quinn looked like a cross between a character from Half-Life and Snake Eyes from G.I. Joe. Leering through his visor, the enhanced vision feature provided Quinn with other useful lenses. In addition, the Corinthian gave Quinn a magnified view of what lay across the dance floor. Unsure if Toy Maker's assassination was Custodial or not, Quinn was halfway onto the dance floor when he heard a halting voice a few paces behind him.

"Quinn!" The voice was a barreling shriek.

This person spoke to Quinn like he was being scolded. The fact the voice was raised demonstrated that the killer didn't want Quinn to take another step. He gave Quinn his back. Quinn had his gun but had chosen not to break it out.

He looked dead ahead.

Seconds after Quinn heard his name, Quinn knew exactly who he was in the company of.

He assumed another Custodian would arrive soon, but not here, at this club. Quinn rotated and stared at the one responsible for the nightclub attack.

Consequently, it was the same one responsible for Toy Maker's death.

Quinn would say this killer was *big*. He was also aware that there were few out there who were bigger than him. In this case, this Custodian from California was. He was an absolute mammoth of a man and Quinn's newest foe. Fearless and powerful, when Quinn spoke his name, he did so with a dutiful calmness; a profound and significant respect.

"Briggs." Quinn faced down another colleague, there was so much more Quinn wanted to know. There was even more Quinn wanted to do. He started with professional courtesy and extended to his fellow assassin a warm and careful greeting. Quinn hoped that Briggs would do the same.

"Hi there, Quinn."

"So...you found me?"

Briggs nodded and smiled. The hulking man was relishing in this discovery, evidently. "Looks like I have," Briggs said, "and also looks like you've got some new gear on ya too. I like it," said Briggs.

"Yeah," Quinn said. "Well, maybe if you hadn't killed the one who made it for me, you might have gotten one for yourself. Now that I think of it, you should have. You're gonna need it."

Briggs chuckled and he folded his arms. Pushing his biceps against his knuckles so he could look all the more jacked, Briggs was the biggest man Quinn had ever seen. He might actually be the biggest man anyone had ever seen.

"Got everything I need right where I'm standing," said Briggs.

"Hmm," Quinn squinted at the mammoth. "I hope so."

Both Custodians were locked in a glorious stare down and each waited for the other to make the first move. Seeing Briggs, Quinn was assessing more than just his weapons but also his measurements. Briggs weighed an easy two seventy-five. He was also nearly six feet, six inches tall and was built with a wide-ass frame. His arms were so fat they appeared to be suffocating beneath his spandex shirt. Briggs had a military background, same as Quinn.

Once a SEAL, Briggs left around the same time Quinn left Delta. This allowed for both men to have some shared experiences. Briggs had crushed skulls with his bare hands, and the reputations of his Custodial exploits were not only impressive, they were gruesome—stomach turning. Briggs was a human chainsaw. If you threw him into a crowd, he was less about precision and more about demolition, *destruction*. Quinn knew this and he hated Briggs because of it. The man was a good killer but a bad professional.

"I take you're here to...*answer the call?*" Quinn asked.

Briggs smirked and nodded. "Yeah, but then...aren't you going to run?" Briggs asked.

Quinn's head shook. He never ran or hid from anyone or anything. No, all Quinn ever did was stand and fight, and now was no exception. "Nope."

"Good," Briggs replied. He flicked his fingers and winked. "Then, what are you waiting for? Are you just going to stand there or are you going to fucking bleed?"

Briggs's hand slid to his waist and Quinn drew his pistol and fired.

Quinn's weapon was easily detachable. He squeezed

the trigger and the giant man lifted his arm and covered himself. Quinn let loose with the top-of-the-line gun and continued to spit rounds that hit exactly where he wanted.

Quinn's aim was top-notch.

He hit Briggs, but each round was absorbed and swallowed by the clothing that enveloped the big man's body. Whatever the material was made of, it allowed for zero penetration. Seeing this, Quinn was reminded how he wasn't the only one who acquired impressive material. Firing again, Quinn marched toward Briggs, who continued to hide behind his bulletproof coat. Now on approach, Quinn twirled his pistol around his index finger like a gunslinger and did not plan to run anywhere.

What Quinn wanted was to flush Briggs the fuck out and then own his fat ass.

Quinn knew he was up against a far bigger opponent. He also knew that Briggs couldn't see where Quinn was at this moment. Quinn shuffled toward the door and vanquished from the gyrating, sweaty bodies. He exploded out onto the street dressed in prototype armor. Quinn didn't care who saw or did not see him. He pressed the button near his chin and the Corinthian folded back to reveal Quinn's face.

On the sidewalk outside, Quinn was lambasted by the chilly night air. Giving the Custodian a tickle, multiple vibrations crawled along his earlobes and up into his nostrils. Devoid of injury so far, this was good, and Quinn marched on, knife out. He could see Briggs's jugular. Like a number at a deli, all Quinn had to do was reach out and take it. Ready to do precisely that, Quinn moved in but Briggs's hand jolted and he wrapped his fat palm around Quinn's blade and squeezed. "Don't think so, boy."

Quinn stabbed with his OTF and Briggs let the blade pierce his hand. He displayed no signs of pain and instead opted to give Quinn a coy smirk. Quinn turned. Suddenly, the Custodian was presented with a new challenge.

"Freeze!" The cops on the scene shouted at Quinn.

He didn't raise his hands because raising hands implies guilt and criminality.

Quinn was neither.

Killing cops was never part of the plan—something Quinn never did. Staring past the boys in blue, Quinn looked at the side of the road, to a sewer grate no larger than three feet in diameter. With this, Quinn had an exit strategy; unpreferred but still it was a way out.

"Put your hands up!"

Quinn rolled to the grate and ignored the uniformed officers. He half expected them to start shooting but this action was cut off by an emphatic voice that addressed the men and women of the NYPD.

"Officers! Officers, please, stop! I can explain!"

An ominous chill crept up Quinn's still body. Seeing one cop's gun drawn, Briggs motioned closer. "I can explain everything!"

"Let me see your hands!" One cop shouted at the big man.

And, as Briggs continued to step, the cop's screeching yells still persisted. Quinn gazed at the firearm in Briggs's possession. It was a weapon well suited to the man carrying it.

Quinn didn't know how Briggs had managed to conceal a gun of this caliber. What he did know was because of Briggs's size, he could hide a number of weapons without anyone noticing. In this case, what Briggs had was an all-black, fully loaded automatic shotgun known as an AA12.

"Please, I can..." Briggs stood two feet before the portly officer. Then, after a heaving swing of his hips, the large Custodian flipped the huge shotgun up and squeezed.

Quinn closed his eyes. He couldn't watch this part.

Although Quinn *could* have shot Briggs, if he were to draw any kind of weapon in front of the amped police, he would have been targeted or worse. There was just no time to secure the safety of anyone other than himself.

The Atchisson Assault shotgun could fire three hundred rounds a minute. It shot twelve-gauge rounds and had an API blowback. It held eight shells loaded into a box magazine and was able to hold up to thirty-two in a drum.

Unfortunately, a drum mag was what Briggs had with him now.

Briggs screamed. Quinn watched as he leveled through the first cop. Briggs blew the officer away like he was confetti. Head down, Quinn had witnessed nearly every form of violence there was, but even he could not watch this.

It was a demonstration of pure carnage as Briggs let loose with the AA12.

Quinn lifted the sewer grate, dropped into the tunnels below, and he ignored the screams and the agony.

Again, he just couldn't watch.

———

Upon escape, Quinn ran into a narrow passageway. His boots sloshed dirty water and he was surrounded by shadow and stink. Quinn raced. Stories about Briggs suddenly returned to the Custodian's mind and Quinn remembered exactly who he was up against.

A loose cannon, Briggs didn't just watch his enemies fall, he wanted to crush them and see them driven before him. When other soldiers returned from war, some had the unfortunate challenge of fighting PTSD, guilt, and loneliness. Briggs returned and went on to work for a demolitions crew while, at night, he'd frequent bars and look for trouble.

Like Quinn, Briggs also worked as a bouncer but was fired for being too volatile. He lacked the temperament, so he was sent home packing.

None of this rang any alarms for Briggs. It had zero effect.

In the end, Briggs was not like most people.

He was a textbook narcissist; a borderline sociopath. Briggs was also the only person Quinn knew who smiled whenever he killed. And, because Briggs didn't seem to care about anything, none of the stories surrounding him compared to one.

Such was the tale that sealed Briggs's reputation. It was the precise reason why Priest had chosen to recruit Briggs into the prestigious unit of expert killers.

One night, Briggs visited the Jersey Shore.

There to hit up the beach and work on his tan, upon arrival, he stumbled upon a few juiceheads. It started as nothing more than a simple exchange of glowers and mean remarks. Briggs told these Guido assholes they should watch where they were stepping but the boys refused to adhere to such advice. There were five of them and only one of Briggs. Yet, the boys' shallow confidence and disrespect pissed Briggs the fuck off because, if there was one quality he loathed, it was no respect. Now Briggs had assured this entourage of douchebags that their behavior would not go unnoticed but then these Guidos didn't buy into Briggs's warning. One called him a *punk bitch* before he sauntered along the shores. Enraged, Briggs overheard how these boys planned to go to a club later in the evening. This presented Briggs with an opportunity he could take advantage of. So, he snuck into this same club earlier the same day and planted various weaponry while pretending to be a repairman. Being a determined man, Briggs waltzed in later fully armed and very pissed off.

Once inside the booming nightclub, Briggs located the boys who fucked with him back at the beach. From there, he commenced what would be known as the Jersey Shore Tall Man Massacre.

The title was a little on the nose for Quinn's taste.

Blowing all the assholes away, Briggs opened fire on the fuckers in a sea of carnage and bloodshed. Though not completing a sanctioned Custodial mission, Briggs behaved as though he was. At the club, Briggs unleashed all his power on the five boys who antagonized him and killed anyone who stood in his way. When low on ammunition, Briggs went for the guns he stashed, and with so many dead, Briggs emptied his AA12 and killed over twenty people total by the night's end. The shooting was solidified in the American history books. The Jersey Shore Tall Man Massacre was not committed by some moron with a gun or some incel who wanted to project his pain onto the world. Contrarily, this shooting was conducted at the hands of a monstrous professional.

But to stop a one-man army, one would need an army of their own.

In this case, this army was two SWAT teams and more than thirty Jersey PD officers. The units arrived just as Briggs began to exit the club. Briggs staggered onto the street. Carrying an automatic pistol, he continued to indulge in the thrill of the slaughter, and basked in the deaths of those who had fallen before spotting another officer.

Briggs removed him the same as he did all the others.

It was at this point that the SWAT team and the Custodian entered the showdown.

They enshrouded the depraved maniac in a cloud of

gunfire. Back and forth, Briggs rolled and absorbed a storm of angry bullets. None of the hits were fatal. None of them were able to put the big man down. Briggs took the cops to the ocean, where he jumped and swam through the cold water. Beneath the surface, Briggs stashed an oxygen tank and an underwater Sea Scooter for his planned getaway.

Even underwater, Briggs was not safe. Having done what he did, he was officially placed on the FBI's Most Wanted list yet ended up getting away on a boat. There was nothing and nowhere Briggs could go whereby he would not be pursued.

This Briggs knew to be true.

Even in spite of being aware of this fact, the man did not tremble or stop grinning. He got the hell out of the Shore and reached for his phone so he could contact the only man who could help him now.

"Mr. Priest, I need to see you right away."

Far from cordial, when he received this call from one of his Custodians who was not on a mission, the Lock Smith was not impressed. Bailing out a mass murderer was not part of Priest's duty and was not why he assembled the Custodians. In the end, Priest saved his favors for when his men were actually trapped in tight spots. He did not intervene if they went on miscellaneous rampages for an apparent or unapparent reason.

Nevertheless, Priest agreed to meet Briggs on a freight transport.

Upon arrival, Priest glared as Briggs casually strolled toward him.

"Thanks a lot there, Priest. You know, I owe you big time. You know how I get. Sometimes I'm a bit of a hothead. I'm a mess. I take things too far, and I know that's not what I'm paid to do, but—" In the middle of his pitiful apology, Priest lashed out and struck the towering man with a clean cross straight to his fat face. Priest knocked Briggs to the ground with another hit to the nose and gleamed with remarkable madness as he stared at his wounded subordinate.

"Ah!" Briggs was hit once and then once more.

Priest did have some solid fighting skills. He pounded Briggs's face into the pavement and knew the behemoth would not resist. What Briggs was experiencing was punishment for the shitstorm he created due to his insolence and ego. Priest clobbered Briggs until the tall man could no longer stand. Once done exacting the necessary consequences, the brooding contractor stood over his fallen man, who was nothing now except a disappointment.

"Next time I call," Priest said, "you better damn well answer, because your next mission is gonna be your worst one yet. You can goddamn guarantee that. And if you refuse, then what happened here will only be just the beginning, do you hear me? You won't be a new man, Briggs, you'll be a fucking dead one."

On his knees, blood smeared Briggs's bruised cheeks. Priest, who defeated his subordinate, said nothing afterward. Once he provided an order, Briggs was so beaten he would be an idiot to dispute or make matters worse.

So, he didn't. He had only one phrase to speak, and that was it.

"I'll be there. I'll be ready."

Tonight, Briggs was.

———

In the sewer, creeping beneath the city, Quinn was assaulted by a putrid stench of rotten eggs and manure in what was a myriad of gross, vomit-inducing smells. In his Phalanx armor, Quinn was mobile as he sloshed the smelly water. When fitted with this protective gear, it aided Quinn during his escape. Quinn marched until he reached a series of new tunnels and the Corinthian helped Quinn navigate his way through the tumultuous underground. Thanks to its many applications, the area was illuminated by the mask's night vision and allowed for Quinn to see through the darkness. Everything Quinn spotted was overcast by an orange tinge and unveiled any and all surprises.

In many ways, Quinn's vision was clear as day. As he hopped across the swampy lair, he headed back the way he came. Quinn flew from Wyoming to New York and left his Cirrus Vision at the LaGuardia Airport. Afterward, Quinn asked for his AMX to be present after he touched down so he could drive through the city. The car was arranged to be brought here by the only contact whom Quinn still had on his side. She was not only his partner, but she was so much more. She was the love of his life and the name he kept repeating to himself over and over like a mantra.

Ally. Ally. Ally.

The last time Quinn saw Ally was back when he infiltrated the underground lab and discovered the truth about Priest's nefarious future plans. It was here Quinn came face-to-face with Priest and his wicked orchestration and it was here he also connected with Ally just days before he left his home back in Wyoming. Quinn began his escape and then he told Ally where he was going and what he needed her to do.

"My car will be in Wyoming. I need you to find the nearest cargo ship and get it to me in Manhattan as soon as possible. I'll be flying there to save time. Do you still have contacts in the CIA?"

"Yes, of course, but..."

When Ally replied, the *but* she mentioned was in fact

a *but* that indicated how, if she did help Quinn, she'd then also be putting herself in danger the same as he was. Priest's reach extended quite far. And, as soon as Quinn was extricated, Priest would be deploying every Custodian he had to hunt Quinn down. And, if Quinn wanted help, it was because he damn well needed it.

Even still, Priest could go beyond Quinn and kill those close to him. Priest could kill her. He could kill Ally, but in spite of the fact that Priest could do this, the question of whether or not he would was unclear. Once Quinn had what he needed, he'd shake his head free of this thought. He did this now as he continued to trek through the sewers. The only reason why Toy Maker was killed was because Briggs was a sadist. He was a man without honor and someone who enjoyed watching other people suffer and die.

Ally, however, was only helping Quinn.

She was the only one who could, and that's why Quinn adored her as much as he did.

Quinn couldn't live without her and didn't plan to. Ally was also wise enough to stay public. She also knew how to protect herself. She was also one of the bravest people Quinn had ever met. He was sure that wherever Ally was, she was fighting too. She was likely waging her own war, and this one was one she refused to surrender, but then, this was why Quinn needed her. And it was why he always would.

He loved her.

Quinn came to the end of the tunnel but the entire time was following a movable icon. This represented Quinn's Cirrus jet, still at LaGuardia. Quinn had lots of ground to cover. So long as he kept moving, then he was further from Briggs.

The Custodians would be coming for Quinn one way or another.

Fortunately, Quinn had a strategy.

He was not going to crawl through the sewers and emerge at LaGuardia. The desired circumstance called for more. This was something Quinn realized the moment he left the Fade. Into the underground, Quinn believed the best place for him to go was the marina.

Quinn sought to emerge as close to the ocean as possible.

Although Quinn didn't have a boat—or a boating license—he was familiar with how to operate a floating vessel. He gained practice from his time in the military. Once he reached this spot, Quinn planned to hop on the first one he came across. It was then he would get to the airport and get back to his jet.

Much to do before then, Quinn raced. He pushed through and fought the terrain of excrement and filth. When Quinn journeyed, the words of Robert Frost accompanied Quinn along his journey.

Miles to go before I sleep.

In another tunnel, a large figure draped in shadow ogled the fleeing mercenary. He gazed from far away and the figure's hands were gripping a small, portable device.

It was a phone. The man stopped and Quinn watched his every move.

"This is Briggs. I have Quinn, and I know where he's going."

CHAPTER 3
NO SAFE PASSAGE

Briggs spoke to Priest, but the man in charge was in a DC office when he received the call.

Keeping a temporary residence there, Priest was waiting for updates about the status of the one known as Kyle Quinn. So far, the results were anything but encouraging.

"Well, what are you waiting for?"

Priest received word from Briggs and had no interest in engaging in witty, playful banter.

Priest ended the call and Briggs remained at attention while in the sewer with Quinn.

He had hiked through literal shit for almost an hour and had gained much ground and was closer to LaGuardia now than before. More than this, Quinn was closer to a mode of transportation. Taking a glance over his shoulder, Quinn saw everything that lay ahead of him, as well as what was behind.

Always in motion, Quinn had no time to stop, turn, or look around. But, damn did Quinn fucking see *him*.

Quinn could fucking see Briggs!

Quinn saw Briggs earlier. Quinn was wise enough to know when he had a tail, especially a tail like Briggs. He had likely come to the sewers right after slaughtering all those police officers. Quinn could only imagine the shitstorm now happening above. He could feel Briggs closing in. Quinn had his suit and he had his guns too, but right now, he hadn't a clue about what else Briggs might have, if he had anything at all.

Quinn stopped to look over his shoulder.

If Briggs was going to shoot Quinn dead in the dark, he would have done that already.

And, even if he did do it, Quinn was armored. He was not as fearful of dirty shots. If Briggs was willing to follow Quinn, then it was because down here, the hulking Custodian believed he had the advantage.

But Briggs was wrong.

He had no advantage.

Trekking further, Quinn halted beneath a circular opening and switched off his night vision. He stepped up onto a rusty ladder that led up to the street and pushed the metal door with a straight arm. The circular disc weighed a solid sixty-five, but Quinn managed. Out to the side, one hand remained on the steel while Quinn kept the other down near his waist. When Quinn emerged, he was struck by a wave of new, less vomit-inducing aroma. Refreshed by this new atmosphere, Quinn had no clue what time it was.

Most often, he would check his Luminox wristwatch to be sure.

But, as the time of day flashed across his visor, Quinn's question was answered.

It was two a.m., the middle of the damn night.

Quinn vacated the sewer and, feeling the rich air coming off from the World Fair Marina, could breathe easier now. Quinn sprinted and was quickly in the company of boats lined up by the docks. His least preferred form of transportation, he didn't care.

He had his ride.

Quinn wanted to get to the airport as quickly as possible. He needed to get Priest before it was too late. Quinn scurried to a speedboat that caught his eye. It was mid-size and its nose still roped to the dock. Painted red, it was Quinn's favorite color and so, he felt an instant connection as he hopped inside. Quinn went for the controls and scoured its systems for anything familiar.

No sign of any keys, Quinn sighed. Of course, he didn't expect to find any so easy!

What kind of bum leaves their keys for someone else to find?

Quinn couldn't hotwire a vehicle like this. He didn't know how to do that. Quinn also refused because he might damage the boat and feared what would happen if he tampered with any of its components. But, given how badly Quinn needed to get to the airport right now, he refused to waste any time trying to jumpstart a boat.

Then Quinn remembered something he had not before. Having snagged a tool from his belt, it was not his OTF or his guns but instead...a *Skeleton Key*.

Such a classification was given to keys with the power to open any doors.

Toy Maker hadn't mentioned this tool to Quinn, but the Custodian noticed the added feature when he first acquired the Phalanx armor. And, unlike everything else Toy Maker was selling, this one item required no background or briefing. Quinn knew exactly what he was going to do with this fine piece of machinery. The Skeleton Key was more than a tool, it was a bloody cheat code capable of gifting any person with near unlimited access. When in someone's hands, they could enter any system and, consequently, any machine.

Forgetting it was on his person, Quinn pinched the key's tail. It was shaped without ridges or curves and was instead straight and thin. A digital tool, a series of codes were built directly into its engineering. And, when Quinn inserted the key into the panel, he breathed a pronounced sigh of relief.

It was too easy and so, Quinn couldn't help but laugh.

"Thanks, Toy Maker. Thank you very much."

Hands on the wheel, Quinn drove this boat away from the docks and toward the airport.

The Corinthian, still over Quinn's face, he was disguised as he scanned the region and absorbed nearly everything that caught his eye.

So far, all Quinn could see were more boats.

And yet, heading to LaGuardia Airport, the possibility of arriving here under the circumstances forced Quinn's heart to skip. Briggs was back and racing in a boat of his own. Neither coincidence nor happenstance that this man was following Quinn, what he was preparing for now was the final round.

It would be just Quinn and Briggs.

The two would come face-to-face in a deadly match to see who could come out on top. Quinn pushed toward the airfield, and with the night still young and the sky black as gunpowder, the thing about airports, Quinn said to himself, *is they're never empty.*

Damn airports never close.

————

Quinn loathed airports.

In fact, he couldn't express how much it pleased him to have a plane of his own. While it did allow him to fly almost anywhere, Quinn was completely non-reliant on pilots, security, or people. All of these things lent to making any trip so much worse but then Quinn left his AMX at the Toy Maker's club.

Someone would find it there and turn it in, but then that's where Ally would come in.

Right now, her role was to be Quinn's collector. She picked up the pieces left behind and made sure they found their way back to him, *somehow*.

Ally promised to stay close. Being Quinn's main reinforcement, she was ready for anything. And most of all, Quinn needed her to be.

Always, he needed her. Right now, Quinn had other priorities.

When Quinn first flew into LaGuardia, he thought Priest would send an F22 and shoot him out of the sky. Priest could do this, but then Quinn did have some solid maneuvering capabilities even in his Vision jet. Should he be targeted, Quinn would simply bail out like he was goddamn Maverick. Granted, Quinn missed his plane. It was not worth keeping if it cost Quinn his life. Considering this as a potential outcome, Quinn recalled a conversation he had once with Priest.

Quinn remembered just how much this man in a suit hated the Air Force.

"Bunch of wannabe Top Gun idiots who wear nice uniforms and who do their fucking killing from the goddamn sky. Bunch of bitches, if you ask me. Really want to kill a man, you do it up close and in their face, not with the flick of some button."

While Quinn didn't give a shit about Priest's opinion now, it was ironic given how he had people killed without raising a single hand. But, when Quinn walked into the terminal, he stared at the long line-ups of people all scattered about in misshapen pockets and looking like messy clusters of misanthropic individuals who wanted to be anywhere but here. Beneath the bright lights of the airport, all was prototypical. It consisted of kiosks and check-ins and Quinn looked at all the packs of families walking hand in hand.

Still in his armor, Quinn swiped a coat from the boat and proceeded through the terminal in a fisherman's slicker. Quinn's face was all bloody and he smelled of shit, and he was in the worst and the best place at the same time.

Now out in the open, Quinn was completely exposed. But anyone who knows anything about airports knows what happens there. Almost as secure as police stations or government buildings, the idea of antagonizing anyone at an airport is a choice made by only a few.

Aware that Briggs was still following him, what Quinn needed now was his jet.

Moving through one terminal, it was here where Quinn remembered leaving it—another one of Ally's vital favors. Again, Ally helped Quinn so much now. When Quinn walked on, he sought to glimpse at the nearby mirrors and check his six.

Quinn spotted Briggs in the busy terminal. He was not far, but what Quinn had on his person was a one-way ticket straight to jail. There was literally an entire arsenal attached to his body. Though the coat did help to keep most of it concealed, drawing a gun here would be like lighting a firecracker at a funeral.

The act was suicide. Still, Quinn's priorities remained the same.

He wanted his plane!

Housed in its own hangar, Quinn couldn't recall precisely how much he was paying for it to stay in this location. Given his time frame, which was about forty-eight hours since his arrival, Quinn would worry about payment another time. It was possible Priest had asked a

Custodian to blow it to shit. No Custodian would pull that stunt at a location such as this.

Briggs was still following Quinn. The giant man would continue to pursue Quinn until he was stopped. How Quinn planned on doing this was aligned with his usual strategy: He would draw out his enemies and then attack them head-on, no pauses, no apologies.

In this case, what Quinn needed was to get Briggs out onto the tarmac and out of sight. Quinn's current environment was inhibiting, so casually he proceeded to the men's room. Quinn saw four men standing by urinals. He closed the door while the men washed their hands in the sink.

"Leave," Quinn demanded.

"Excuse me?" snapped one man.

"Get out, now."

How Quinn managed to get these men to notice him was because of his bloody and beaten appearance. Quinn also hoped it was because he also looked a little like a cop or a repairman. Whatever the reason, with the men leaving, Quinn had, in effect, saved all their lives.

He continued to stand close to the door. Once all was clear, Quinn made sure it stayed open. Moving toward the sink, Quinn soaped his wrists and his neck. The act of cleaning himself free from the stenches now clinging to his body became an enchanting practice and Quinn did what he could in the short time he had.

When the door did open, Quinn didn't have to turn around to know who had stepped through. He was now in the presence of a gigantic silhouette that could only belong to a man twice Quinn's size. When Quinn heard the door slam, the merc stepped back and had a look.

"Quinn."

"Briggs."

Briggs's suit was covered in dark patches and each one was more putrid than the last.

"So...you had to go through the sewers, did you?"

Quinn shrugged. Unaffected by Briggs's disapproval over the choice of exit, in fact, Quinn had a reply of his own he felt was better suited to the question.

"So...you had to kill cops, didn't you?"

Briggs chortled as he motioned across the bathroom and approached Quinn.

"You do what you have to do," said Briggs, "or did you forget that staying alive is the name of the game? It's the same game you're still playing, or maybe you forgot that too."

Quinn shook his head and replied. "I forgot nothing."

"Good," said Briggs. "That's good."

Quinn examined Briggs. He tried to see what he was carrying. The fact that he hadn't pulled a weapon yet indicated that he might not have one. It was in this way Briggs sought to attack Quinn using only his hands and feet. Nevertheless, Quinn opened his hand and spread his fingers—*ready*.

"I heard you got Suloco?" Briggs said to Quinn.

Quinn didn't expect this to be a question, but then Quinn also didn't know where Briggs had heard this or why he chose to mention it now. "*I did.*"

"Looks like you're taking your extrication seriously."

"More or less," Quinn said.

"Killing a Custodian is no joke, though," said Briggs. "Then again, you *are* a Custodian, or at least...you used to be."

"I still am," Quinn declared to the man who had come so far to kill him.

"Sure," said Briggs. "Right, but I gotta say, I was really impressed with what you did back at that club. You still haven't lost your touch, and given how much the game has changed, I gotta also say...it's, well...it's good to see your new outlook on life hasn't affected your skills. Didn't expect that either, to be honest."

"Glad you're impressed."

"I am," said Briggs. "Well, sort of. Not totally enthused about me being here, though. An airport is a shitty place to die."

"Doesn't have to be," Quinn said. "You could let me walk out that door and get on my plane. We could let bygones be bygones and just go our separate ways."

Briggs snickered at the request and stood with his hands pressed to his waist and he smirked as Quinn stood five feet in front of him. Still, he was assessing what could be a *possible* opponent.

"Ah, well, you know I can't do that," Briggs admitted. "You know I *won't* let you do that, Quinn, old boy."

"I thought maybe, just this once, you might want to be better."

"Nah, you know me," answered Briggs. His eyes rolled back and his lips pursed until they turned white. "I ain't built for better."

"Then make your move," Quinn said. "'Cause I got a plane to catch."

Briggs gradually slipped off his jacket and laughed. Quinn found it amusing that Briggs was willing to take off his coat before the fight. The gesture showed his lack of fear as well as his eagerness to get on with the hands, fists, and blood. Quinn unzipped the coat he stole from the boat and tossed it into one of the stalls.

"Nice armor," Briggs commented, noticing Quinn's Phalanx hidden beneath the jacket. "You're gonna need it."

"We'll see."

"Same old, Quinn," added Briggs. "Still think you're never out of your league, are ya?"

"Same old Briggs," Quinn rapidly replied. "Still

spends more time talkin' than he does workin'. You wanna bore me or do you want to fucking throw down while you still can?"

"Hope you don't plan to use any of those guns," Briggs said. "This here is a full-on fistfight, a test of strength and will. You respect that, yeah?"

"I plan to."

"Good."

Ending with the mutual nodding of heads, the two Custodians both accepted their fate and role in the forthcoming battle. They were broken down, with only their fists and their minds to guide them out of the approaching storm. Now, it just became a question of who was going to make the first move in the rain.

For Quinn, he handed the choice to Briggs.

And why not? He was the one who was going to lose.

Briggs started off the fight by throwing his coat at Quinn. A crappy attempt at a distraction, Quinn instantly saw the jacket flying toward him and he raised his arms to knock it away like it was nothing. Quinn didn't fall at all for Briggs's pitiful attempt to throw him off.

For a brief second, it did obscure Quinn's vision.

Struck by a swift kick with immense force, the Custodian felt like he'd been slugged with a battering ram.

"Ah!"

The Phalanx deflected most of Briggs's blow, but the impact done to Quinn's chest made it difficult for him to breathe. Quinn rolled back and pressed his hand against the tiles and stared at Briggs.

Now up, Quinn charged with his fists ready. Briggs was set too. "Come on, Quinn!"

Moving in, Quinn began with a series of leg sweeps. He spun and swept his right leg and then his left. He did this to try and disrupt Briggs's stance. He was aware of his opponent's size and so, Quinn leaned into his creativity.

As he delivered more sweeping kicks, he aimed for Briggs's shins. The hulking Custodian, however, squeaked by. Then, Quinn lifted his leg while Briggs shuffled. Quinn couldn't connect at all with his rival attacker.

In spite of this, what Quinn did next was more interesting. It was more enticing.

Quinn flipped and cartwheeled to complete a double-kick upside down. It was a common move in the Brazilian martial art known as Capoeira. This was not Quinn's main area of expertise but he was somewhat fluent in some of its basic techniques.

Quinn flipped his leg up and around and clipped Briggs just below his chin. Having grazed the fucker's fat jawbone, Quinn pushed Briggs back. The tall man waddled and Quinn was back on his feet, dishing out some new punches. He hooked, chopped, and jabbed, and the two men traded shots like two boys in a school yard.

Quinn's stance was Jeet Kune Do basic. For this fight, he sought to test his power and his strength. Briggs was a big guy, but then, Quinn was a big buy too. They continued to trade. Punching Briggs in the chest, Quinn ducked so he could pop Briggs's ribs.

"Ah!" Hard and fierce, Quinn entered into full-on *show-no-mercy* mode.

Quinn clobbered Briggs like a boxing champ defending a title.

Briggs wanted to deliver a similar jab. And, though Quinn could see it coming, he leaped and dodged the blow. Briggs's fist slipped past Quinn's chest. Out of the way, Quinn swiped hard and blocked again. He knocked Briggs's fist. Escaping. Snapping elbow, Quinn smacked Briggs's right cheek, moved back in, and stepped. From here, Quinn completed a step-in throw. Summoning the power from his hips, Quinn kept both arms locked out. He pushed as he moved hard into Briggs's space. Quinn knocked his opponent off balance and sent him into the bathroom sinks.

"Bah!" Now Briggs's balance was terrible.

Being a big guy, Quinn wasn't very surprised by this. What Briggs had in strength, he lacked in flexibility, in control. A brute, he was a fighter who relied mostly on power. Quinn was aware of this. In most cases, when combating opponents such as Briggs, they were the easiest to take down.

At least, they would be on any other occasion. This was not *any* other occasion.

Even one was too many. A strike of only partial accuracy still hurt much.

And Quinn was hurting.

"You little worm!" In an act of frustration, Briggs placed his hand on Quinn's head and squeezed.

Without the Corinthian, Quinn's skull was vulnerable. And Quinn never let someone hold his head with such an *ironclad* grip. Briggs tossed his fellow mercenary aside and Quinn was not knocked back hard enough to fall, thankfully.

Standing back, Quinn gawked.

Briggs, now by the sink, leered at Quinn with a shit-eating grin. Quinn was ready to take this big man down to the floor so he could grapple him like a Gracie. On the ground, an opponent like Briggs would be out of his element. Lost. Should Quinn get him where he wanted him to be, then he could roll. Quinn also wanted to put Briggs in a solid rear naked choke and then stab him in his fucking heart. Once he had Briggs in said choke, Quinn would break out his OTF. He'd stab Briggs under his left arm, puncturing his heart, and completing what would be a solid kill, no doubt. It was the same as wrestling a fucking boar and then gutting it with a Bowie.

What Quinn wanted to do was roast Briggs on an open fire, which he planned to do .

One step, then another, and then another, Quinn completed three wide footsteps directly into Briggs's space. Pushing his knee into Briggs's side, incrementally, Quinn dragged him closer.

This was the part of the fight where Quinn would usually go for the pin.

In Yoshinkan Aikido, an Ikkajo is the first-control pin. It happened when the opponent's arm was placed flat on the ground and secured within the attacker's hand. If Quinn could get a big guy like Briggs in said position, then he could then break him down afterward. Quinn would break Briggs the way he deserved to be broken.

Forcing Briggs's arm up and around, Quinn pressed as hard as he could. Now relying on the strength of his shoulders, Quinn was doing all he could to break Briggs's arm. Still not one hundred percent certain he didn't already, Quinn felt like he did. He felt this as soon as he touched it. Briggs delivered a solid Tyson cross into Quinn's jaw. Hands looped around Briggs's arm, it was impossible for Quinn to deflect, block, or avoid from here. He took the punch like a champ. Quinn felt like he'd been bashed by a baseball bat or, worse...a Japanese kanabō.

Briggs plowed into Quinn head-first like a bull.

"Nice try, Quinn. Nice fucking try."

Quinn raised his hand to strike but to no avail. He tried to do more locks and more pins, but they weren't enough. Knowing he could not fight back the way he wanted, Quinn was as shaken as he was cold. He returned to the fight with a push kick that nailed Briggs dead center. It knocked the big man down onto the slick tiles and, flipping backward, Quinn rose right away.

Briggs vehemently reentered the fight. Now in a feral state, he exploded into the altercation in a kickboxing versus kung fu show of action, a strange combination in Quinn's mind. Although, Quinn's was more Jeet Kune Do than kung fu.

Still, Briggs charged.

If locks weren't going to defeat this beast of a man, then Quinn understood there was only one other way to. When Briggs's leg shot out again, he smacked Quinn, who did his best to block. The kick forced Quinn's blocking arm to hit his side. Then, Briggs grabbed a handful of Quinn's hair, pulled the killer up, and punched him again. Quinn used his elbow as a shield and Briggs's knuckles connected with the vertex of the Custodian's bent arm. Bone not broken, thankfully, Quinn stayed loose and the throbs produced from such high levels didn't just remain in Quinn, they flourished throughout his whole body.

Punching Briggs high in the chest and then again near the groin, all rapid and succinct, Quinn delivered one after the other and did not stop once to distribute these blows. Suddenly, Quinn was back in his basement, standing in front of a post laced with rope and pounding away as his father screamed.

"Faster! Harder!"

Doing the same now, Quinn pounded Briggs. But it made no difference. He was hurting the leviathan but he was not breaking him, so Quinn was not owning. He was *not* winning.

"Ah-ha!"

Exhilarated by pain, Briggs laughed and absorbed all of Quinn's hits like he was getting a massage.

"I love it!" Briggs rejoiced. He struck Quinn's shoulder and wrapped up Quinn's neck and squeezed. Quinn was being held like he was about to receive a classic Choke Slam. Briggs pivoted. He pulled Quinn up like luggage and stomped to a row of stalls.

Shit.

The barrier to the first stall was down and off its hinges. The rest fell like dominos. Briggs struck the walls and roared with near uncontainable laughter because he was now bringing Quinn on a ride he would not forget. Together, the two Custodians had laid waste to the men's restroom at LaGuardia Airport. Quinn was trounced by the pieces. No matter what he did, he could not break free.

Strong as an ox, Briggs was tilling fields with Quinn's body acting like he was a fucking rake. Drawing to the end of the stalls, everything was left bludgeoned and destroyed.

"Ya!" Briggs finally let Quinn drop onto a heap of fallen doors and busted toilet seats.

Briggs chucked Quinn into the adjacent wall. Having shattered bowls and plastic dividers, there were so few instances whereby Quinn felt weightless, like a goddamn toy. Going up against an opponent like Briggs, Quinn was whipped into the mirror and shards of glass rained down onto his aching chest.

The fight produced a cacophony of sounds.

How no one heard what was happening eluded Quinn. This didn't amaze him as much as how he was going to get out of this mess.

"Can't win, Quinn. No matter what you do, you're just too damn small."

Briggs tried yet again to snatch Quinn's throat. Although wounded and slow, Quinn held his own. He cracked his neck and locked Briggs's arm in a straight arm pin. From here, Quinn regained some control. In the midst of spinning, the Custodian pounded Briggs back with a swift uppercut into his chin. He clattered the bone and Quinn could actually hear Briggs's teeth chattering. A sweet sensation, Quinn swung Briggs around into the sink, and at last, did what he thought he could not do.

He brought the big man down.

"Fuck you, Quinn!"

Tall man down, Briggs changed his tactics.

He retrieved one of the shards from the floor. Selecting the largest piece he could find, Quinn wielded a makeshift knife while Briggs himself was armed with a contemporary weapon. Executing a series of sloppy, haphazard cuts, Briggs sliced, but Quinn would be damned if someone was going to hold a blade with his hands being empty.

No fucking way.

Quinn's hand slid to his belt and he drew his OTF.

At long last, Quinn was gifted with the opportunity to use said knife. Holding it taut, Quinn jabbed. Like joined in a dance, both Custodians were engaged in a virile, surprisingly immersive knife fight to the death.

Quinn cut one way, Briggs another.

Both were aiming for the other's vital arteries before slipping back and reestablishing position. Quinn cut again and Briggs's hand moved down and then around. He was not the best knife handler, but Quinn reminded himself what Briggs had in his hand was not actually a knife. Nevertheless, Briggs was doing well. He was fairly competent with what he had in his hand, despite it not being much at all.

"Bring it, Quinn!"

Quinn made figure-eight motions before bringing the knife to his forehead. Briggs spun and tried to stab, but the extricated Custodian jerked. Then, with Quinn's hand free, he was taken off guard when he heard a shouting coming from the door.

"TSA! Open this door right now!"

Quinn looked at Briggs, who smirked. Both men were still holding knives.

"Do you want to answer or should I?" asked Briggs.

Quinn's answer was nothing more than a shaking head. He knew Briggs would do something terrible to these men as he had killed so many innocents already. Still, Quinn refused to see more people die because of him.

"Do it, Quinn."

Quinn lowered his OTF. For now, there was to be no more bloodshed.

"I said open up!"

Knives out—literally—Quinn and Briggs stood in front of a door bombarded with fists.

Standing by his *no-cop* rule, such was a hard and fast one for Quinn. Priest used to say: *you can kill almost anyone in this game, except a fucking a cop.* Nearly all Custodians adhered to the rule, all except for Briggs. This was why Priest hated him. Though no longer an *official* Custodian, Quinn insisted he stay true to this law.

Not here to kill cops, and no, Quinn was not about to start now.

Quinn clicked the OTF and returned the blade to the handle. Once this was done, he took a deep breath. Controlling all his adrenaline and stress, Quinn used all his concentration in order to return to calm.

He stepped back and placed his knife back onto his belt. Briggs let go of the glass shard/blade, and both he and Quinn were now totally unarmed.

"Nobody move!" shouted one officer. "Do you hear me?! Everybody stay where you fucking are!"

Briggs raised his hands and Quinn did the same. Quinn counted the heads of the men who had moved in. So far, he saw only four.

Just four.

"Show me your hands!"

The men had thick accents. They sounded like they were from Queens or maybe Brooklyn. Their hair was black as shoe polish and they smelled of cheap cologne. If they only knew who Quinn really was, they wouldn't have been so rough when handcuffing him.

"What the hell did you two assholes do to this place?"

Quinn looked at the decimated room.

All parts were either upturned, knocked down, or broken, there was nothing for him to say. No, Quinn just waited to get the hell out of the room so he could escape to a more public setting.

"Got out of hand," said Briggs. "I hope you have insurance."

Briggs said this as two more TSA officers secured his hands behind his back. Quinn observed the lecherous look displayed by his opponent. Neither shaken nor broken, the only reason Briggs surrendered was so he could thieve the cops bare.

Briggs eyed Quinn and the big Custodian looked dead ahead. With despondence and dislike, Quinn knew what Briggs was about to do.

"Goddamn," expressed one officer, "this guy's wrists are fucking huge."

"That they are," responded Briggs. Gleeful staring at Quinn, Briggs's wrists were yet to be cuffed.

"Come over and help me!" exclaimed the officer. "Jesus Christ."

Another officer came in to assist and Quinn bowed his head and looked away. He loathed the ruefulness that was Briggs's personality. The man was gearing up to make another bold move; a course of action not a single cop was prepared to face.

"Stop resisting!"

The force of Briggs's thrust provided an instant knock-out. The cop was down. Quinn focused on the floor. He didn't hurt cops but was too far to help.

All of these men in uniform were dead. They just didn't know it yet.

Briggs snagged the officer to his left. He gripped the cop's neck and pulled. With an effortless twist, Briggs snapped the cop's neck and cackled. During the second cop's execution, Briggs snatched the keys off his belt and flashed the access card. Bragging a little, Briggs had what Quinn did not.

"Freeze!" The cop pulled a gun and Quinn shut his eyes.

The last thing you wanted to do against someone like Briggs was draw a weapon now. Briggs smoked the cop with a clean cross and took back his weapon. For someone like Briggs, all of this was just too fucking easy. The other officers left Quinn to attack and the Custodian again found himself trapped in yet another helpless situation.

He continued to look away.

With only two cops left, both reached for their sidearms. Upon approach, Briggs pulled the trigger and delivered two clean shots to the officers' heads. Each one fell and Briggs laughed again. Quinn's hands were still behind his back, and as he shook his head, he liked none of this. When Quinn interlocked his fingers, he commenced with the removal of his handcuffs. He removed a pin—a steel one—and inserted it into the slit of the cuff. He jiggled until he heard a snap. The steel loosened. Quinn slipped his hand out. Briggs, though prepared to execute the former Custodian, Quinn was already preparing for his next attack.

Without cuffs, the first act of defense committed by Quinn was to hit the floor and roll.

Hearing a shot cracking inches above his head, Quinn activated the Corinthian and his eyes glowed a reddish hue. Only a feature of the helmet, it was also reminiscent of the aggression now burning inside the best of the best Custodian.

Armed with two OTFs, Quinn had transformed into a dagger master. Arms extended; Quinn curved the blade. Even if Briggs were to concentrate his gunshots on Quinn's center, he didn't care. In fact, Quinn's invitation was simple:

Go on. Do it, motherfucker.

Quinn lunged. He swiped, and Briggs—using his hand —deflected. The first three were prevented. They were also the three Quinn never intended as fatal. They were only a distraction.

"Ah!" Briggs unleashed a grunt of displeasure and steadied.

He hobbled like he was going to fall but soon after, Briggs recovered. He looked down at his chest. Across his torso was a perfect line one inch in diameter. It oozed a color that could not be mistaken for anything else. "Fuck you, Quinn." Briggs gazed at the cut across his not-so-clean chest.

Quinn waited for Briggs to go down. His cut was perfect. If Briggs didn't get immediate medical attention, he would be as dead as the cops he'd slain in cold blood. Head shaking, Briggs watched with a grimace. Pints of blood dripped from his head and to his chest. It was clear now his options were limited.

Waiting for the next move, Quinn inverted the blades and then he leaped. And Briggs—in a final act of sheer fucking will—knocked the Custodian right back down.

Quinn was not incapacitated, not in the least. In the seconds between severing and puncturing, Quinn was a hairstylist, clipping and chopping away at all the extra strands and doing whatever he could to shed the weight. A silly comparison, by the time Quinn was done with Briggs, the man was a Jackson Pollock painting. Covered from head to toe in clean cuts, Briggs fell to his knees in a dramatic show of defeat.

Finally, Quinn had earned the upper hand in this brutal fight that ended only in death.

Quinn had chosen to let Briggs die with dignity. He left him to rot in a bathroom filled with blood and debris and then marched down the terminal, back to a man who had walked literally through shit and simply couldn't take anymore.

He was out the door, bumping into random people as he stepped.

Quinn didn't want to be rude, but he was.

It was like he said from the very beginning. After all... he did have a plane to catch.

——————

"I'm sorry, but could you please repeat that?" Vice President Lament made this request while sitting in the West Wing of the infamous White House. Facing the window in the presidential lair, and with a phone pressed to his ear, it had been a full week since he'd spoken with SAC. And, although this newest division wasn't quite associated with SAC, it also wasn't disassociated with it either.

"How bad?" inquired Vice President Lament. "Well, like what? You mean like...on a scale from one to ten?" Lament waited for a moment and thought he would have something to understand by now. Instead, Lament heard nothing on the other line, nothing except for the grim sounds of inconvenient silence.

"A twelve, sir. I'd say...*at least a twelve.*"

The call ended after.

Lament offered thanks to the man on the other end of the phone. He was a CIA agent tasked with following the crime scene created by the Custodian gone rogue named Kyle Quinn. Lament, who contacted a station chief down in NYC, apparently, there was a brutal shooting that happened at a nightclub there. Many were killed, including ten NYPD officers. In addition to this story, there was also another one describing an attack at LaGuardia Airport. TSA officers were murdered during a vicious altercation that happened in one of the bathrooms.

All Lament wanted to know was the motive.

He demanded a line of consistency that indicated a pattern and desired anything that might let him know who was responsible. It was hardly a shooting or an act of brutality without purpose or reason. No, what Lament had here was an act of serious rebellion: one man's rage against the machine that was the United States of America.

Knowing this, Lament reached for his phone. He dialed a new number.

Halfway across the country now, Priest was a fucking nomad.

He drifted from place to place, scoping and dealing, talking and planning, and it was in this way he found things to report back to Lament and inform him who should be the target for the next *cleaning*. This was the way it was always done in the Custodian program. Now that it was falling apart, when Vice President Lament called...he damn well wanted a solid, comprehensible answer.

As he glanced at his communicator, not even the POTUS himself would know what was happening. Lament, rubbing his hands through his greasy hair, hoped the situation was contained. He hoped not a single credible source knew what was actually happening. And for him, this was the way it needed to stay, for now.

No more terminals to see, Quinn was out.

In fact, he was out for good.

Vacating the airport, it was only a matter of time before more police and more men in uniform came in to make arrests and ask questions. While they would only take Quinn into custody, he could not kill them like the rest of his pursuers. If Quinn was not in control of his freedom or his mission, then he might as well be as good as dead.

He hurried across the runway and searched for his jet. Quinn's plane was outfitted with a top-of-the-line security system installed by the same contractor who worked on his home. The entrance to the jet itself was accessible only by Quinn's fingerprint, and as a result, there was zero chance of anyone tampering with his prized possession.

Quinn shuffled up to his Cirrus Vision and, in the distance, heard the harsh shouting of sirens. Having stayed in New York for too long, Quinn's jet was parked exactly where he left it. The sky was black but seemed to be brightened only by the lights shining from the aircrafts that were sailing by infrequently.

Quinn checked his watch.

In full armor, for now, this felt somewhat normal. Quinn no longer felt like he was wearing body armor, but instead, felt like he was wearing ordinary clothing and Quinn liked this feeling.

He liked being normal if it was only in a slightly, partially acceptable kind of way.

Quinn pressed his thumb against a pad by the door. Then, he watched as a narrow staircase gracefully fell from inside. Quinn boarded. Once in, he hopped into the pilot's seat. Quinn examined the setting to check if everything was safe. So far as he could see, the jet was empty.

With six spare seats, the plane was high on fuel and ready to fly. Quinn remembered this was how he came to this state. He flew in his jet, dropped down, and arranged for the AMX to be there when he was. All of this was due to Ally and right now, Quinn missed her.

Right now, Quinn wished he was with her.

The extra space was occupied by chests filled with additional weapons and gear.

Quinn checked what he had. He lost a few weapons, but this didn't matter.

There was only one thing that did, and that was to take off before it was too late.

Quinn skimmed the panel and checked and re-checked his comms and switches. He performed an engine check, a fuel check, and then, finally, a security check.

Still no cause for concern.

In the pilot's chair, Quinn strapped himself in nice and tight. He touched his arms and felt the moisture absorbed into his armor. The Phalanx was crafted from impressive material: matrixes and Triweave fibers. Quinn was wet and then suddenly, he was dry. For a reason he couldn't determine, he was also far less smelly than before.

This was also strange.

Once everything was deemed safe and functional in the Cirrus Vision, Quinn started the engine as vibrations coursed through his steady hands and firmly planted feet. Uncertain if it was adrenaline or excitement or maybe both shaking him up a little, in under ten, Quinn would be wheels up and sky high. Quinn pushed back and the Vision rolled. During the jet's initial movements, nothing happened that irked Kyle Quinn. His hand stayed on the stick and he glanced at all the other planes flying by. Quinn drove the jet like a car.

Damn, he thought to himself. His AMX was still in New York!

"Later," Quinn said. He said this and then he said something else. "Ally."

Quinn pushed the throttle and waited for his turn to roll down the runway. He hoped ATC would give him the go ahead soon. Listening to the hissing static from his headset, Quinn glimpsed at the tower.

Two men were there and they were staring at Quinn and his jet. Their stares were hardened and cunning. Such heated gazes indicated to Quinn that they did in fact see him. Therefore, getting permission for takeoff became increasingly less likely.

No, Quinn was going nowhere.

"Private charter, this is LaGuardia Tower. You are currently not cleared for takeoff. Do you comply? Over." Quinn heard this voice through his radio while continuing to power the jet forward.

He moved to the nearest runway and did not care at all about the warning he just received. He was gone.

Sure to it, he was perfectly gone!

"Private charter, I repeat, this is LaGuardia Tower. I said you are currently not cleared for takeoff. Do you comply? Over."

"No," Quinn said to himself, without having any contact with the tower at all. "I do not fucking comply."

Now prepared to accelerate the runway and hit the skies, in the distance, Quinn was greeted by the tiresome yelping of a hundred police vehicles. Patrol cars on approach, Quinn knew right away he was done.

"Son of a..." Mouthing these words, without a second to spare, Quinn pushed.

Quinn's Cirrus was small, but damn was it fast. It was easily maneuverable due to its modest size which enabled Quinn to take off faster and to fly easier. And, while it was not *exactly* a weapon, it could be—in the right way—used as one.

Quinn thought this might be a situation that called for that kind of handling. Nevertheless, Quinn continued with his push.

"Private charter, I said this is LaGuardia Tower. You are currently not cleared for takeoff. If you do not comply, we will be forced to prevent your departure. Do you understand or do you still not comply?"

Quinn stopped listening because now...now, he was presented with a path needed to take off. With no other planes in sight, Quinn's Vision was like a sprinter ready to bolt at the sound of a gunshot. In no more than three seconds, he sped along the tarmac. In a merciless show of rebellion, Quinn was responding to the tower's warning. The Vision fired across the runway and Quinn's grip on his controls eased. Quinn's jet began to lift but starting its descent, the Custodian spotted something far more terrifying than police.

"No fucking way."

And there he was, Briggs, bleeding in his suit, and somehow...still breathing. In one last attempt to try and fulfill his duties, Briggs had somehow found his way back to Quinn.

"Fuck you, Quinn!" Hearing Briggs, Quinn glowered.

Watching his fellow Custodian lift his shotgun and point it at Quinn's aircraft, it was then Briggs began to unload. Shooting one round that managed to clip the jet's window, the hit caused a few sparks to flare at the nose.

Quinn flinched. He had his own weapons, but to choose to use any of them now, while his jet was in midflight was not a wise decision.

All Quinn could do now was keep going. All he could do was *fly*.

Briggs fired again. The next round pinged the same window while Quinn gave a gaze of peculiar intensity at the monstrosity of a man who was still somehow alive.

If he shot again, then...

Quinn heard more sirens and then he increased speed. Wheels up, the jet was just beginning to make its ascent.

Then, Briggs shot again.

"Fuck you, Quinn!" Briggs shouted a second time.

Quinn accelerated. He retracted his landing gear and at last, was finally in the air.

"Guh."

The fact Quinn was up now demonstrated the success of making his daring escape. It was something only referenced in the pages of pulp fiction novels and men's action adventures. Quinn looked at the police vehicles parked haphazardly along the tarmac. And, before he could finish what he started, Quinn had one last task to cross off the list.

Quinn barreled his jet straight at the tall man and ran Briggs down like he was in a snowplow. Doing this, Quinn basked in the glowing relief as his once solid grip over the controls began to desist. He was able to let loose and breathe easier now that he was up and gone and also alive. Quinn's eyes closed and he reflected on what his next step was going to be. Due to his extrication, wherever Quinn went, there would be another Custodian waiting for him.

In New York, Quinn already encountered two: Suloco and now Briggs.

How many others were in operation? Right now, Quinn was trying to remember the rest.

He wasn't in contact with many. If Quinn had to guess, there might be at least three more about to come knocking on his metaphorical front door. Yet, Quinn's priority was not on his fellow Custodians. No, his goal was —and always would be—Priest and KEYS.

Quinn sought the annihilation of both of these entities.

He had his next route mapped out and ready. Still on

the hunt for Priest, there was no sign of him in New York, unfortunately.

Nonetheless, Quinn could not stay in the city. So, he was now heading to a new city, and in this case, that city was Washington D.C.. When Quinn learned of Priest's paramilitary groups operating in various bases in different places across the country, from what Quinn could recall, there was only one possible base he was made aware of.

Quinn's ETA was set for three hours.

Now, D.C. was not that far from NYC, but Quinn would be damned if he was going to drive there. Always safer in the sky, and so high up, he was now looking down at the numerous cityscapes below. From twenty-thousand feet above, Quinn thought of a life beyond this wreckage and terror. It was the same life Ally had once mentioned. He tried to imagine a time whereby he could simply fly away and not have to think about whether he'd be shot down, killed, or hunted. He reflected on a time when he could return to a world where there were people in it who didn't want to see him dead. Quinn considered this to be only a blissful thought at best. Quinn's fingers tingled. The jet, for some reason, was drifting. It was not *off balance*. From what Quinn could determine, it was not flying straight.

Detecting a modest tilt—a lazy drift—Quinn seized the controls.

Sailing through an unblemished sky, there was nothing ahead that provided a challenge. Based on what Quinn could see and feel, the coast was clear. Even so, something was compromising the Vision's trajectory. Something was weighing it down and altering its balance. Quinn checked to see if any flaps were opened. Maybe there was a problem with the landing gear after he killed Briggs. Quinn would be surprised if there wasn't, actually.

Quinn inspected and then re-inspected but was left to no avail.

All was normal, all was—

Quinn felt a shudder and then a tumult course through his entire body.

Eyes exploding with shock, Quinn turned toward the window. Experiencing a drop near the wing, Quinn was now fixed on the source of this alteration. What was weighing down on the jet was nothing more than a sight that—if Quinn had not been present—he would have never believed.

The sight left even an experienced Custodian like himself awestruck because this...this was impossible!

But, as Quinn insisted to himself, impossible was nothing now.

For Custodians, everything was possible.

"You gotta be fucking..." When Quinn witnessed such an unconscionable sight, he blinked again and again. Unable to believe his eyes, what he saw was Briggs.

Still alive, he was now here: Briggs was right there...*on the fucking wing!*

"Quinn!" A belligerent roar sounded from Quinn's gaping mouth and actually penetrated the window.

Briggs was somehow connected to the wing because of something built inside his suit. This had to be the case. No normal man could hold on now. Quinn didn't know what that something was, but he didn't care. Although it was mind-blowing for someone to stay on a jet while in flight, one of Briggs's hands was on the wing while the one opposite wielded a Glock.

"I see you!"

From this distance, Briggs might even shoot Quinn. At this altitude, however, the wind would disrupt the bullet's trajectory. Even at point-blank range, there would still be interference. Yet, this wasn't a factor for someone such as

Briggs. He made it this far and was prepared to make it even further. Quinn played the most common trick in the flying handbook. He curled the Vision again and tried to force Briggs off the wing. Now Quinn was doing this as safely as he could, but the Cirrus was a solid aircraft and even still, it did not possess the same maneuvering capability as others.

It was ideal for transportation.

Quinn knew the risks. He was careful, but Briggs needed to get the fuck off.

Quinn continued to feel a solid tilt and the plane continued its downward shift. Still tight on the controls, Quinn fought longer and harder to get Briggs off the wing of his plane, but Quinn doubted himself the entire time he attempted to make this happen. All it would take was one slip for Quinn to lose control. One change and Briggs would have the shot he needed to peg Quinn square in the face.

Quinn, choosing to remain calm, breathed in and felt waves of air pushing through his lungs as he glanced out the window.

Suddenly, Quinn had an idea.

Briggs lined up again and this show was close, too close.

The Cirrus Vision stayed steady. Eyes shut, Quinn felt ready for the next part of his plan to take effect. Quinn was no daredevil, sky captain, or a fucking maverick. No, he was just a mercenary who also happened to be a pilot.

He was nothing more than that.

"I got you, Quinn!" yelled Briggs. Crawling across the wing, and magnificently still holding his gun, again Quinn couldn't help but shake his head.

How could someone be this strong?!

"Do you hear me, Quinn?! I got you; do you hear me?! I got you!"

Hand on the controls, Quinn looked at Briggs with a crooked eye.

"No," Quinn said, "what you got is...*one less hand*."

It was at that moment Quinn channeled his inner hotshot pilot/badass Maverick. He held the wheel and turned it far to one side. Now feeling the jet starting to turn again, it kept turning until it was completely inverted, until it was upside down!

"Ah!" Another scream inched its way out of Briggs and the huge man finally peeled off. Briggs detached from the private charter and then glided through the air. Quinn watched his enemy sailing across the sky, and the rival Custodian screamed as he fell from twenty-thousand feet.

Out of the game, Briggs was now crossed off Quinn's kill list.

Having executed another, Quinn steadied the craft and let out a long and exasperated exhale that scraped his throat and forced his tongue to curl. He had never used his jet to kill a man before. So, this marked Quinn's first initiation into actually using an aircraft as a weapon. This was not surprising, however. When Quinn removed his hands from the controls, he calmed himself by listening to the sound of his own breathing. With his adrenaline pumping profusely, Quinn ground his teeth while uttering the phrase, "This is still my aircraft." As if it would grant him more authority over it.

Contrarily, the more Quinn said this, the less power he acquired.

The Vision was once again not flying the way it should.

"Shit."

Quinn gasped at a blinking light. It would seem something else happened while Quinn was fighting Briggs. Some damage was sustained to the Cirrus's left engine. Not significant, it was enough, nonetheless. Sustaining this damage, Quinn would not make it to Washington. He could not keep flying it in the state it was in. Quinn couldn't risk losing this plane.

Always, this was Quinn's main exit strategy.

And, if he continued to push, he'd sustain even more damage. And this was a change Quinn could not afford. He adjusted his grip and lowered the Vision down further. With the nose dipping, Quinn began to approach the runway of Dulles Airport. He reached for his phone but remembered it was synced to his Corinthian mask/helmet. Making calls much easier, Quinn spoke clearly. "Call Ally."

The Corinthian dialed her number and Quinn waited for the comforting sound of Ally's voice. Quinn hated asking for help. But when he asked Ally for anything, it never made Quinn feel weak, incompetent, or for that matter...ill-prepared. In fact, it was the strangest thing. Quinn didn't just want her...he *needed* her.

"Ally, it's me. I have my location," Quinn spoke slowly. He wanted to appear as calm as his body would allow.

Yet, he wasn't that calm.

In fact, he was pretty fucking uncalm.

"I need you to meet me as soon as possible. I need you, babe. *Really badly.*"

CHAPTER 4
THE COMING OF THE RED KNIGHT

EVEN WITH A DAMAGED AIRCRAFT, QUINN successfully traveled from LaGuardia to Dulles.

Quinn hit the runway, but had little time to dawdle, think, or do anything other than move like he had a goddamn purpose. Having been asked to land in a private airfield, this was something that was provided to Quinn by Ally: another favor in her longlist of favors.

For now, this would keep Quinn under the radar, literally. "Affirmative."

Quinn maintained secrecy while speaking to Ally on a secured frequency. When Quinn brought the Vision to a steady landing, he found a space, and then looking across the runway, saw Ally as she raised her hand and waved.

Struck by déjà vu, Quinn remembered the first time they became more than just "colleagues."

This change occurred back in Louisiana, when Quinn was sent to eradicate the sinister child-abducting cult called the Brotherhood of Cyn. Today, Ally stood with her hair tied in a ponytail and Quinn recalled the past with absolute clarity. Back then, Ally was wearing a black jogger's outfit and looked so adorable Quinn wanted to squeeze her. After Quinn stepped off his jet now, he looked like a man who had just been to hell and back.

He was bent, broken, and bleeding.

"Hey," Quinn said as he stood in his Phalanx armor.

"Jesus. You look like you just staggered off Normandy, or you survived a goddamn bombing, or maybe it was both," Ally said. "I guess that makes sense, which is why you're wearing what you are now, huh?"

Ally, obviously referring to Quinn's new set of armor, his Phalanx, she couldn't take her eyes off it.

"And also carrying," Quinn specified, and he raised his hand and gestured to the weapons on his person. "Don't forget that."

"Right," Ally said. The two then began walking toward Ally's car. Quinn's AMX was not here...yet.

"See you couldn't get your hands on my baby." Quinn was referring to his ride.

"Not yet," Ally said. "But it's on its way, I assure you. Couldn't leave something like that out in the open, could I?"

"Thanks," Quinn said. "I appreciate it and everything else."

"It was going to be impounded obviously," Ally said, "but I did have someone in NYPD transfer it to the Bureau, and the Bureau was asked to fly it out for an inspection by us, CIA, so..."

"Inspection?" Quinn asked. "Inspection by who?"

"Who do you think?" Ally smiled and then she pointed at herself. "It should be here soon, like I said. What took you so long flying, by the way?

"I had a...*weight issue.*"

"Weight issue?"

"Yeah," Quinn said. "*Big* weight issue."

Quinn was despondent. His knees felt weak and his balance was almost disrupted.

"Nice armor. I take it that's new to you as well?" asked Ally.

"It is."

"It's nice."

"And functional," Quinn said. "Lost weapons too, not many though. Gonna need to restock before the next Custodian arrives."

"Well, we can have that arranged, I think," Ally said. "What is your next stop?"

"Re-arm," Quinn said. "And wait for more to come."

"More?" Ally said, again pretending like she didn't know.

"They're still coming for me, Ally. They're *all* coming for me."

"Right," Ally said. "But by now, I don't know if you heard, but it's all over the news, the attack that happened in NYC."

Quinn sighed. "Son of a bitch. Do they know it's—"

"You?" barked Ally. She interrupted Quinn to completely occupy their conversation. "Not yet, but..." Ally was solemn. Her eyes were sunken and her cheeks sucked back into her face.

"There will be others," Quinn said. "Wherever I go, they're going to come and find me, which is why I have to try and get to him...*while I still can*."

Quinn reached for the door handle and pulled. The car they shared was a Silver Acura. Compact and gleaming as if layered by a new coat of wax, the car looked spanking new despite not being so new. Quinn didn't imagine it was. He hadn't entered this vehicle yet. He would soon.

"How many?"

Quinn shrugged. "Don't know."

"Okay," Ally said, "but you did say something about weapons, about getting... *restocked*?"

Quinn nodded. "I did."

"Well, I can get you your new weapons," Ally said, "but first...I think we should have ourselves a little pow-wow, yes?"

"Agreed." Quinn opened the door of the Acura, but Ally hadn't moved as of yet.

She was paused for whatever reason and Quinn listened to the grumbles of her hard exhales. She was breathing deep and fast, but her body continued to stay still—frozen.

"Ally?"

Waiting for her to get in the car, her silence left a repugnant taste in Quinn's mouth.

Sad?

Conflicted?

Afraid?

All were the qualities a Custodian could give to someone like Ally. Now, Quinn was looking across the roof of the Acura, and was waiting for Ally to speak.

"Ally?" The second time Quinn called out to his love; Ally stopped. She stopped and raised her left leg and began to enter the vehicle before slamming the door behind her.

"What? Everything all right?" Ally's question was redundant.

When Quinn examined the woman he desired, he waited for Ally to turn. Blue to the point of melancholy, Ally always had something to say, but now she didn't say anything at all.

"I..." Hesitant to speak, the response troubled Quinn. And, when she did turn to face Quinn, she replied rather meekly. "I need to talk to you about something."

Quinn nodded and gave Ally his undivided attention. One hundred percent present, Quinn waited to hear what Ally had felt compelled to say. Suddenly, Ally's hand shifted to her stomach and rested there, just above her naval. "I'm—"

In the midst of disclosing to Quinn exactly what was bothering her, a screeching, harsh-sounding whistle echoed from all around; this as well as the crumpling of shattered glass intruded to ruin Quinn and Ally's moment. Quinn flinched as a clean shot pierced the windshield and he pulled Ally's head down while, at the same time, followed the trajectory of the single bullet. Nearly hitting the woman next to him, Quinn immediately went for his Triumph Glock

"Shit." All Quinn could see behind him were three cars. Uncertain if they were SUVs, RAVs, or Escalades, whoever had taken the shot, they were fucking solid. It was then abundantly clear to Quinn exactly what was happening to him and to Ally.

The hunters had returned—the arrival of another Custodian.

"Damn it."

Quinn and Ally sped away from the Vision jet. Ally drove despite being shot at and Quinn had no idea what was going to happen to his jet, but he was leaving it right there on the airfield after a new pack of hunters managed to track his location. With its built-in security and Ally's injuries, Quinn had made a clear choice of what he cared to protect. Aside from blowing the jet to smithereens, Quinn was willing to leave it where it was. The last thing he was thinking about now was his plane.

Ally...was hurt.

"Hold on," Quinn alerted.

The Acura soared down a two-lane road and Quinn watched Ally's hand wrap itself around the steering wheel. Doing her best to hold on but was leaning too far forward, it was so far Ally was practically hunching over the driver's seat.

"You okay? Goddamn it, speak to me!" Quinn yelled, hearing Ally's breath scraping against her throat. Not stable and possibly hit, she sat up, shaking.

"You hit?"

Quinn could feel Ally's doleful eyes watching him from behind a line of reserved tears. Hand up, she showed her palm to Quinn.

"No," Ally said, cheeks glazed with sweat. Ally's lip quivered and she fought to give Quinn his answer. What happened to her was because of him.

It was all because of Quinn!

"Shit." Quinn looked at Ally's palm, glazed beneath a layer of syrupy red.

"I'm...I'm okay."

"No," Quinn said, "you're not. We have to get you to a hospital. Where's the closest one?"

"You can't go to a hospital." Ally's face was a rictus of pain. "Too dangerous."

"What the hell are you talking about?! We're going to a hospital!"

"I can go," expressed Ally, her head oscillating. "But you...you can't."

"Well, I'm not letting you go alone."

"But..." Losing her words again, Quinn glared at Ally's wounded side and inspected the bloody region. The pancreas seemed the most likely place where the bullet might have entered. One to the belly is a sure-as-dead injury and there's only so much time before the person bleeds out. Quinn could not determine if this happened to Ally. What he did know was the hospital was the only place for her to get help.

It was also a place Quinn could not go.

"Just hold on," Quinn said. "It's going to be okay."

———

The one who shot the Acura was the latest Custodian to join the fight and his name was Onix. Letting the efficiency of the shot weigh on his cold-hearted-killer ego, the Russian mercenary needed time to assess what he did and what else needed to be done. Onix, who had been notified of Quinn's extrication the same as the other Custodians, was also provided of his location by the same man who hired him.

Based on the bodies left behind, Quinn was quite a difficult asset to acquire.

Right now, Onix was wielding a Cooey Model 600 and the sniper rifle, which was only an updated version of the Remington model, Onix did not fancy himself as much of a sharpshooter. And even so, he clipped the person in the passenger's seat—someone who was a friend of the one he had come to kill.

"Boss? You good." The man speaking to Onix was Grigor, Onix's right-hand man.

Being former Spetsnaz, Onix was born in Russia, where he served in the country's Special Forces. All of this had happened before he emigrated and before Onix had moved to America to *find better work*. When Grigor addressed him now, he did so while in the company of a brigade of other bad guys. All of them were here to fulfill the exact same goal:

They wanted to chop Quinn's head off his body and hold up his severed head like a trophy.

As Onix held his Cooey rifle, he watched the vehicle vanish into the cold, soon-to-be dreary evening.

"Is that him? Boss," asked Grigor. "Was that Quinn?"

Onix stood in a checkered suit. Being a boss in the Russian mob, Onix never went out in public unless he had a good reason to do so. In this case, the incentive was not only to answer this *custodial call*, his fight with Quinn was a personal one.

Before Onix became Onix, he was first only the son of two wealthy Russian aristocrats.

His father was an arms dealer, and so, his parents were not just rich, they were *super, disgustingly* rich. They didn't just own things, they had control over the lives of others, of people. As a result, Onix was the heir to this decadent lifestyle. Throughout this life, Onix witnessed both disturbing and disgusting acts committed by his parents. Raised to rejoice in the demise of others, his mother and father's social gatherings were christened with the torturing of their guests. Often this was done by publicly humiliating them or paying for others to beat them or, in rarer cases, eat them alive.

Indeed, Onix's parents actually ate people.

While only a boy at the time, Onix observed all of these occurrences as if they were daily rituals and common practices. Both his folks were status-obsessed, but as Onix grew, he developed entirely separate traits. Becoming a volatile specimen, in the end, no one was safe from his outbursts or his hatred.

And, as Onix enlisted in the Red Army, he tested well and performed very well.

Due to this, Onix was assessed at the highest level. He was in good condition and knew his way around a rifle and was also well versed in the Russian fighting styles of boxing and Sambo.

Tough as he was unforgiving, Onix's commanding officers saw much potential in the spoiled heir. They enjoyed seeing how far a cadet like himself was willing to go in order to be called the best.

Although Quinn was recruited to Delta, Onix had also served in an elite unit. During his enlistment, Onix participated in several kill missions. He executed and he rescued. He took and he defended, the same as Quinn did. A suitable soldier, Onix's time spent in the division was only a means to an end for the cretinous human being.

In the military, the two attributes Onix enjoyed most were the respect and the admiration he received for being a soldier. Enjoying being idolized, in Onix's mind, there was nothing greater than a soldier serving one of the most powerful nations on the planet. Onix heard stories about a Bratva outfit operating out of New York City. There, Onix sought to develop his own crew. As Onix moved into a country he wasn't fond of, he did this because he felt it would offer him new, better opportunities, or so he thought. Having crossed into America, there, Onix connected with a peculiar man who had only one name.

"Priest."

Based on the initial exchange, this person was aware of Onix's brutal and, frankly, grotesque reputation.

"I have been following you for quite some time. I have a proposition that I think will be of some interest to you."

"Interest...to *me?*" Onix waited before hearing Priest's voice again.

"Yes, Mr. Onixana, of interest...to you."

From there, Onix was welcomed into an enhanced branch of the American military.

In a sect known for employing assassins and other extractors, the division consisted of men who did everything well but did it entirely on their own. This Priest fellow, whoever he was, was someone giving Onix the chance to show off his skills and the opportunity he had come to America to find. He was, in fact, granting Onix an entire field to sprint down and all the Russian maniac had to do was say yes. All Onix had to do was agree to rebuild and to destroy. All he had to do was become the elite of the elite—a Custodian.

Onix liked the name.

He liked even more the duties and the expectations

that came with the new job. Onix knew enough to pinpoint how the title could be interpreted. Onix was able to do whatever he wanted so long as he left the scene spotless. They didn't care about methods or boundaries. Now as one of the more unconventional Custodians, Onix did establish some relationships with a few of the others. Some of them Onix didn't mind, but others he downright despised. But of all the Custodians whom Onix knew, there was one who bothered him more than the others. A tall man, tough and skilled, this man reminded Onix of the classic American military types he heard about while in Spetsnaz. This one was a Canadian, a good fighter, a crack shot, a really tough bastard and crazy son of a bitch. He was one known for being multi-faceted in his approach to the Custodial ways.

During a mission to eliminate this Italian gangster, Giovanni Tulva, who was the head of the Tulva crime family, Onix had a meeting with this new and dangerous Canadian killer.

Mr. Tulva was not quite a gangster. He was more someone who was sticking his nose where it didn't belong. Interfering with unions, he tried to make a play against a democratic governor, and by doing this, caused a chain reaction that would make things very difficult for the party in power.

And so, Priest ordered his Custodians to wipe out the entire Tulva organization.

For this execution, he called upon two Custodians to complete this job.

What Onix wanted was to parachute in with the best weapons money could buy and then *do his thing*. Later, after he was told how this would be a poorly executed plan, it was Quinn who took the liberty of offering such an opinion. "Your plan is a waste of time."

And, ever since that day when Kyle Quinn embarrassed Onix because of a truth he could not accept, animosity ensued between the two professionals. And, when both men met again, they eagerly awaited to see who was better.

There were countless tests and epic face-offs between Onix and Kyle Quinn, which did not all end in Quinn's favor.

"Is that *him?*"

Onix returned to the here and now and he was back to the deathmatch still approaching. He was back on the field where Quinn's plane had landed and was back to staring through the scope of his Cooey while his right-hand man stood next to him.

"Was that...Kyle Quinn?"

Onix grinned. The leader of the Bratva and former Russian Special Forces and newest Custodian stared at where the car used to be. "It was." Letting his gun go to his waist, Onix ejected one shell slip from the weapon. "Rally the men. Bring them all...*to me.*"

"Aye," said Grigor. The men deployed from their SUVs.

Outfitted in full tactical gear, these men were carrying automatics and loaded with body armor. Each one was tall, stocky, and oozing with a torrid, almost offensive masculinity.

"And the jet? What should we do about that? Just sitting there. We should take it."

Onix, head shaking, he gasped. He didn't buy into this whole notion of the jet being an innocuous mode of transportation. "Destroy it," Onix ordered.

Grigor moved his chin and signaled to the other men. He walked toward Quinn's Cirrus and he and the others circled the aerial vehicle. All of them pulled grenades from their belts and chucked them through the jet's windows. Sprinkling the inside of Quinn's plane, a cloud of blinding fire exploded in the Cirrus, and all that remained after was a plume of flame and a waft of flailing ashes.

Onix's smile penetrated the thick wall of smoke. Excited, he was looking forward to seeing Quinn die.

He was picturing it already and it was goddamn beautiful.

———

Now in the lobby of another hospital, the last place Quinn wanted to be was in a place like this.

Trapped in an ocean of bodies, he slipped into the congestion and could see the cameras and new people who eyed the Custodian as he entered. Being a man covered in blood, Quinn was also with his hurting partner.

Not a good look.

Right now, Quinn couldn't think of a worse situation, yet his survival came second to Ally's. Of the two of them, only one deserved to die.

"Help!" Quinn tended to Ally's wound as best he could. She shuffled alongside Quinn like a sick child clinging to her parent or guardian. "We need help!"

Two nurses sprinted through the hall and gallantly approached the frantic twosome.

"Okay, okay. What happened? What is it? Was this an accident?"

"Yes," Quinn lied. He knew what would happen if he told these nurses the truth. "Please, just get her to emergency as soon as possible, please."

"Yes. Okay. Come on. Let's go."

The nurses then took Ally away and Quinn made his way into a new hallway. Quinn wasn't used to seeing Ally so frail, so unable to stand. His heart bled for her but as Quinn stood by himself, he was busy with his own thoughts. The whole time, he continued to see Priest flashing through his burdening and incrementally painful subconscious mind, and Quinn, who tried to fight through these many intrusive and burdening feelings, swiped his hand across his stone-cold visage and cursed the man who almost killed the love of his life.

He thought about the sadistic fuck who was now pursuing him.

And, with a chance to take out his primary target, this rival Custodian chose to pop Quinn's passenger as well. There were few so monstrous, pitiless, and vindictive as this. Indeed, Quinn knew of such people. He had crossed paths with the worst of the worst many times before. The greatest scum in this world is nothing compared to the one who shot Ally.

But this round came from a professional. It came from only one man.

"Onix," Quinn said. "Fuck you."

———

Quinn didn't want to think about how many news outlets were in possession of his picture. Quinn knew how he looked. He also knew enough to establish some form of tradecraft to avoid being noticed. He placed his Phalanx armor into a gym bag before taking a trip to the bathroom. He covered the contents as best he could and inside this bag were Quinn's tonfa, his Triumph Master Glock, and his OTF.

Quinn then paced around for hours and thought about Ally's wound, about exactly where she had been shot. Relentlessly reviewing whether or not this area was significant, Quinn knew of all potential areas. Still, he did not have the time to properly assess the urgency but was at the same time unable to imagine a world without Ally. He refused to do this. Still pacing back and forth, at the end of the two-hour mark, the nurse came by. She told Quinn he could see Ally now.

"Thank you." Quinn didn't waste a second.

He hurried after her and couldn't remember asking the nurse for a room number.

He would find it on his own.

"Ally!" Quinn called out like a father in a maternity ward. He shouted Ally's name as a resounding voice echoed from behind an opened door. He was at last welcomed by a face he longed to see.

"In here."

Quinn burst into the room; his Vipers screeching the tiles as Quinn looked at Ally as she lay in a wrinkled, grimy bed. "There you are. Jesus. You're...you're..." The right words had managed to leave Quinn unexpectedly. He was frazzled and yet, all of this was very new to Ally. She chuckled after seeing such a formidable man so flummoxed.

"I'm okay."

"Right. You're..." Quinn struggled to speak while in Ally's presence. It was so heartbreaking Quinn had to sit down.

"What happened? How bad is it?" Quinn leaned in and waited for Ally to answer.

"Not terrible. Missed my pancreas, but only just barely. I've been stitched up all right, apparently. It's actually a miracle when you think about it."

"A miracle?" Quinn said this one word with skepticism clinging to every syllable.

Not a word he would use to describe what happened. In his mind, miracles didn't exist.

They never would.

"Yes," Ally answered, looking down. "It's a miracle."

"Right," said Quinn, bypassing the notion entirely.

"How are you doing?"

"Don't worry about me," Quinn replied. Rapidly shifting his head in either direction, he fought the question away like he didn't want to be anywhere near it, and he didn't. "I just want to know if you're going to be okay, and that's it."

"I am."

Air expelled from Quinn's nostrils as if there was a pump built directly into his face. "It's my fault. You being here. It's my fault."

"No," Ally said. "Don't say that."

"I have to," Quinn said, "because it's true."

"No, it isn't," Ally said. "I came here on my own because I wanted to help you. I understand. Priest...what's he's doing...it needs to be stopped."

"You just think I'm still part of your job," Quinn said, "but I'm not. This is my fight, my undoing, and I dragged you into it, and I shouldn't have. And now, look at you. You're in a hospital. You're hurt. You almost died, and none of this would have happened if I didn't make the choice I did."

"But the choice you made was the right one," Ally said. "I know you know that. You just can't hold onto it or believe in it because you're...you're...*broken*."

Quinn's heart skipped a beat. Never did he hear anyone referring to him as *broken* before. In the end, that was the perfect way to describe Kyle Quinn, who he was, his state of mind, and why he was the way that he was.

In the end, he *was* a broken man.

"None of this is your fault. Do you understand me?" Ally stated. "You wanted to stop Priest. You wanted to stop what he wants to do. You know the consequences of his actions better than anyone. You know what will happen to these children once they're born and what will happen to our country if we lean into the madness that

Priest is selling. Others might see us as a nation that likes to break things and fight, but I know better, and so do you."

Quinn, sliding his hand across Ally's bed, rubbed her dainty fingers. He felt the warmth of Ally's soft, gentle touch.

"Back in the car," Ally said, "I wanted to tell you something, but I didn't have the chance. I think I have it now," she said. "I still want to tell you, if you're willing to listen."

"Of course, I'm willing to listen," admitted Quinn.

Ally sounded shaky. It cracked when she said what she did before. Quinn couldn't tell if Ally was happy or upset. Perhaps she was both.

"Tell me. What is it?" Quinn watched Ally's eyes starting to shift. Touching her stomach again, moved her hand in concentric circles so he could soothe her body. Quinn gazed.

"It's about us," Ally said.

"Us?" Quinn replied.

"Yes."

"What about us?" Quinn asked.

Ally closed her eyes and stopped moving her hand. After doing this, a tingling sensation crawled up Quinn's back and over his shoulders. "I'm pregnant, Kyle. I'm pregnant, *and you're the father*."

Burdened by waves of this inexplicable and paralyzing revelation, it was astounding. Yet, so brutally cliché, Quinn was a character in a bloody sitcom as every muscle in his stunned body became encased in a frigidness he could not get rid of. Feeling like he had fallen into a deep pit, just because it was well suited to a dramatic storyline didn't mean Ally wasn't telling Quinn the truth, and fear was only the feeling that Quinn felt.

Amid all the strangeness and oddities, Quinn paid

close attention to Ally's expression, vastly different from his own. Although he was shocked to hear this news, when given the opportunity to actually think about it, Quinn began to feel a slight, comforting warmth. He envisioned what was now growing inside of Ally, a woman he adored, and who was now bearing a child—*Quinn's child*.

"The father?" Quinn didn't want to pose his response as a question but that's what he did.

No, all Quinn really intended to do was repeat back what was said. He did this so it would seem more lucid, maybe all the more real. Quinn had been with Ally many times before. Sometimes he used protection, sometimes he didn't. Quinn didn't because, subconsciously, he felt it made him feel closer to her.

And there was nothing closer than sex.

"Yes," Ally said. "I know what you're going to say. I know you don't—"

"No," Quinn interrupted.

Before Ally said more, Quinn glowered. He insisted on showing intensity because he refused to abandon his new role as a father and possibly as a husband. To turn his back on the pregnancy was to turn his back on Ally, and Quinn would die before he ever did this. For now, Quinn had a reason—a real reason—to stay alive and to fight.

"Don't," Quinn said to Ally. "Don't do that."

"What?"

"Don't tell me we can take care of this," Quinn said, "and that it doesn't have to be this way."

"But...you...me...we've never...and you've never..." Ally trembled.

She tried to find the right words, but in the end, she was just as nervous and as uncertain about the news as Quinn. He decided to take the reins of the situation and knew precisely what he was going to say. He knew what needed to be done.

"I know," Quinn said. "I know we never talked about this or about that, but there's a lot we didn't discuss. Still, we fought through it. We made the best of it, because... when a fight comes," Quinn said, "we don't run. We charge forward and we push on. We rise and we fight ... *together*."

"Together?" Ally said. Tears spilled out from beneath her stolid eyes.

Quinn could see she was on the verge of crying. While in Quinn's company, there was no need for either. Quinn wanted to cry too, if not more than Ally at this moment.

"Always."

"I..." Ally couldn't speak. Right now, Quinn's mind was a whirlwind of complicated and complex ideas that leveled his thought process to the point where everything was sundered and reduced to a storm of uncertainty built around unchartered territory. All he really wanted was to sit and think about his next move, and during his time of equanimity, Quinn felt compelled to get up and leave.

Still, he was a hunted man.

"I love you." Ally's hand stayed tight against Quinn's. He lifted her wrist up to his face and kissed it. It felt so warm and light, even Ally's hands felt perfect. Holding onto her, Quinn's focus shifted and now he thought about Onix, wherever he was, if he was close or on his way. Quinn considered how quickly another Custodian could track him and Ally. They could kill him and her without any warning whatsoever. Quinn rested Ally's hand on the mattress and gradually started to rise. His posture was tight, his body rigid, and his face burning with uncontrollable determination and power.

He was ready.

———

It didn't take long before Onix's men arrived at the hospital.

Ten minutes after exiting Ally's room, Quinn walked through the lobby with his head down and there...he saw two men waiting for him.

"Hiya, fellas." Quinn snatched the collar of the first Tango. Getting to work immediately, Quinn used the power of his back, and smashed the Tango with a furious headbutt. Quinn marched to the elevator. His footsteps dug into the surface. Spotting the two useless oafs who were too easy to locate, Quinn delivered a hook kick and then a spinning back one.

The man fell and Quinn punched his tiny balls.

No stops in between. Quinn connected one and then another and another. Then, Quinn withdrew his OTF and decided to have a little fun with this man's gonads.

Slipping in between the man's legs, Quinn cut the fool's testicles and jabbed him in the back. This man was sure as dead. Quinn couldn't stop himself from going further.

He kneed the man in the backside and put him down for good.

Quinn finished by slitting the man's throat and watched as he bled out onto the floor. Quinn went after the man he recently hit in the face. The man's nose continued to bleed and he waited there with his head down. The man raised both his fists but Quinn was having none of that. A one-on-one was not in the cards now. Quinn booted the man in his knee and rattled him almost until he was unconscious.

Quinn could have done worse, but he didn't.

Men down, Quinn shed himself of all inhibition or reverence.

Out of the hospital, he had only a limited amount of time to get going before the police arrived. Already short on time, Quinn held the man by his shoulders. He cursed at Quinn in Russian before he was thrown into a mound of garbage. Quinn pushed the blade deeper into the Russian fool's neck and the fool shrieked like a poltergeist while Quinn's body stayed turned.

Even he couldn't watch this next part.

"Where is he?" Quinn waited for the fool to speak.

How deep Quinn was willing to go with his knife had remained to be seen. But, if the Custodian pushed just a little deeper, inevitably, he would puncture the fool's brain and he would bleed out and die very painfully. To experience even a fraction more would leave him incapacitated. Quinn was now giving him his only opportunity for mercy.

Talk or die, there were no other options.

"Tell me...now." Quinn pushed the blade in. Blood gushed out of the man's ear like jelly. The man's voice went higher and the foolish Russian spewed words that, at last, finally had meaning.

"South building! Peterson Street! High rise!"

Quinn brought his face closer to the man's lips. He heard him loud and clear. Quinn made the man repeat himself because he wanted to extend his suffering just a little longer. He had come to this hospital to kill Quinn and to kill Ally, so why not take a few more seconds to make his pain more memorable? It was deserved.

"Thank you." Quinn stepped to the side. About to move, when Quinn altered his position, the Russian began to rise up. Quinn, though turned, was not done. He inverted his knife and jabbed to pierce the skull of the Russian who served Onix. Finished with his moment of savagery, Quinn left the knife inside the man's head. Quinn then kneed the man in the gut and dropped him into a messy heap of putrid garbage that would be his grave.

Now done, Quinn shuffled down the alley, left the hospital, and pursued the address.

Onix, penthouse, street, and place.

All Quinn needed now was a car, his AMX.

Where was it, and how would he get to it?

Only Ally knew the answer to those questions.

Quinn rushed back to Ally's room. Covered in blood and sweat, Quinn knew Ally would ask him what the hell happened. Quinn skipped over this topic entirely and looked at Ally with a firm, unbreakable stare.

"Where's my ride? I got somewhere I need to be."

Ally didn't hesitate. She gave Quinn what he asked for, smiled, and lifted her phone. "It's wherever you want it to be."

————

Ally called her contact, whoever they were, even Quinn didn't know. As if performing a magic trick, Quinn's AMX was two kilometers from the hospital.

Who arranged for it to be there, Quinn hadn't a clue.

Whoever they were, they were Quinn's guardian fucking angel.

Before Quinn could chase Onix, he needed new weapons and new gear. Back in the hospital, Ally handed Quinn a card with a new location. This was where Quinn could go to get a new batch of firearms, he could use against his Russian adversary. It was a secret space. Actually, the location was a storage locker not far from the hospital.

Again, who was this person, Quinn asked himself?

It wasn't Ally, so who else could it be?

Quinn was unable to determine the identity of this *other* person. Nevertheless, when Quinn arrived at the place Ally told him about, he was now standing in front of an old storage unit. Quinn hustled past a perimeter fence and checked the code written on the back of a card and punched the numbers into the brass padlock.

It was four-digits, easy to remember.

4, 4, 4, 4.

With a quick yank, the door opened and Quinn was presented with a new and glorious arrangement. He was now in a space with wall-to-wall weaponry that was a supermarket of weapons and firepower. Quinn examined the vast assortment of elite firearms. And it was then that Quinn embraced the truth surrounding what this place really was. The guns were either impounded or confiscated, but whatever the reason for them being here, Quinn liked what he saw.

In fact, he downright adored what he fucking saw.

What Quinn really wanted to do was replenish the guns he had lost.

The first model he came across was a SIG-Sauer MPX carbine. It was fitted with another Trijicon MRO sight, a +11 base pad, an adjustable stock, and a fat magazine. Quinn closed the door and recovered the rifle and was instantly enamored by the elite tool.

After the MPX, Quinn selected a Benelli M4, his favorite. He grabbed shells to go along with the magnificent shotgun. Granted, Quinn *did* like the Beretta, but he liked going back to the classic more. Quinn passed the other compartments carrying firearms and spotted an item that captured his interest. It was a colossal tool of epic proportion. What rested on a shelf was a fat grappling gun the size of a missile launcher. Quinn brushed the gun's hook and felt the cool touch of its tempered steel.

Quinn traced the cables back and saw they were attached to a gas tank, which felt oddly light.

Quinn examined the other tools in his vicinity and was now on the lookout for something that would match well with the projectile. Quinn was curious about how far it could send the hooks connected to it. In order to ride this beast of a tool, one requires more than just a cable and a target. Quinn grazed the cluster of plaited rope. He was now attempting to assess the textile strength of this long strip of metallic twine.

What he had now was a way *into* Onix's penthouse.

And it was one even a bad guy like him would not expect.

Quinn grabbed the gun and the cables and held them all together.

Quinn darted back to his AMX and tossed everything he had into its trunk. Quinn's Phalanx armor was still functioning well and his Corinthian was also in good shape, which was a decent break all things considered. With new weapons registered with his new tech, Quinn had all he needed for the next execution.

He took whatever he could fit into his hands and proceeded to the front seat of his muscle car.

"Nice assembly," said a man standing near Quinn's car. Quinn went for his sidearm. On guard at all times, before Quinn could draw his weapon, he stopped because the Custodian was relieved. The person before him was not an attacker or someone whom Quinn had expected.

No, the person standing in front of Quinn was more. This person was...*a friend*.

"Heinreich?"

Looking at the man who was his ally for most of his previous mission, Quinn couldn't help but smile and feel glad. The last time he saw Heinreich was back when he helped Ally at the other hospital. This was after Quinn first engaged with henchmen who belonged to the enemy organization known as KEYS. At the time, Heinreich was hurt too. He also knew things, but he said he'd be back, that he'd see Quinn again, and now here he was. Back.

Feeling grateful, Quinn was impressed to see Heinreich return. Evidently, Quinn had more than just Ally helping him. Contrary to what Quinn always thought, he did have friends. There were people out there who cared about him.

"You're..."

"*Here*?" said Heinreich. Nodding, Heinreich gave Quinn a sly grin. The Custodian's expression stayed the same.

"Yeah," Quinn said. "I thought you were injured."

"I was," replied Heinreich. He limped away from the AMX and Quinn assumed his leg was still on the mend. It might have remained fractured from the last encounter. "Got busted up pretty good, but thanks to your girl, I've been steadily getting back into shape."

"Right," Quinn said. "How did you—"

"Find you?" Heinreich answered. Already, he had guessed everything Quinn was going to say.

"Yeah." Quinn's smile grew. Still, he couldn't help but feel warm and fuzzy. He liked Heinreich. He liked him because he was a good man, a far better one than Quinn.

"Well, who do you think has been giving you the hook-up all this time?"

"You mean..."

"Yep," said Heinreich. "I'm Ally's contact. Alive and well, at least...*I am so far*."

"Right," Quinn said. Happy as he was, Quinn looked past Heinreich and at his AMX.

If not for Heinreich, this car wouldn't be here, but it was.

"See, now you got your vehicle back to you in one piece," said Heinreich. "You're welcome."

"Yeah," Quinn said. "Thank you for that."

"Yeah, well, figured it was the least I could do," said

Heinreich. "Just take good care of her. She's a beauty, as you know."

"I do know and I will."

"Also, in case you're wondering, this is going to be my last favor. Priest knows me, and well, since I'm on his shit list too, I'm...you know."

Quinn nodded. He did know. How many people were willing to risk their lives to help him was astounding. Heinreich was brave to do what he did. Therefore, Quinn had only one way of thanking him.

"I can't thank you enough for this," Quinn said. "So, I won't even try."

"Don't," said Heinreich. "Just do one thing for me, will you please."

"What?" said Quinn.

Quinn stepped away from his AMX and Heinreich backed up. The man continued to express his pleasantness with smiles and carefree laughter.

"Finish it," he said. "Finish *this*."

"I will."

"Good."

Quinn made his declaration while at the same time reviewed his plan for how he was to going to *beat* this rival Custodian Onix. Quinn's plan was to lure the bear with the trap. All of this was the embodying philosophy of nearly every single Custodian, so an experienced one like Onix would be aware of it.

Had to be.

But now that Quinn had Heinreich, the Custodian hadn't thought about how many people wanted to see this conflict come to an end. Quinn didn't think about how many other people wanted Priest dead. Thinking it was only him, now Quinn knew different. Now, he was called for a higher and better purpose.

"Good luck, Quinn," said Heinreich. "And Godspeed."

"Thanks," Quinn said. He nodded at Heinreich like he was still a soldier. To Quinn, he was and always would be. "See you down the road."

———

South building, Peterson Street.

This was all Quinn knew and all he wanted to know as he embarked on his quest to get even with Onix. Arrived at the location, Quinn looked up at the highest level of this one building and recalled what he was told regarding said location. Supposedly, Onix was held up in a luxury high-rise penthouse here. On the rooftop of the building that was across from Onix's, Quinn hid behind the air vent and gazed through his Corinthian visor to observe what he could through the penthouse's massive window.

Keeping the grappling canon stored in a fat leather bag, Quinn held the burly shaft of the colossal tool. What Quinn could recall about Onix's past wasn't substantial. He admired a fellow Custodian still. And, as Quinn hunkered, he didn't intend to keep himself hidden for long.

Onix was not viewable among the other men standing in his penthouse.

Those Quinn could see clearly were wearing suits and smoking cigarettes, and before Quinn initiated his plan of attack, he reflected on exactly what he wanted to do.

He lifted the grappling gun and retrieved the cables, harnesses, and hooks needed to connect to his Phalanx armor. When Quinn was all wrapped up and secured, he considered the weight of the approaching stunt as well as its outcome.

It was crazy. Absolutely crazy!

The cannon was pushed against Quinn's shoulder and it felt like it weighed a decent fifty pounds. Holding it with two hands, Quinn aimed at the roof, seized the handle and then, with a clear line of sight, had what he needed.

Now, he was ready...ready to take the shot.

Exhaling a deep and profound breath of air, Quinn's Corinthian automatically provided distance and time. Quinn aimed from the ledge. Firmly squeezing the weapon, the hook exploded from the mouth of this gargantuan tool as a solid burst of gas ejected shortly after.

Quinn could smell the fume before a howling whistle reverberated from the weapon. Its beast of a claw flailed from one building to the other and flew before landing on the roof. Quinn struck the target dead on and felt the instant brace from the talon of this mean-ass hook. Gripping the cable, Quinn pulled until it was taut, but he also managed to lift the clamp and connect it to the steel rope.

Now ready, Quinn raced to the ledge with his body braced. Adrenaline flourished throughout Quinn's stiff torso. A diver about to leap from the high dive, when he opened himself up like a starfish, he leaned into his panache. Quinn was fueled by his desire to propel along this rope, yet the hook straggled as it lagged. It was loose, yes, but as Quinn whipped from one side to the other, what he was now...was a fucking beast!

He raced as if he was precious cargo and the Corinthian mapped out his incoming targets.

Quinn squeezed.

Now fifteen feet from the window, a flashing icon blinked at the corner of Quinn's visor. The purpose of this was to emphasize the sheer danger of the stunt the Custodian was now performing. Protected by armor, the Phalanx could stop a bullet, so a window was nothing.

Unsure if any of the men saw Quinn propelling toward them, the wind brushed under the Custodian's arms and he was encased in a cocoon of searing heat.

A meteor headed toward the earth; Quinn read the notification:

Three seconds.

Two men pointed at Quinn's soaring body before he exploded in through the window and hit the ground hard and fast. Covered in glass, Quinn rolled between two-armed men and then kipped-up to his feet. Quinn didn't reach for any of his guns.

Alive as he, he was safe, and still very ready.

After hitting the penthouse, the Custodian added another skill to his list. Now he knew how to crash into a building. Powered by the appreciation of the daring act, Quinn felt encouraged by his own ability to defy death at what was an alarming rate of return. When Quinn charged at Grigor, Onix's right hand, he grabbed him by the wrist, and pushed with his elbow. Quinn then flipped Grigor down and knocked him into a set of round tables. Quinn push-kicked another Russian henchman into a sculpture poised on a platform. The man, who fell into the rubble, gasped as Quinn wasted no time moving to another.

Quinn was dependent on his hands and his feet to do most of the work.

Quinn didn't bring the Benelli here for no reason. He retrieved his shotgun and pushed the stock into his shoulder and felt enlivened by the sheer power of the weapon. Quinn cocked the gun and eyed Grigor. Wide awake, Quinn smoked him dead center and reloaded. Quinn aimed for the chest and legs, struck one Tango in the neck with the shotgun's barrel, and finished the fool off point blank.

The exit wound was juicy. Quinn spotted another and pulled three shells from his belt.

The room descended into chaos and Quinn was smackdown in a shitstorm of miscellaneous sounds, phrases, actions, successes and failures.

Most of the men who could ran.

Those who didn't were left to cower behind nearby posts and pillars. These measly attempts did little against the power of Quinn's Benelli. Shotguns blow things apart. Often, one's aim with this weapon doesn't matter. Point and shoot and anything that stands in your way is mincemeat. Quinn had executed ten so far by his count.

"Quinn!" Now slaying all the men who served Onix, the leader soon made his long-awaited appearance.

Standing in the doorway, Onix wore a checkered suit and looked much more refined than Briggs and Suloco did, like the gangsters featured in old movies. Onix's grin spread conspicuously to reveal his white teeth. He was happy to see another Custodian standing with him, for Quinn was a man who had literally fallen out of the sky.

"Onix," Quinn said the other Custodian's name with a heavy breath. Squeezing his Benelli, Quinn showed his stoic mug and continued to stay tough.

"You found me," said Onix. "You *fucking* found me."

"Well, it was you who found me first," Quinn replied.

He was referring to how Onix tracked him down. At the same time, it was also Onix who shot first. He hurt Quinn's woman, who was now in the hospital because of what Onix did.

"That I did, and now you're here to finish what you started," Onix said to Quinn.

"No," Quinn replied, "I just want to stop you. I know what you did or what you *tried* to do."

Onix smiled a vampire's grin. Amid the mess of the

slaughter, he was completely unaffected by what he'd done to Ally. "Not sure what you mean."

"Yeah, you do," Quinn insisted. "Yeah, you fucking do." He was now standing at the top of the steps that led down to the main level. While there, Onix looked unarmed, much to Quinn's chagrin.

"Oh, you mean...when I took the shot?" asked Onix. "Why'd I choose to shoot her instead of you?"

When Onix admitted his cold and disgusting truth, it hurt Quinn desperately—enraged him as he displayed an unrelenting glower.

"You could have hit me, but you chose not to," Quinn said. "You could have killed me, but you didn't. You didn't, because...*deep down*...you didn't want to."

"Is that what you think?" Onix chimed.

Quinn glared.

"That's what I know," he said. "You like to twist the knife, Onix. Always have. You hurt people because you can, and it's the entire reason why you and I never saw eye to eye. You don't care about the code or about me leaving the order, you just came to settle old scores and to see me suffer."

"Sounds like you got me all figured out," said Onix. "But then again, you brought this fight to me, didn't you? I mean, you slaughtered my men, and now you're here to do what, *take me down*? Not much else to your plan other than that, is there?"

"No," Quinn said, shaking his head. "No, that's about it."

Onix snorted. He was displeased, his former pleasant-ness was gone, and yet Quinn eyed Onix and felt the same storm of rage brewing from inside. Soon, their time for staring would be over.

Onix was right there, right where Quinn wanted him to be!

Benelli up, Quinn cut to the chase. He fired one round like he was a farmer protecting his herd. Onix did nothing to stop it. In the seconds before Quinn pulled the trigger, the Russian Custodian booted the ground and pulled up a shield!

"Goddamn." Quinn loathed admitting this to himself, but he was damn impressed.

The shield was confiscated from a statue that Quinn smoked during his epic crash. And, how Onix had acquired the improvised weapon was a fascinating counter-offensive. Not even Quinn had thought it was possible.

A shotgun shell dinged the brass and left a severe mark in the disc's center.

Quinn pumped his Benelli. Although still impressed, he wasn't going to back down now.

Onix could retreat to a fucking bunker and Quinn would still unload his shit until the base thrashed or worse, it was left as a heap of scrap metal. Quinn treated the shield like it was a moving target. For now, he was aiming primarily for Onix's legs. A somewhat antiquated strategy, Quinn sent three shots into Onix's makeshift shield, and then he cocked the gun and fired again.

Side-stepping, there was seven feet between the two Custodians.

Quinn stepped over the bodies while Onix hastened. Quinn quickened but stayed low to be clear of gunfire. It was Onix's goal to avoid being shot and Quinn was amazed at the amount of strength needed to wield this heavy makeshift object.

Pushing closer, Quinn reloaded.

Observing Onix's lunatic gaze, he peeked out from behind his shield. Taunting Quinn, the madman's expression was one of joy and delight.

"That all you got?"

Quinn dropped his Benelli. He had plenty more.

Stripped of his primary weapon, Quinn leaped. Delivering a solid kick, Quinn hammered Onix's shield and hit and clobbered it until it fell. Somehow, the Russian maniac kept hold of the disc. Onix countered with a roundhouse kick that moved Quinn back. He hit the pillar and his head bounced. Quinn felt instant whiplash after making contact with the tall post. Onix's taekwondo was damn impressive.

At the same time, however, Onix was arrogant. He was brash.

He cared more about flash than he did about strategy. And although this was good news for Quinn, it was also followed by some very bad news. Having crashed the window, Quinn's joints were agonizingly sore. His tendons ached and, while he could still fight, Quinn would be lying if he said he was at one hundred percent.

In fact, he was far from it.

Quinn swung Onix and hit the Russian twice. Quinn swiped, cut, and finished the combination with a flying knee. Quinn grabbed Onix's shoulder and threw his Custodian brother into a giant portrait. Hitting the wall, Onix cackled.

"Nice hit, Quinn. Care to continue?" Onix's lip bled and his front teeth appeared glazed with red.

Quinn could see Onix smiling and he wanted to puke. It also wanted to punch harder and faster, if that was even possible. Delivering a straight punch, Quinn's next strike was executed with equal parts fury and ferocity. Onix laughed hysterically. A sadomasochist, the more pain instilled, the higher his arousal and the deeper his pleasure center. Quinn, who added a spinning back kick no man could have sustained without experiencing a heightened degree of pain, it still wasn't enough. Onix's chuckles soon turned to high laughs before his hand reached for his revolver.

The moment Onix drew his gun, Quinn dove.

Gunshots spat, but all were inaccurate and unimpressive.

Quinn hid behind a dented pillar and then he peered at Onix who was wielding not one but two revolvers.

"What?" Onix said. "You're willing to fight only with your fists? The moment you see a gun, you scurry like the fucking rat that you are. Is that what you are, Quinn? Are you a fucking rat?"

Quinn looked at Onix's Smith & Wesson. Powerful as these guns were, Quinn loathed them. Revolvers had too much recoil and kickback. And any man who chose to wield two was nothing more than a poser. He was an idiot pretending to be a gunslinger.

Onix shot and another bullet clattered and more debris sprinkled Quinn's shoulder. Quinn flinched as he bit down on his lip.

"Come on, Quinn! Let's do this!" Onix delivered his playful invite for Quinn to come and join the fun. A crack shot, Onix rarely missed his target.

But could he miss?

Everyone does.

Could he do more with what he had?

Absolutely, thought Quinn.

He removed his Glock 34-Triumph Master from his thigh rig. The ammo count was registered on the Corinthian. In spite of Onix being the superior shooter, he was *not* the better Custodian. Quinn felt the full brace of the shot which hit only inches from his face. The Corinthian folded back over Quinn's forehead and he squeezed the Triumph nice and tight.

"Hit me!" yelled Onix. "Show me you still know your way around a piece!"

A piece was slang for gun.

"No fists, no feet, just powder and ash, bud! Bring it!" Quinn fired one round and aimed for Onix's face.

Ducking again, Quinn pushed. He and Onix were two kids in a snowball fight now.

Quinn loaded a fresh clip into his Triumph. Its flared magwells made reloading an effortless task as Quinn fell to his side and fired again as he rolled. Seeing Onix holding his revolver, the cocky Russian was fanning the Wesson like a hot-ass cowboy.

He fired at Quinn and did so while sprinting across the now obliterated penthouse. Shots crackling, Quinn reluctantly took cover. He still wanted a taste of this madness! Quinn soared and brought his second hand back. He clutched the handle and returned to holding his sidearm the way he originally intended. Quinn treated it like it was all a game as he dodged bullets, looked ahead and then...he spotted an opening in Onix's armor.

Unexpected, what Quinn found was a straight path to Onix's heart.

The armor carried with it a specific design flaw because what Quinn spotted was an open patch. Though small, the padding in Onix's chest was chipped and weak, and as Quinn's gun felt light and portable, he had but one shot left.

Quinn and Onix had challenged each other to see who was the better shot.

Quinn was solid, no doubt.

Whether he was better than Onix was a test not yet conducted.

Quinn wouldn't know until it was over. Only one would get to walk away. Taking a second, Quinn remembered words from the person who taught him how to shoot, someone who was *not* his father.

"*Patience,*" instructed Quinn's mother, back when he

was only ten-years-old. *"Patience and deep breaths. Don't rush. The right shot will present itself to you. Just takes time."*

Quinn recalled his mom's advice word for word. He could still hear her like she was standing next to him. Back then, Quinn did exactly as his mother told him to do. He breathed and he waited for the right time as well as the right shot to come. And, when he did decide to fire, he did so with both eyes closed. Soon after the shot was taken, the bullet struck Onix in his chest and penetrated the Russian's armored torso. Onix gasped and spun and was forced to an abrupt halt. For Quinn, it was as if Zeus hit Onix with a lightning bolt. He hit exactly where Quinn wanted to hit.

"Nice shot, Quinn. Very..."

Falling down, Quinn could have put Onix out of his misery right then but opted to let the sick man die slowly. This wasn't for Quinn; it was for Ally. She almost lost her own child, and that was worth what Onix was experiencing now. It was a pain he deserved because it was a pain earned.

"I'll be seeing you around, Quinn," said Onix. "You know I will."

Quinn was about to step into the elevator and thought he'd have more to say.

But in that moment, he had nothing, so all he did was raise his hand and bid Onix one final farewell, which he was owed despite being owed so little. "No," Quinn said. "You won't."

CHAPTER 5
NEVER THE PLAN

HOW MANY ARE DEAD?

Priest returned to the Capitol to meet with Vice President Lament.

Once there, this was the first question Priest was asked. After parking his black Range Rover, Priest was ordered not to meet at the White House but was instead asked to go straight to the Pentagon, and though he was pleased to meet there, Priest was granted near unlimited access when proceeding through the complex. Inside, he passed a stretch of rooms, floors, and pictures, and everyone he saw was suited and badged.

They were, but he wasn't.

No, the only badge Priest carried was the classic American flag pinned to his lapel.

Sauntering along, the Lock Smith never felt more American than he did when in this building. The White House is nice, but it's too regal, too esteemed. In Priest's mind, the Pentagon is the place where one feels like the Lord's work is really getting done.

Here's where you know your country is being protected and made safe.

"Excuse me, sir, this room is restricted access," said the man guarding the door. "I'm afraid I need to see some ID before I let you through."

The agent was tall—towering, in fact.

"My ID?" Priest said. "Is that what you want to see?"

"Yes, sir."

"My ID," Priest said and he refused to make eye contact with the nameless man standing in front of him. "My ID is," Priest went on, "get your hand out of my fucking face right now before I break it in two pieces and stick it where the sun don't shine."

"Excuse me?"

Priest stepped closer to this man. His footsteps were loud and abrupt. "You heard me." Priest stomped at the guard, who immediately reacted to the derogatory comment, but before anything significant could transpire, Lament's voice emerged from behind the door. "Enough! Let him in!"

"You heard him, Chief," Priest said, shooing the guard aside. "Let me in."

Priest entered the narrow room with filing cabinets, a podium, and some photos of current cabinet members. The lights were off and the only brightness in the space had come from the windows, yet the blinds were closed.

"Welcome." Howard Lament stood at the head of the table, across from Priest.

"Howard," Priest spoke with no emotion at all.

The room was occupied. It wasn't just Howard here, but those who worked alongside the President himself. Being men of great power, each one controlled a fraction of the country's resources and authority. They were owners, traders, players, and gatekeepers. All outranked Priest, yes, but that didn't make them more feared, resourceful, or capable. And so, Priest was not afraid. In fact, he felt irritated that he had to see them. He was the conductor of the group known as KEYS. He was not its proprietor or its benefactor, but he was, so far as these men knew, another name. He was just another member of the amalgamation of all the country's armed forces.

"What the hell is going on here, Priest? What kind of psychopath did you let slip through your fingers?" The question came from a man with curly hair and a fake tan. He was moonfaced and Botoxed to shit.

"Nothing I can't handle," Priest said to this idiot of a man. "As I said to you before, it's all under control."

"Under control?" snapped the man, who was called Peter Wade. Peter Wade was a billionaire and someone who worked with KEYS to settle finances and to acquire resources. "Is that what you call what's happening out there now?"

A response to his question, all Priest did was scowl. He hated billionaires. Priest was annoyed by men who thought of themselves as powerful when all they were was just rich. Rarely could they be considered the same. In Priest's world, they never were.

"You can understand why we're so insistent now, can't you?" asked Lament. "This situation you said you had under control, but it's continuing to spiral *out* of control, and we would all like to know—"

"Exactly what you plan on doing about it?" intruded Wade.

"I have contingencies in place that are being executed as we speak," Priest said.

"Your former employee is still turning out to be quite a problem," said Lament. "There was an attack again, this time, in a hotel not far from here. As you can see, he's getting closer."

"That he is," said Wade.

"Closer he can be," Priest said. He looked ahead and didn't care about what both Lament and Wade had to say regarding the situation. Priest also refused to call it a situation. "But up to full strength, not hurting or wounded, no...he is not." Priest was staring at Lament only now. What he said was meant for him and no one else. "Quinn will not be a concern for much longer. I already have another one on him as we speak. He should be encountering him within the next few hours."

"But these others, they aren't like him...are they?" asked Wade. "They're not products of the system—the compound like the one we're trying to integrate into all of the new subjects? Kyle Quinn was the first to have it tested on him, is that also correct?"

"It is," Priest said, "but it never was the sole contributor for why Quinn can do what he does. He's a gifted killer, indeed, but he's no more gifted than the others I have under my employ."

"And how many," asked Lament, "of these operatives do you currently have...under your employ?"

"One," Priest said, gazing with hawk-like focus at the vice president. Priest's eyes were sunken. A certain darkness lurked in his pupils so pervasive it nearly dominated his entire gaze.

"One!" exclaimed Wade. "That's it?!" Wade glared, and Priest's fingers curled into his palm and made a fist. He was furious in the presence of this asinine carnival barker.

"Yes, and that means there's more."

"And you said you have *one* on him now, yes?" asked Lament. He returned the room to its former calmness. "Right?"

"I do."

"And how long before they intercept him? Where is he going anyway?"

"It would seem that Quinn is trying to do two things simultaneously."

"How do you mean?" Lament asked Priest.

"Well, based on his movements," Priest replied, "he's coming after me, and then, as soon as another Custodian emerges, he stops and focuses only on them. He's delaying taking me out, but in doing so, he's—"

"*Hunting his hunters?*" Lament said, understanding the greater implications behind what was happening.

"So it would seem," Priest said.

"So...*your operative*," Lament gulped. "Who is he? How long will it be before they have this Kyle Quinn in custody?" Lament demanded further details. The brutal man in charge known as Priest snickered. He hated the question.

"The last I heard," Priest said, "my man was following Quinn out of the hotel after he slaughtered the last Custodian. He'll know he's being tailed, but even Quinn won't be prepared to face this next rogue. Trust me, we'll get 'em."

"And if he fails, like all the others have failed?" asked the vice president.

Priest shrugged. He sheltered his emotions and kept a solid poker face. Truly, he didn't know what was going to happen, if this next Custodian would not be as capable as he was promoting him to be.

But Priest was clear. This "other" Custodian would *not* fail.

"We'll cross that bridge when we come to it," Priest said. "For now, let the professionals do their jobs, yeah?"

"Are you talking about yourself there, Priest?" Lament asked, "or are you talking about *him*?"

The insult was subliminal. Priest and Lament glared during this final moment of meditation. When this improvised meeting was adjourned, the men sitting around returned to their daily tasks and duties. Priest walked out the door and left the occupied Pentagon. Although he was interested to see what happened next, the entire time he envisioned the face of Kyle Quinn. If Priest's next Custodian did fall, then there was only one option left.

It had been some time since Priest saw battle.

Fortunately for him, he was equipped with a secret weapon. It was inside his body—literally *flowing* through him as he spoke.

CHAPTER 6
BREAKING

RONIN IS THE CLASSIFICATION GIVEN TO SAMURAI who, during feudal Japan, were stripped of their masters and left without a leader, cause, purpose, or creed. Now, the last Custodian among Priest's ranks was the one Quinn feared most of all.

He was that. He was a Ronin.

And who was Ronin?

Like Quinn, he'd been trained since birth.

What did he desire?

What Quinn once had: Ronin fought to obtain the title of being the most reputable killer on the planet.

Where did he come from, who trained him, and where was he now?

From what Quinn could recall, there were many stories surrounding this man once known as Reddick Rada. Despite Quinn having no time for tall tales, the reason why he feared Ronin most was not because of narrative or parable. It was because Quinn knew himself. He knew how the two rogues' lives were intertwined by complex, familial expectations burdened by trauma, pain, suffering, and death. Being the son of a Yakuza gangster,

Boss Rada, Ronin began his training at the age of four. Undergoing programming designed to sculpt him into a deadly killer so he could be his father's greatest creation, he was prophesized to lead, to destroy, and to change... everything.

Ronin was going to grow up to be strong, and he was.

Very strong.

Ronin's father was Japanese, while his mother was as American as apple pie. As a result, Ronin grew to have a different build than the other children. And consequently, he lacked flexibility and speed. Finding that this required more effort and pain, Ronin had to break free from the confines of what most thought was impossible, yet in time, he had come to deliver on his desired abilities. He had grown into a winner.

Ronin shaped himself to be precisely as his father intended.

He trained in all the martial arts that were the pillars of Japanese fighting culture, lived among the Samurai, and was educated in the philosophy of Hagakure. Ronin took in all the principles and teachings glorified in the East and, later, moved west so he could learn their ways as well. Afterward, Ronin enrolled in the US Navy, where he passed BUDS training and was welcomed into the elite unit, the SEALs. Once enlisted, something changed in Ronin that would fulfill his destiny. It would secure his reputation as *the one without a master*.

Ronin hoped to obtain security and friendship in the military but his stoicism and skills garnered jealousy and resentment from the other candidates. His high performance, his origins, as well as his willingness to bypass orders, endangered some of his many missions.

All of this was done in favor of his advancement.

The other soldiers had come to loathe Ronin and wanted to make him pay for his insolent behavior. More than this, they wanted to make an example out of him. Ronin, who had extensive knowledge of firearms, his main weapon of choice were his two ninjato swords. Being the weapons of the ninja, the infamous hunters of the Samurai, these blades were shorter and more concealable than their bladed counterparts. They cut quickly and sliced much faster than most other swords.

The furious SEALs came for Ronin's head, then he was only Reddick. He was still a warrior who abandoned his masters. Not afraid or unprepared, the men were so concerned with attacking him that they were immune to what was about to transpire.

Ronin made the first move as two SEALs charged. Being a master evader, Ronin parried in a series of rapid movements. With his sword, he sliced and diced, severing heads and limbs and killing all the SEALs who chose to resist and fight.

If they wanted blood, then blood they would receive.

Using silence and camouflage, what Ronin expected was an ambush. To prepare, he ensured the room was totally dark, and thus, he made the shadows his weapons and his chief tool in the slaughter. It was not long before the massacre was discovered by the colonels in charge. Afterward, the commanding officers stormed the space and there, they encountered the most brutal sight any of them had ever seen.

Priest was informed of the one man who killed ten Navy SEALs by himself.

For obvious reasons, he was interested.

"You've been *excommunicated*," Priest said to Ronin at the time. The rogue killer was in solitary when Priest came to visit. "Now...you have no sergeant or master, but should you want to escape the mess you're in, you will follow me and I will give you a new purpose. I will give you...*your freedom*."

"And just who the hell are *you* to give such a gift?" asked Ronin. He was chained and was about to be executed for his crimes.

"I am Priest, and you...you will be my new altar boy. Welcome to the custodians...*Ronin*."

Ronin was the only other Custodian classified as a level 5. It was him and it was Quinn.

No one else.

When Quinn left the hotel after terminating Onix, he quickly spotted an approaching rider in black. Quinn knew who it was because it could only be one other Custodian.

Ronin was here, and tonight...he was here for Quinn.

———

Quinn should have turned his AMX around and charged at the lurking specter.

Instead, Quinn chose to race onto the nearest street and thought not of this approaching assassin, as he knew who they were, but of Ally. Quinn remembered where she was and how she was not safe.

So, when Quinn returned to the hospital, he sprinted to the elevator and hurried to Ally's floor.

He had not yet notified her. He had no time and Ronin was not far behind!

Quinn couldn't go anywhere without knowing Ally was safe. To make sure of this, Quinn dashed through the hallway, his footsteps fervent and sporadic. He didn't care how he looked or who noticed him. He shouted Ally's name like she was Quinn's lost child.

"Ally! Ally! Ally!"

Midway down the hall, Quinn passed by one of the nurses. As a voice called out to him, Quinn saw Ally standing there barefooted and with her shirt buttoned just above her breasts.

"Ally," Quinn said.

"What are you doing here?" While in the hospital, Ally was understandably not in the best shape she could be in. And yet, here she was, wide-eyed and amped, alert and ready.

"We have to get out of here," Quinn said. "Now."

"What?" asked Ally. "What do you mean?"

"Grab what you can," Quinn ordered. "We're leaving."

"Okay." Ally scavenged to grab what she could and assembled most of her things.

Quinn had been to so many hospitals since his extrication that they were now all beginning to merge as one agonizing, despondent setting.

"Ready," Ally said, holding a generic bag.

"Good," Quinn replied. "Let's move."

Quinn and Ally scurried to the elevator. Hand in hand, Quinn and Ally checked every corner, every narrow space, but few could escape Ronin.

"Where are we going?" Ally asked Quinn.

"I can't leave you out in the open," Quinn said. "I won't." The elevator chimed and opened its doors, and Quinn was suddenly in the garage where his AMX was parked. "I was a fool for thinking I could."

"You're not," admitted Ally. "You're not a..." Ally said this and then she stopped abruptly in the garage. Soon as she and Quinn entered the bituminous underground, twelve paces in front of both of them, stood the stoic rider in black.

"Who the hell is this?" Ally asked.

Quinn glared.

Haunting as a Lovecraftian specter, Ronin stood before Quinn, armed with two swords, the handles of which appeared just above his shoulders. Donning a sleek black trench coat, the jacket clung to Ronin's sculpted body. Slick hair, with flared nostrils, two individual scars appeared etched across Ronin's crooked eyebrows. Absent of expression, soon as Quinn saw Ronin, his hold on Ally's hand tightened as it secured.

Quinn said nothing.

He looked at the next Custodian he was about to do a tango with and grunted.

"Ronin."

"Ro...*who*?" Quinn let go of Ally's hand and walked toward his greatest rival.

"Quinn." Ronin's voice was in fact quite calming. He was an ASMR artist ready to tingle his viewers. Neither intimidating nor conventionally scary, he was a man who could just as easily read to children as much as he could murder them with his cold hands.

"Answering the...*call*?"

"*Owning* the call," Ronin clarified to Quinn.

"You know you don't want to do this," Quinn assured Ronin. The only weapon he possessed right now was his tonfa. The rest of Quinn's arsenal was stashed inside his AMX, which was not here.

Ally had arranged for the car and Heinreich had arranged for the arsenal.

Quinn was thankful of both as he approached Ronin.

"And you know as well as I do," replied Ronin, "that is *not* true."

Quinn watched Ronin remove his pistol. Instantly, he fired three succinct shots at Quinn. Although the gunshots were instant, Quinn dropped. Hand in hand, he and Ally blitzed around the corner and raced after the AMX. Seeing the car, Quinn raised his voice and ordered Ally to get in. Quinn slid over the hood like a cop in one of those lame nineties television series. Unlocking the vehicle, he hopped in. Ally sat too, yet was slow to move and only quickened once Quinn revved the AMX and rocketed from the parking space. Along the way, Quinn burned rubber and thick tendrils of white trailed as the car skidded across the pavement.

Quinn reached into the slot next to his seat and removed his Triumph.

The gun was loaded, yet the AMX wasn't Quinn's only weapon now. Gun in hand, he blasted Ronin, and the rogue "ninja" jumped as if he was a trained high jumper.

Soaring above the car, Ronin lithely glided across the AMX. He skittered up to its hood and Quinn moved like he was weightless as well.

Still, Ronin's speed was impressive.

He was so light and so fast that he appeared only as an absolute blur. Quinn stared through the windshield. Wielding his ninjato, Ronin stabbed both blades into the back of Quinn's car. He pushed the swords in and Ronin began to claw his way toward the front of the AMX.

Quinn fired three rounds.

Amid gunfire, Ronin snaked alongside the car without being hit once. Doing all of this as the vehicle stayed in motion, Quinn was utterly baffled as he asked himself how? How was Ronin holding on despite the torque and the whiplash?

Then, Quinn had a thought. *Ronin was the only one as good as himself.*

He blasted his own windshield in an attempt to knock Ronin off. And, though unsuccessful, the slick Custodian known as Ronin crawled against the AMX like a spider in a web. Using an adhesive unbeknownst to Quinn, Ronin gripped his blades and punctured the transport again. Jamming his weapons through the side of the AMX, Quinn watched as another sword penetrated his car.

"Hold on!" Quinn turned the AMX down a random corner and skidded in a near-perfect circle.

A gallant and risky move, it was what some might call a *Tokyo Drift*. Grinding the AMX's rear wheels in another occupied road, the stunt was something Quinn had done a hundred times in the past. Usually, he was alone when he did.

Now with Ally, and still holding on, Quinn looked toward the back window.

There, Quinn watched Ronin creep closer to Ally's seat.

Taking one hand off the wheel, he turned to shoot Ronin as he once did. The assassin had disappeared from Quinn's sight. It was only half his sight to begin with. Quinn kept one eye on the road and the other glimpsed at the back of the car. Against an opponent like Ronin, during their encounter, Quinn could not drive and execute the assassin at the same time.

It didn't take long before Ronin disappeared. Quinn estimated he was still near the car.

The question was...where?

Quinn had yet to discover, but he was anxious. As he approached the exit, he rolled along the narrow street in D.C. Quinn and Ally were going somewhere none of them knew.

"Do you see him?" Ally asked.

Quinn watched her as she turned to the only window left unshattered.

"No, but—"

Quinn was interrupted again. The last window was smashed when Ronin rammed his fist straight through it, now going for Ally. Quinn kept one foot pressed against the handle for leverage, and Ronin squeezed Ally's throat.

"Ally!" Quinn stretched his arm but struggled to get the right shot.

The AMX steadied. Quinn's focus was on the road. With the love of his life now in the clutches of this psycho killer, Quinn jerked to pull Ally's hand. Using her as a shield, Ronin was covered behind Ally. Her throat was locked in his grip, and looked on vigorously. Appearing flushed, the veins in her neck bulged, and even still, Ally was neither helpless nor beaten, and Quinn be damned if another man was going to put his filthy hands on her.

Ally wrapped her mitts around Ronin's wrist and clamped until her attacker's grip was broken. "Let me...go, you..." It was during Ally's moment of threat and fore-warning that Quinn fired another round that ended Ronin's ability to stay connected. He flew through the air when, from out of nowhere, a Ducati sped along the road.

It drove until it aligned with Ronin's falling body and the bike literally caught Ronin before hitting the pave-ment. Ronin, using his elite technology, summoned his motorcycle using a remote attached to his forearm, a stunt which impressed the hell out of Quinn. He had heard of these cycles before, the kind that could be driven via remote. When this bike moved, Ronin landed on its seat. With both ninjatos sheathed, he seized the handlebars and reentered the chase.

Now, he had his own ride!

Both vehicles exploded into the occupied D.C. street.

Quinn's AMX versus Ronin's Ducati, each moved into oncoming traffic, and the streets were brimming with random vehicles and gawking civilians. Being midday in fucking Washington, swarms of working D.C. folk flooded the road. Now in the first lane, Quinn's foot steadied over the brake.

He slowed.

"Well, this guy is..." Ally said. She was referring to Ronin. "*Interesting.*"

"He's Ronin," Quinn added.

Now among a sea of cars, the Custodian brought his hand to his lap. "Ally?" Quinn said.

"Yeah?"

"You know how to drive a stick?"

Ally's response was a sly smile. Quinn's strategy for how to take Ronin out was another stunt made up of incredible chutzpah and absolute fearlessness.

"Take the wheel." Quinn scooched to insert himself in through the broken window. Almost out of the AMX but still clung to the roof, he removed his body from the seat and headed to the spot above.

"Don't slow down," Quinn said to Ally as he gripped his gun.

What he was doing was not only risky and dangerous, it was downright insane. Given Quinn's most recent activities during his extrication, being crazy was what kept him alive. Quinn couldn't drive the car and battle Ronin at the same time. Fortunately for Quinn, Ally's unique set of skills, particularly her driving, proved useful, if not also essential.

She and Quinn were partners, after all.

Quinn nodded at Ally, who lifted her foot and slipped in to take control of the car.

Keeping one knee down, Quinn opened himself up as best he could. His hand stayed on the roof and Quinn used the other to wield his Triumph Master Glock. Aiming at Ronin as he rode, both Quinn and Ally were trapped in this turbulent setting. So much torque was generated by the AMX's engine that Quinn's only way to stabilize was through his strength and positioning.

Nothing else.

Quinn's hand shot up and he stared through his pistol's modified scope. Ronin glimpsed back and Quinn imagined he knew a number of maneuvers. Rather than moving in a complicated way, Ronin remained. His head stayed turned as he stopped to gaze at Quinn.

With an unbreakable stare, Ronin exuded a cunning, predatory confidence.

He grinned because now...now he was begging Quinn.

Take the shot, motherfucker. Take the fucking shot.

Gifted with a clear invitation from his arch-nemesis, it was an act of cordiality to Quinn, and something granted by men who adored rivalry and relished in the thrill of competition.

And, in the presence of this wanted sight, Quinn did as Ronin asked him to do.

He shot once, and though Quinn was a solid shot, the setting didn't help.

Among the unsteady rocking of steel lashing concrete, Ally was still a suitable driver.

She struggled with the clutch more than Quinn. In spite of this, Quinn still kept a suitable position and managed to cut the fabric of Ronin's trench coat. Quinn was now shooting a blanket hanging from a wire. The bullets smoked and dented, but none penetrated. And, because Ronin was still in motion, his jacket was wrinkled.

It was a cape! It was his shield!

Quinn continued to fire, but right now, he needed his other hand. Only a few rounds had grazed Ronin and so, Quinn holstered his Glock as he stood on the roof.

Dead ahead, Quinn could see Ronin's Ducati approaching.

Quinn observed the traffic and felt Ally swerve.

If the triangular nose of the AMX was faced in a head-on collision, the neighboring car would fly above and clip Quinn where he stood. While not inevitable or likely, Quinn was cautious. So long as Ronin was on his bike, he would remain clever, cunning, *adaptable*.

This was but another reason why Ronin was considered the best.

He was a warrior without a master. He served no cause other than his own and yet, it were these same principles that Quinn once applied to himself. Ronin would not stop riding his transport unless someone had the balls to knock him off it. Fortunately, Quinn had such balls. He had red hot big dick energy that propelled him in places most men would dare not go.

In this particular case, where Quinn wanted to go was after Ronin.

Leveling up, Quinn assessed distance and space. If he timed it well—just well enough—Quinn could hit Ronin and they could land on a nearby sidewalk. The only way for Quinn to beat Ronin was to once again take him off the bike. After that, it would be a straight fistfight. And a straight fistfight, Quinn could work with.

In fact, a fistfight was exactly what he wanted.

"Quinn!" Ally's voice was a nerve-pinching shriek. As long as Quinn could see Ronin on the bike, then he could also see where he might land.

"Ah!" Quinn jumped and hit Ronin with a clean bodycheck but did not push the bike over as intended.

No, Quinn overshot his stunt by a few feet.

He collided with the rear of the Ducati, and then—gripping the back of Ronin's jacket—Quinn held his rival's sleek coat and dragged Ronin sideways. Quinn squeezed but it was not his hand, his wrists, or any other part of his upper body that proved the most challenging. No, as Quinn was towed behind Ronin like a tractor-trailer, the soles of his Vipers ground the pavement more than the tires of his elite American Muscle vehicle. The road sawed the base of Quinn's boots and left plump streaks of rubber strewn across the tarmac.

Quinn couldn't hold no more and he glared at

Ronin. The rival Custodian peered back, fuming with a palpable, lip-quivering contempt. Ronin knew he was pulling something. Ronin looked to the man he wanted dead while Quinn gripped his enemy's jacket taut. Quinn's Vipers continued to grind until they were almost gone. Also, he could hear Ally screaming. She continued to maneuver Quinn's AMX as much as she could.

"Kyle!" Ally yelled.

Quinn fought to be more than just dead weight.

Watching Ronin curve his bike and alter the vehicle's trajectory, he was heading toward a stone balustrade. It was a robust location, a place epitomized to meet the glory that is Washington D.C. Swerving in and out of cars, Ronin was taking Quinn for one hell of a ride through the country's capital.

Soon as Ronin changed direction, Quinn heard the screeching tires of his own AMX.

On the Ducati, Quinn and Ronin advanced toward the park called Meridian Hill. While Quinn did manage to get some traction, Ronin's bike slowed as it entered the greenish section of the park. Now facing down several fleeing people, Quinn and Ronin neared the park's famous stone steps.

They collided with these stairs and rolled down one bumpy step at a time.

With Quinn still behind Ronin, he leaped, wrapped his hands around Ronin, and bear-hugged the deadly killer. Quinn squeezed.

"Argh," Ronin grunted to express displeasure.

He rolled over more steps and, on way to the balustrade, Quinn reached back around, and snagged the bike's handlebars. He pulled to the right and veered. Both Custodians were locked in a fight to see who would hold the reins of this high-octane machine.

Quinn yanked one way but then Ronin pulled another.

Engaged in a game of tug-of-war, both men bumped shoulders before Ronin hit the brakes. The squealing sound of tire grating stone echoed from behind the motorbike. The foul, rank smell of gasoline and smoke filled the air and the Ducati lambasted the railing and catapulted both men forward.

Now in midair, Quinn was mid-fall when he tried to seize at least one of his tonfa.

Wanting to be armed after he landed, but burdened by the drop, Quinn made sure to stay relaxed on the dive. Ronin, he imagined, would try and do the same. In spite of both falling off this one bike, each landed in different positions at different times, yet did fall in the same place.

Both Custodians tumbled until they fell into the thirteen-basin fountain of Meridian. Among streams of water spilling in multiple sections, Quinn and Ronin traded blows until they both came to the communal pool below. Both of these killers thrashed the third level before plunging into the sappy water. With one going over the other, both killers were like two foolish dogs duking it out for a bone.

Quinn was the first to land in the pool of tepid, filthy water.

The fountain contained mildew and sudsy pockets of putrid bacteria. Quinn swept his legs up and around and performed what is known in breakdancing as a *helicopter*. Quinn whipped his right foot and then his left and hooved Ronin square in the jaw. Quinn relied on his limited knowledge of capoeira. He was not an expert in this discipline, but it did feel good slugging Ronin using one of its illustrious and flashy moves. Nearly every blow Quinn delivered—so far as the Custodian was concerned—was a job well done. It was a solid step in the right direction.

And yet, after landing a successful and effective blow, it was not enough to stop him.

Quinn knew this. He returned to his basic stance, and for once, it was not one introduced by any martial art. At last, Quinn had come to craft his own starting position. Acquiring something that was a combination of aikido and Jeet Kune Do and karate, Quinn opened his hands, shifted his fingers, and performed the classic inviting gesture.

Quinn returned the favor to Ronin. Now he was the one inviting him into combat.

It was as Ronin did back when on the Ducati.

Ronin's style was different from Quinn's.

It did, nonetheless, consist of symmetry and balance.

Keeping his legs bent and his body square, Ronin lowered himself down and bent one arm. He slid this arm in front of his chest and straightened his hand so it was the same as Quinn's, who closed his eyes and meditated in the grim silence of D.C.'s most illustrious park.

There were no words as the two men stood toe-to-toe. And, with nothing done, each waited. Then, after the moment passed, both charged at precisely the same time. Quinn and Ronin trudged the water in the style of two kung fu masters heading for a showdown.

Quinn studied Ronin's position but couldn't make a clear decision about what he was going to do. The capable martial artist's reaction was instantaneous and Ronin did something not even Quinn expected.

As Quinn went in for the strike, Ronin's head dipped to dodge the blow. Quinn missed Ronin only by mere inches, but he never missed. Fast and cunning, like a panther, Ronin's fucking face was a serpent's. He was so rapid, so quick, that even the most impressive striker could not hit.

Quinn observed his hand as it slipped and passed Ronin's grim face.

The killer of all things pivoted—Ronin's back leg glided in a loop and snatched Quinn by the wrist. Ronin's defense was a mirror image of Quinn's.

With a firm rotation, Ronin bent and curled Quinn's wrist.

He flipped Quinn into the water using a kotegaeshi! It was a real and deadly kotegaeshi!

So far, Ronin's movements were solid. What was most threatening about aikido was its means of defensiveness. Quinn knew other martial arts just as well but was taken aback by all of this. As well, he was disturbed by the fact Ronin was familiar with a style that, until now, belonged mostly to Quinn.

"What?" Ronin said.

Quinn stared shockingly at him. He was on his feet, rubbing his wrist.

Ronin's kotegaeshi was fantastic!

An agonizing technique, Quinn preferred not to experience it again.

"You think you're the only one who knows the way, *your way?*" Ronin asked coyly.

"No," Quinn pretended as if Ronin's stunning knowledge didn't bother him. Truthfully, there was nothing that bothered Quinn more than another fighter who knew his ways. "But surprised you do."

"You weren't the only one taught the old arts," Ronin claimed

"You're good," Quinn replied. "But let's see how well you hold up."

"*Hmm.* Against what?" asked Ronin.

Quinn ogled Ronin as if he were an interrogator.

He knew aikido better than any other Custodian, Ronin included. Quinn knew its strengths, but then, also... he knew its weaknesses too. Every martial art has them. Regardless of how respected and appreciated the art is, always, there are compromises—areas whereby the art can be exposed or, at the very least, reduced to its least effective point.

In this case, Quinn charged, and pushed Ronin to the ground. Rolling through the water, again, Quinn understood the discrepancies in aikido. It was excellent for handling someone who was a powerful striker, yes, but what it lacked was a profound floor game. There were some techniques accessible should a fighter find themselves on the ground, but even so, aikido did not thrive in such an environment. Most practitioners are taught to avoid being swept or knocked to the floor, so the lack of exploration of this territory fits into its lack of understanding. When up against a certain opponent, the practitioner of this art could fall too. They would have to rely on other techniques not germane to their experiences. Quinn speared Ronin and the two rolled around, yet here Quinn had found a solid spot to exploit. Ronin was good at many things, but like so many fighters, grappling was his Achilles heel. There were few who actually knew how to fight on the ground, there were even fewer who knew how to fight well. Now, Quinn had Ronin. The two wrestled and exchanged blows and blocks with precision and power.

They slapped each other's fists like they were swatting fireflies and they used their knees and elbows to absorb whatever strikes came after. Quinn's focus was on one move only. He wanted the classic, unbeatable death blow and the sole solution to winning his fight against Ronin.

What Quinn sought was the infamous Rear Naked Choke.

If Quinn could get Ronin here, then he would squeeze his throat until his eyeballs popped out of his head. *Once you get that RNC, it's lights out for thee!*

Quinn assumed Ronin had some defense in place should he encounter said technique.

In the end, Quinn didn't care. Wrapping the rival assassin's slim arm, he initiated a killer choke. The entire time, Quinn felt like he was wrestling with one of those boyish mannequins made out of steel and plastic. Soon as Quinn's bicep began to clench around Ronin's tight neck, the rogue killer activated the deadly defense. Quinn's arm touched Ronin's throat and the Yakuza killer nudged his free hand from Quinn's choke.

Now stopping Quinn from getting the grip he needed, a crafty motherfucker, Ronin read the pin. He knew it was coming!

Quinn fought to be more furtive, at least as furtive as he could be under such ugly circumstances.

He fastened his feet around Ronin's shins and enveloped Ronin like an anaconda. Quinn didn't get the choke he wanted, but he'd be damned if he was simply going to let it stop. His window was narrowing and Quinn needed to apply the pressure here and now...while he still could.

Quinn engulfed Ronin and seized his wrist.

Like a noose tied around Ronin's body, Quinn's jaw locked as he gave it all he could.

Did Quinn have Ronin in a choke?

Yes!

Was it the best choke Quinn ever produced?

Not even close.

With no space to move, the issue was not the lock. Instead, it was the setting where it was being applied.

In almost two feet of water, Quinn was also on his back.

If he lost only an inch, he would dip below the surface and drown. So, head up, Quinn fought to stay keep himself above the disgusting water. During this fight, he continued to push and fight. Amid the strangling moment that was his to own, Ronin's body didn't go limp like it needed to. Flexing his body using so much needed energy, Quinn enfolded the man he was trying to make into a dummy.

Quinn's arm was only close to where it needed to be.

He squeezed and asphyxiated Ronin. Still, this did not lead to the conclusion he wanted.

Somehow, still going on, Ronin was still fucking breathing!

Ronin, gaining strength and traction from his feet while inside the water, Quinn had to ask: how?

How was this possible?

Quinn remembered who he was fighting. Ronin was no mere man.

He was like Quinn. Almost...

Flipping back, Ronin's shoulders jammed into Quinn's. Should Ronin get behind, then the Quinn might as well go home and cook himself a steak well done because that's exactly what he'd be!

Done.

Quinn heard the commotion from all civilians as he battled Ronin in the fountain of the very public park. Quinn was not back in the club facing Briggs or in the subway handing Suloco a piece of his own ass. No, Quinn was now fighting in an open space. He was also a wanted man. Quinn knew he would be greeted with more cops, more reinforcements.

And so, it was now or never to wrap this thing up.

Quinn did. He did know how he was going to end it.

Although he was unable to maintain his choke, and Ronin had found a way to flip out of it, even in water, Quinn could still kip-up. It was not his best kip, but Quinn was up straight away and then, reaching over his head, recovered his tonfa. Twirling the weapon into his forearms, Quinn pressed the button on the handle and ejected the blades. Now armed with a pair of swords, the length of Quinn's tonfa razors were twelve inches—more than long enough to sever a limb or decapitate a bastard.

Quinn wielded the tonfa in the natural position and glowered at Ronin.

His rival reached for his ninjato and glared. "Modifications?" Ronin said about the change Quinn had made to his signature weapon.

"A few," Quinn said.

"Why ruin a classic?" asked Ronin.

"Because," Quinn moved in, "sometimes an upgrade is not just better, it's...necessary."

Quinn spun one tonfa, circled it backward and then frontward, and attacked.

Quinn cut.

With the tonfa's blades still out, it was going to be a surprise for Ronin to see which end he would face. It could be the blunt side or the one sharp enough to cut his face clean off. Quinn delivered all his strikes in rapid succession and targeted vital sections of Ronin's body.

The ninja was now in the presence of someone who wielded these tools as if they were his own body. Now at the climax, Quinn and Ronin attacked and deflected. While mirroring each other's movements, Ally raced down the steps. Arriving at the scene, tangentially, Quinn was aware of her approach. He could see Ally had taken some time to arrive, but then she was also still healing from her recent surgery. She called out to Quinn, as she always did, yet the Custodian did not take his eyes off Ronin for a second.

Ally's change in tone was distracting for Quinn.

It coerced Quinn into making a slip while, immediately after, Ronin changed his position.

He rotated and switched his hands as well as the place of his sword.

"Kyle!" One call from Ally was all it took for Quinn to take his eyes off Ronin for only a second. Still, that was enough for Ronin to get his window. With a nimble stab, Ronin got him.

He got Quinn!

"Kyle!" Ally's voice went higher and she pulled a revolver.

But it was too late. Quinn was already stuck!

Stabbed by Ronin's blade, he jabbed Quinn in the shoulder, in the scapula above his chest. Without armor, Quinn was exposed and so...he was hurt, badly.

Ronin's sword penetrated Quinn and the ninja twisted the blade to further open the bleeding wound. Widening the agonizing cut, Quinn grimaced. Stabbed before, never was it with a blade this thick or done in such a painful, grueling section of the body.

Ronin hissed and grinned, with relish. "*Hehehe.*"

Ronin twisted the knife again and Quinn's wound gushed as more carmine drops spilled from the incision. The pain coursed through his entire body now, and Ronin pressed the ninjato in further. Quinn looked at the eerie face of a man who was savoring every moment. Ronin, who was a more reserved and careful sociopath, leered back at Quinn's glower.

Still writhing, Quinn wrapped his hand around the blade. He clamped down and pulled it slowly from his shoulder.

"*Uh...*" A sigh of relief squeaked out of Quinn, and Ronin gallantly waved his ninjato about. Preparing for the next cut, in the midst of this execution, Ronin halted after two shots were fired near the fountain. The gunfire forced the rogue warrior to backstep and then to backflip.

"To me! To me!" Ally shouted like a new cop on the

block. She continued to open fire. Ronin's hand pushed into the ground and he flipped again. Another sight that left Quinn utterly fascinated, he hated to admit it, but he was a little envious of his rival's abilities.

Ronin was dancing his way into combat and delivering some exceptional executions.

Fleeing the park, Ronin called his bike. From out of nowhere, the Ducati bolted toward its master. It looped, and Ronin jumped and landed smoothly on the seat. He skidded and burned out in a perfect circle as the Ducati spiraled. In a great show of skill, it aligned well with all of Ronin's previous gestures of panache and spectacle and then raced out of the park and was gone in a flash.

In this case, however, it was more like gone...in a cloud of smoke.

Ronin disappeared in the foul air. Ally shot and so, broke the cardinal rule in Law enforcement: don't draw your weapon when civilians are present. Also, you definitely don't shoot in a place as public as a fucking park. And yet, this didn't stop Ally from spitting a few rounds and fighting to try and hit the guy that had almost murdered Kyle Quinn.

Quinn could have done the same thing but Ally was here to protect the man she loved.

Whenever someone does this, then all the perceived rules and regulations fade away.

On his knees, blood spilled down Quinn's chest, from a wound that burned differently than the many other sustained throughout his life. It was long, deep, and open, and Quinn wanted nothing more than to disinfect and to stitch, but he was compromised by a lack of wherewithal as well as levels of sheer and utter shame.

Quinn and Ronin had dueled almost to death.

Both were so compatible they were in perfect sync and rhythm.

In spite of their shared gifts, Ronin did find a way to escape. And, it was Quinn who failed to kill his notoriously equaled Custodian. Every Custodian had a name and a number.

Quinn killed the others before they could kill him, but was not true when Quinn watched Ronin vacate the park. Inevitably, Ronin would return. He was tired, but he was not done or defeated. At this point, Quinn was the only one who was. He grimaced as he stood. Still holding his tonfa, Quinn flipped the weapon back to the slot where it belonged and listened to the racing slaps that were Ally's footsteps.

"Kyle, damn it. Jesus Christ. You're hurt."

Quinn continued to feel the blood pouring from his cut. Worse than hurt, his self-image was bruised, and it was bruised badly. Quinn respected Ronin both as a fighter and as an assassin and believed he should have—could have—done more.

In the end, Quinn should have won.

"Yeah, he cut me real good." Quinn's eyes clenched into a cluster of squiggly, broken lines. Ally scurried. She placed Quinn's arm over her head.

"I'll be stitching you up again." Ally guided Quinn away from the fountain and, consequently, away from the scene.

Quinn appreciated the help, but he didn't need it. He could walk, and he was more than willing to do this now. With Ally's assistance, Quinn was thinking about what to do now that Ronin had escaped.

"Déjà vu, huh?" Ally said.

"Yeah," Quinn said.

"Come on. We have to get you out of here. I can already hear sirens. The cops will be here soon."

"Yep. *Ah.*" Quinn's throat felt scratchy and worn. Fighting through the intermittent throbs that burped into his body as he moved, with one foot in front of the other, the AMX was parked on the street adjacent to Meridian Park. Catching sight of his car, Quinn hustled.

"Come on. We gotta go." Quinn hobbled up to the vehicle and motioned along the driver's side but was in no state to drive. He could barely lift his arm without feeling excruciating pain in that shoulder tendon that was cut and bleeding. He stopped and reached for his belt. The Phalanx armor had done an incredible job of keeping Quinn's possessions secured. He found his keys and tossed them to Ally.

"You drive." In the AMX, Quinn had never really sat in the passenger's seat.

"No hospital." Ally inserted the key and started the engine.

Quinn listened, head resting against the window. Even now, he could hear sirens. They were drawing closer and will soon become unavoidable and so, what Quinn and Ally needed to do was get the hell out of this place now, while they still could.

"Absolutely not," Quinn said.

"All right then. Now, the roads are gonna be tight," Ally said, "and this car isn't exactly inconspicuous."

Quinn cracked a smile. If he wasn't burning so badly, he would have chuckled at the comment.

"We have to go through some backstreets. I know a couple." Ally said this as she proceeded to another street.

This began her and Quinn's secretive departure using the roads mentioned. Quinn didn't doubt Ally's abilities. Having done well so far, when Ally said she was going to get something done, then she damn well got it done. True to Ally's word, she was in fact much truer than Quinn could ever hope to be.

"We can get out there, but how long it will be depends on where we're headed. Where are we going, Kyle?"

Head against the window, Quinn was a sick child. It was Louisiana all over again, and when Ally asked where they were going, Quinn could barely speak.

There was only one place left to go.

"Kyle?" Ally asked again.

Quinn thought of what he was going to say about where they were actually going to go. He had planned to return to this long-forgotten place one day. He just didn't expect the day to be here or now; to be for these reasons and under these circumstances...yet it was.

"Where are we going?" Eyes shut; Quinn dared not speak of this destination.

Yet he did anyway. He did because, deep in the bowels of Quinn's subconsciousness, he wanted to go back there. He *needed* to go back.

"Kyle, where are we going?"

After too long a pause, Quinn finally answered Ally with a gruff and deep voice.

"*Home.*"

CHAPTER 7
THE YOUNGEST

WHEN BRODER QUINN TRIED MURDERING HIS SON BY blowing up his trailer, a.k.a. the safehouse, the grizzled military man returned to the only place that would accept him, and that place was oddly...Saskatchewan, Canada.

In this province, Broder Quinn was just another American, but through channels arranged by Priest, Broder could return to Canada, where he would be free from arrest or prosecution, or so Priest had claimed. At the very least, Broder Quinn would be dealing with the bare minimum of his problems. If he stayed in the US, however, he would be dealing with more—a lot more. But finding his way back, Broder Quinn was not left unscathed or unmarked.

Nearly killing his own boy, Broder absconded through the back of Quinn's mobile home but did so with markings and many, *many* scars. Half of Broder's back was scorched while his flesh was left perforated by various indentations leaving his left eye transformed into an opaque sphere of pure white, much to Broder's chagrin. However, Broder refused to go through life with such in his head. In doing so, Broder opted to have his dead eye replaced by one crafted from black marble. Despite Broder's sight being somewhat limited now, he was on the lookout for something better. He hoped Priest would show this to him, but when he completed his narrow escape, Broder was smuggled out of America and sent to the place where he had once raised his family and it was the same place where Priest had, ironically, set up his new base of operations.

Broder once thought the KEYS headquarters would be positioned somewhere known.

But this was actually not true at all.

It was in the place no one in America would ever think to look.

"No one ever suspects fucking Canada. Peacekeeping nation and all that other bullshit. Might be the best place to set up our new shop. Expectant mothers go in, we keep 'em happy and comfortable, and then we inject them with our new magic sauce and wait to see what pops out on the other side."

As Priest articulated this to Broder, the former military instructor had a job, and it was to train whatever it was that *popped out* of these women and this was a responsibility he was prepared to fulfill. Broder understood the acronym.

KEYS stood for Kinetic Enhanced Youth Supplementation.

Sometimes Priest would say *program*, but Broder refused to call it this. For him, it didn't quite have the same ring and didn't acquire the same meaning either.

But then, what was this other organization, TAURUS?

As Priest outlined in *Phase Two* of his *Building Better Worlds* plan, the phrase stood for Tactical Augmented Universal Recon Usurper Sentinel (Unit). KEYS was the new organization but TAURUS would be the *new* Custodians, and today that newer Custodian was whatever type of soldier Priest could acquire that would serve him as he began to rebuild the next phase of his newest program.

So, the *new* location where the training would occur consisted of prototype TAURUS operators—the ready-to-go, upgraded army of...*Kyle Quinns*.

"They will take power from those who are too irresponsible to wield it." Saying this, the word *usurper* didn't have much meaning for Broder. Frankly, his vocabulary wasn't very extensive. Still, it was a word included in the vast index of military terminology and lingo. Broder was told everything he needed to know upon his escape. And so, after arriving in Saskatchewan, Broder was given asylum, so to speak, and was also given...*a job*.

In the earliest stages, Broder expected the location of TAURUS to be like the other military camps he'd visited in his past. But, when in Saskatchewan, Broder was driving across untilled plains in search of a top-secret location. He owned a map, which was granted to him by Priest, and as soon as Broder Quinn did arrive where he was sent, he found himself in an endless field of green.

Not at all as expected, Broder was sure to check the map again.

He tried to see if his longitude and latitude coordinates were correct. In the end, Broder Quinn was exactly where he was supposed to be. Conversely, there was nothing around him that indicated a base. No hoots of men marching in unison or the grinding axis of transporting military vehicles, the hollering of drill sergeants castigating their men for better movement and performance. No, Broder was in the middle of nowhere, and reaching for his phone, he dialed for Priest.

Broder Quinn was not one to ask for directions, but with his eyes up, a whistling echoed overhead. Broder glared at a suspicious cloud formation. Eerily, he inspected this new cluster of white puff. Through its rents, Broder could see something lingering in the haze, creeping along as a low-sounding grumble bellowed before a monotonous silhouette formed in the sky. Shaped as a perfect circle, this *thing* resembled a giant face in the sky. Once it penetrated the clouds, the fog parted. After, a great ship rose from inside the crisp blue and was brightened by the hidden sun.

"Well...I'll be..." The headquarters that Broder Quinn was searching for was not angular in appearance but was, in fact, a floating structure of epic proportions. Ululating like a wife in grief, the ship neared and Broder observed its design. Outlined with starlings and swathed in layers of crimped metal, Broder could swear he was staring at a ship constructed to resemble a bull.

Broder thought about the technology required to power this kind of machine. The engines and propulsion systems capable of keeping the massive vessel afloat were beyond anything comprehensible, but when it landed Broder was welcomed aboard to examine the ship's interior.

The Bull, as it was officially called, consisted of multiple sections, all accessible via a staircase.

Within the grand ship, every facet of its interior was prepped for the training of new and improved soldiers. Arranged in serried rows were mats and weapons racks loaded with automatics and semi-autos. There were barbells, weights, ropes, and body bags for those too weak to survive. These TAURUS men, called Steeds, were to be commanded the way a Matador commands his bulls.

Was this Priest's responsibility, or was it his? Was it Broder's?

Once Broder Quinn entered, he was told by Priest to prepare for the *new birth*.

Priest had foretold every chain of events happening so far, Broder didn't care to dispute any of them. Whatever he was in, the Bull hovered above the clouds as a floating city unseen or unknown to anyone.

"How long do I have to be in here?" asked Broder.

"Until I say otherwise," Priest said with a grin.

Broder nodded. Those were his orders. They were clear. He had spent almost six months inside the Bull. There was enough food and water to last for weeks, and there was no one else there except for him. Broder was assured he would have company soon. In the end, TAURUS was gearing up for something big. Broder knew there was only one other person who could spark that level of response.

"Stay there and await further instruction," Priest said to Broder. "I need to first find out where he's going."

"If you're looking for *him*," Broder declared, knowing well who Priest was looking for. "I might know a place he's likely to go to."

Broder knew Priest was referring only to his son, Kyle.

Granted, Broder Quinn had not seen Kyle Quinn since Louisiana. And it wasn't until Priest told Broder that Broder's other son, Cane, had died that he reconsidered the fate of his oldest boy. Broder mourned in his own time and in his own way, but as a man comprised of little feeling, there was still some left buried deep inside.

Although Broder was aware of what Kyle Quinn was up to, he was impressed by his decision to leave Priest. Quinn had purposefully put himself in an epic fight for his life. Of all the skilled mercenaries, none had taken down Broder's boy.

In the end, no one was a match for the Quinns.

Broder was told Kyle was on the run and Priest said he was tracking him. Priest also informed Broder Quinn that his son was heading north, away from D.C.

Why Quinn was heading in this direction, Priest didn't say.

He didn't say because, Broder suspected, he didn't know. In fact, no one knew, no one except for Broder.

"He's going to see...*her*."

"Who's her?" Priest barked.

Now Broder knew there was only one other person in Quinn's life who *might* be able to help him. It was the only one he could be driving toward now. She was also a person whom he knew...a long time ago.

"Her?" Broder said nothing to Priest. Everything else was best left unspoken.

Broder refused to tell Priest a goddamn thing.

So, Priest stood, grinning madly in the dark. With no explanation given, nothing said or unsaid, Broder considered Quinn's destination and a twinkle glinted in his solemn gaze.

In the Bull, Broder thought about what came next.

It was to be a family reunion, which was a pleasant thought worth some of Broder's time.

But was that where Quinn was now heading? Was that who he was going to see?

Broder knew the answer. Like it was an order, it was clear.

Absolutely.

———

So, where were Quinn and Ally going?

After the fight that happened in Meridian Park, both had escaped using the city's service roads and side streets and did their best to stay "under the radar." Ally avoided any and all traffic stops. But then nothing stood out more than Quinn's AMX. Ally asked if they could get back to Quinn's Cirrus Vision, yet Quinn refused. "No more jet. Stay in this car and just head north."

Proceeding out of state, Ally drove along the I-90

when she was done using side streets and service roads. Quinn slept most of the time. The bandage over his wound was thick. He was eventually awakened by the sound of the radio. It was from the music Ally selected while behind the wheel.

Quinn thought it was a great selection choice. The sound of Creedence blared from the speakers and sparked the Custodian's abrupt awakening.

"You okay?" Ally asked.

Quinn nodded. "I think so."

"How's your shoulder?"

"Burning," Quinn said.

Ally let out a crass chuckle. Concerned with Quinn's wound, she grazed the bandage. Quinn remembered his own scars. Some hurt worse than others.

"And yours?" Quinn said to Ally.

"Mine?" Ally replied.

Quinn glimpsed at Ally as she shrugged and blushed. Always light and carefree, even under these recent circumstances, Ally's slight operation happened only one day earlier. She neglected to complain about what was gestating inside her, the pain that a child brought to a woman's body. A miracle Ally didn't give birth right then and there, the doctor said, but then Quinn had no idea how far along she was. Later, Quinn gave his head a shake and then remembered how the something inside his woman was as precious as it was growing.

"I'm fine," Ally admitted.

"Fine?" Quinn asked, concerned.

"Yes. Completely fine."

"No, you most certainly are *not* fine," Quinn said to Ally.

Ally went quiet as if she'd been scolded. Quinn was beginning to sound more like her father than a possible husband. Still, this didn't matter. Quinn was right about Ally. She was many things, but fine she was not.

"Yeah, but for now, I'm functional, and I'm alive, right?" Ally said. "That's enough."

Quinn grinned. Ally's response was sensible, he supposed. Yes, she was functional, the same as Quinn, but was that enough? *Time would tell.*

"Are you?" asked Ally. "Are you okay?"

Quinn inspected his wound. Still bleeding and still hurting, fine was the key word in the conversation. It was also far from what Quinn was now. "I'm going to make it."

"We should stop, though," Ally said. "I need to get you stitched up better."

"Any stop we make will cut into our travel time and that will draw more attention to ourselves, put us more out in the open. Can't have that."

"We also can't have you bleeding out before we get to wherever it is we're going," Ally said. "You need to be at full strength," she said. "We need you wide awake and alert. I know some over-the-counter stuff that might help."

Quinn grinned.

He knew what Ally was referring to, painkillers such as Tylenol, opioids, or an anti-inflammatory. Some of this would help, but Quinn wasn't sure if this was his best decision to make right now. What they needed to do was stay on the move and prepare for what was ahead.

"Your call," Quinn said. "You're the driver."

"I am." Ally said this before she reached for Quinn's hand.

The moment his fingers touched Ally's, Quinn's pain dwindled, almost to the point of leveling off. At peace, for a time, Quinn returned to rest. Easy as he was, Quinn looked at all the passing cars and reflected on the forthcoming location. Where he was going and what was about to happen, he hadn't told Ally about. For now, Quinn wanted to do as suggested. He and Ally drove for ten hours because where they were heading was actually Michigan.

More specifically, where they were heading to was Bay City.

"And who do you know in Bay City?" Ally had asked this already. She did shortly after Quinn told her what exit to take. Quinn declined to answer. Right now, they were in Ohio, and there, they stopped at a nearby pharmacy.

Ally parked on a hidden street, and thankfully, the AMX wasn't as noticeable here as it was back in D.C. In this city, American Muscle cars garnered respect rather than suspicion among other car kin. But, as Ally parked where few could see, she told Quinn to wait.

She said she was going to grab some 'materials'. "You're going to be okay."

Quinn said nothing. He knew he would be.

"Just stay. I'll be back soon."

Quinn nodded.

Ally exited the car and Quinn leaned back in his seat while wearing the prototype mask that allowed him to hear the directions via an earpiece built inside. The address he entered into the controls was done through the device on his wrist. This was super convenient. Quinn hoped he had it right. The last time he was told where his *friend* was living happened five years ago. Quinn didn't exactly remember the circumstances of how the information was disclosed, but she was there. The drive from D.C. to Michigan was not the worst drive ever. If Quinn and Ally kept going and did not stop, then it was manageable. Quinn imagined Ronin was back with Priest now.

Maybe Priest was in D.C., *or maybe he wasn't?*

Maybe he was in the air or on the move.

Whatever Priest's location, there was nothing comprehensible about Quinn's past overlord. All Quinn knew was Priest was alive and the Custodians were now almost all dead. And where Quinn was going was to recruit one last member of his team.

This was the outcome he could only hope to occur.

Quinn had yet to share any of this with Ally. Maybe now was the time to do so.

Ally walked out of the pharmacy carrying a plastic bag filled with several items. Quinn could guess what they were based on their shapes. He noticed a box of bandages, some Gauze, a bottle of disinfectant, and a haphazard collection of needles and thread. Quinn, who had no idea how Ally retrieved all of this so quickly, then again, Quinn didn't visit a CVS very often.

He only went there as a last resort.

Oddly, Quinn did most of his shopping at Wal-Mart. They had everything a person needed, at least everything someone like Quinn would need. Quinn opened the door and stretched out his legs. Pushing his shoulder deep into the chair, Quinn felt the slick rubber digging into his tender muscles.

Burning yet at the same time irritating, Quinn felt more dispirited than he did tired.

No matter, as Ally approached, she rolled up Quinn's sleeve. He stored his Phalanx armor in the back along with his tonfa. Quinn held onto the rest of his weapons.

"How are you feeling?" Ally asked Quinn. She was kneeling next to him.

"Better," Quinn said. Lying through his teeth again, Quinn was not good. He was actually quite horrible. The burning persisted; Quinn fought the pain.

Ally pulled open the bag and removed more of these bandages. "How is it? Is it swelling?"

Quinn glanced at his throbbing stab wound. To answer Ally, it was excruciating. Quinn could move his arm, but not as much as he should be able to move it and would need to move it when the time came.

"You tell me."

"Here," Ally said. She wet the bandage with the disinfectant and waved her hand. "Let me have a look."

Quinn gave Ally his arm. So maternal and kind, this could easily be Ally treating her very own child. Quinn gazed at Ally as she continued to wet the bandage. Head up, she stared at Quinn's wound.

"I would tell you this is going to sting, but I know you already know that."

"Just get it over with," Quinn said.

Ally nodded. As she tended to the mercenary, Quinn was struck by déjà vu. Before he could say more, Ally spoke again. "Louisiana all over again, huh?"

Quinn was stone-faced as Ally dabbed his wound with the wet cloth.

"Whenever I'm hurting," he said, "I can always count on you to come and get me."

"Well, one of the perks of being with someone who worked in a trauma center unit," Ally said, "before they started working for the government."

She reached out and tapped Quinn's wound. Not feeling much, Quinn adapted to this new level of discomfort. And, given what he experienced, this wound was merely added to a collection of others. Quinn couldn't distinguish this or set it apart from others. All were the leftovers from the fights Quinn lived through and won.

"That's not the *only* perk," Quinn looked at Ally like she was a painting. He stored all her characteristics in the confines of his solid memory. Quinn was thankful for so much he didn't know where to begin.

"So this...*guy*...the one you fought in the park," Ally said, "I take it you...*know him?*"

Quinn nodded. "Well."

"Right," Ally said. She continued to clean Quinn's wound. "Who is he?"

"Exactly who you think he is," Quinn said. He exhaled so harshly that his breath carved away whatever phlegm lurked in his throat and removed whatever residue was still left there. "He's the last Custodian to come to kill me."

"Yeah, well," Ally answered, "that part I figured already. But, so far as I know, that's what, like the third guy who's come for you now?"

"Fourth, actually."

"Shit," Ally said, surprised to hear the number as she wet Quinn's bandage for a third time. Ally assisted Quinn while in the passenger's seat. His legs were spread and he leaned forward. He was being taken care of by the best person he knew. "And how many more do you think there'll be?"

Thinking this violent thought through, Quinn could only shrug when he stopped considering the last remaining Custodian. "Don't know. Like I said, though, I'm hoping Ronin was the last."

"Ronin?" Ally replied.

"Yeah," Quinn said.

"That's his name? The one in the park, on the motorcycle, his name is fucking Ronin?"

"Yes."

"Sounds fearsome," Ally added.

"You have no idea," Quinn added. Truly, Ally did have no idea.

Few knew what made Ronin so dangerous. But, as Quinn was prepared to explain, he turned and watched his future wife reach again into the same plastic bag. Pulling a needle and a thread, this next part Quinn hated most of all.

"And he what, works for Priest as well?" Ally asked.

"They all do," Quinn said.

"Right," Ally said.

"Each one packs a helluva punch too," Quinn said. "Killing a Custodian is damn dirty work."

"And you sure there aren't many left?"

"Of the order?" Quinn asked.

"There was an order?"

"There was."

"How many?"

"Don't know exactly," Quinn replied. "Started with six, I think..." It was at this point Ally's arm extended as she pinched the needle. Quinn's wound was now all cleaned, she poked his skin and began to sew. "Some died," Quinn said, "but of all the others, he was the worst."

"And by he," Ally said, "you mean this Ronin character we faced earlier?"

"Yeah," Quinn said, "and I wouldn't say he's much of a character."

"What would you say he is then?"

"As easy as I can put it," Quinn replied as he flinched as Ally threaded the needle. "*Lethal.*"

"Right," Ally replied. "Obviously."

Working her way through the wound, she stitched, and Quinn's arm remained steady. Quinn ignored the singes erupting after each weave, each pluck, each delicate pull. Ally laced the string in and out without taking a single break.

"We're fine now," she said. "I didn't see anyone following us, and I was checking, as I'm sure you were as well."

Quinn didn't admit whether he was or wasn't checking. From what he could recall, he did check to see if anyone was tailing him and Ally. But being gassed from the fight, Quinn hadn't checked as much as he should have or wanted to.

"Rather somewhat," Quinn answered. "But it won't matter. He'll find us either way. No matter where we go, he's going to come for us, which is why it's so important that we—" As Quinn was about to say more, the pain from his stitching stung his very nerves. Feeling a burning, this sting interrupted his thought process and Quinn stopped mid-sentence. He hoped Ally would not inquire further, but she did.

"Important, we do what, Kyle?" It was then Quinn felt he had to tell Ally the truth. He had the perfect window, and it was time for him to take it. Right now, Quinn wanted to say everything. And, if he could have, he would have. But immediately hit by crippling feelings of guilt, what Quinn was thinking, was unanimously linked to his greatest and most significant regret of all. It was something that weighed on him each and every day, so much so that it blackened a fraction of his soul.

"What, Kyle?"

Eyes closed; Quinn had suddenly gone numb. He glared. "Important we keep going."

"But you still haven't told me where it is we *are* going," admitted Ally.

Pulling the thread, Ally approached the end of Quinn's stitching, and he felt further pinches and more burning but, for some reason, it didn't hurt as much. Ally sealed Quinn's cuts in a process that was getting easier, albeit in the most uncomfortable ways.

"I think I have a right to know," Ally said.

Quinn's jaw locked. His gums swelled and he looked at the thread Ally yanked from his shoulder. What Ally said was absolutely true.

"You do," Quinn said, "but..."

Quinn was about to tell Ally exactly where they were going. He just didn't know how to phrase it or how to describe it, not in the right way.

"But what?"

"I don't know how to say this, but I guess...it's...it is *complicated*."

"I'm sure that it is." Ally was pulling on a string now—both figuratively and literally in Quinn's case. "Doesn't mean you keep things hidden from me, though," she said. "We don't have secrets, right?"

Ally, in effect, had ignited the first spark in her and Quinn's plans for a possibly long-term relationship. Before being informed of Ally's pregnancy, she and Quinn were only two people engaged in a casual, not-so-serious courtship, and this was something done because it was mutually beneficial to both parties. And yet, now that they were going to raise a child together, everything was about to go to a whole new level.

This level would consist of new things, the top of which was trust, and though Ally and Quinn did trust each other, with almost everything and more shared and disclosed, they hadn't mentioned trust, which is what they were doing now. "I know, it's just...it's better if you don't know, not right now."

"Better for me?" asked Ally, eyes up. Her once patient stare had now altered. She was now looking at Quinn with a narrow gaze.

It was a prelude to a glower done to fully express her displeasure. "Or better for you?"

Ally ceased stitching. She finished after she plucked the thread and cut it with her teeth. Now that the job was done, Quinn had a peek at this wound. What he saw were a series of interconnected threads looped around a dark line carved into his skin and tightened into a sloppy, broken smile, reminiscent to how Ally appeared now.

"All you need to know is...where we're going...will be good for us."

"*Us?*" Ally said, justifiably doubtful.

"Our situation has taken a bit of a turn," Quinn said. "As I'm sure you can already see." Quinn was referring to everything that's happened to him and to Ally. Calling it *a turn* was a nice way of classifying the impending doom that was their growing, constantly unfolding relationship, which was pushing them to the brink of their capacity for love and care. "And we need to convene with someone who understands."

"Understands? Understands *how?*" asked Ally.

Quinn rotated his arm to test the efficiency of Ally's repair. There was a tightness in his shoulder, but Quinn wanted to see if he could move it, and he could. The fix was good—solid, actually. "Understands me."

"Okay. Hard to imagine it getting worse than it already has," Ally said.

Quinn chose to remain silent again. Ally was right. It was difficult to imagine anything getting worse, but as Quinn had come to learn through his years of experience, no matter how bad things seem to be...always, they can get worse.

"But, if you say it's in our best interest," Ally said, "then I believe you."

"Do you trust me?" Quinn asked.

"No doubt I do," Ally said. "But, in this case, it's less about trust and more about how I have no choice but to trust you, see? I *have* to believe you. I *have* to trust you."

"Right."

"Looks like you're good to go here, though," Ally said, referring to the stitches. "Should be all right until we get to...wherever it is we're headed to." Ally clapped herself free of dust or dirt. White flakes covered most of her palm, but after a few light smacks, she was back in the front seat of Quinn's car where she didn't wait for him to come and join. No, she opted to start the car and gave Quinn her cold shoulder.

Quinn could detect a rancor so strong he could smell it.

Their first fight? *Nah.*

It was just the first time whereby Quinn was made aware of Ally's disapproval. And, although he didn't take this personally, Quinn did find himself questioning what he was about to do. Ally and Quinn were equally involved in the challenges that awaited them. They were each going to raise a child together so, the least Quinn could do was share the truth surrounding their heading.

While Quinn wanted to do this, in the end, he didn't know where to start or how to explain.

He didn't know what to say other than... "I'm sorry."

Into the car, their drive continued. The entire way, Quinn refused to sleep.

Throughout the duration across the country, Quinn did nothing other than stare at the woman next to him. He hoped to see her return to her flavorful, more sprightly self, but Quinn received none of it.

And so, they drove for six hours without saying a single word.

Quinn supposed they were in a *relationship.* They fought and nearly died together, and for him, that made two people more inseparable than a pregnancy.

———

Quinn didn't have much to say about Bay City, only that he could never see himself living there. It was a typical suburb, condensed and cubic, and in Quinn's opinion, the neighborhood they were in looked like a box of crayons strewn across Bristol board paper. With all of these structures popped up, each acquired its own unique shade and accent. Now Quinn, who preferred to live in more rural areas, drove through the suburb where he was struck by the smell of gasoline and burned rubber. At the same time Quinn also received a notification. His Corinthian informed Quinn they were almost at their destination and he hadn't told Ally any of these instructions. Apparently, she could also hear the instruction provided by Quinn's advanced tool .

"Hey," Ally said. "Healed?" asked Ally.

Quinn flexed his shoulder. "Surprisingly, yeah."

"Good."

"You?" he said. "How have you been doing with all the driving?"

"Well, I would have preferred if we switched every couple of miles," Ally said, "but given your condition, I'd say it's good we stayed where we were."

Quinn rotated his wrist and rolled out his shoulder.

He did feel better. He agreed with Ally because he shouldn't be driving. At the end of the short road, Quinn was assaulted by a cascade of bloody images, all of which he didn't think he would ever see again. All were buried deep in the perils of his subconsciousness, and Quinn knew what they were as well as what they were affiliated with.

A deep exhale shot from his nostrils, and yet, Quinn didn't intend to make his breathing sound so loud. Venting the way he was, a great release that was essential was expelled.

"You okay?"

Quinn examined the street. He remembered the last time he was here, when he was told to go and never come back. Despite this being years ago, Quinn believed he had changed a lot since. There was so much he wanted to offer, but not much he actually had to give.

"Fine."

"Are you sure?"

"Yes." Quinn looked out the window. He saw the

streets as they were and recalled when he'd seen them all before.

It was so long ago, but Quinn felt like it hadn't been as long.

For Quinn, this was due to the fact there are scenes from a person's past that don't appear unless they're drawn out. Such can happen either by circumstance or by choice. What drew them out for Quinn were the colors. Quinn observed things he would never see in Wyoming. Then again, Quinn didn't go here looking for places that weren't Wyoming. He never would.

"We should be coming up to it soon."

"Yeah?" Ally said.

"Yeah," Quinn said. "Very soon."

Driving the AMX, the car was a pencil moving in a straight line. Beyond the survey was a collection of modest-sized homes all leading to a clearing surrounded by a dense ravine. Guarded by trees with overgrown branches as well as a gathering of mossy bushes, when Quinn saw the house at the end, his heart beat hard.

The Corinthian's GPS allowed Quinn to hear the sound of his monotone voice. This was a small detail that Ally herself had shared with Quinn while on the drive. He could hear it now too. He just didn't care to mention it.

In all honesty, Quinn was more overwhelmed by the reveal that now lay ahead of him.

"I think this is it," Ally said. She proceeded along a straight road to a house at the end of the street.

It was so distant the house itself was practically on an island. The patches of grass entrenched the residence like a moat. A house so quaint, it could be in a motel's portrait or featured in a children's storybook. Unlike Quinn's own house, this one was squared and included three windows, a perched roof, a three-car garage, a veranda, and a rivulet peeking out from the end of the driveway. The whole scene sparkled and Quinn smelled the appetizing aroma of homemade cookies and scintillating mowed grass.

Right now, Quinn heard the rumbling of a lawnmower as Ally slowed to the long, deep driveway. Approaching two congruent posts, Quinn looked at a mailbox with the name of those who called this place home.

"The Murphys. Who the hell is named the damn Murphys?" Ally asked.

"Normal people," Quinn said.

The AMX proceeded and Quinn meditated. Pain and guilt and shame still lingered deep within the Custodian. Most of these emotions had deepened. This was the life Quinn wanted and one he could still have, someday.

"Nice house," Ally said.

Quinn concurred, but his response was a simple reply. "It's perfect."

Having marched to the front door, after taking in all aspects of the charming home, stepped up. Along the way, Quinn heard Ally exclaim. "Hey, you're not carrying anything. Do you know that?"

By carrying, Ally meant that Quinn didn't have any of his weapons on his person.

As of now, Quinn had his MPX carbine, his Benelli, his Triumph Glock, his OTF, and his tonfa; the many gifts from his old friend Toy Maker. In the end, Quinn had enough guns and ammo to take on an entire army. All of this stayed inside the vehicle. Still, Quinn would never go anywhere without something to defend himself.

In this instance, he didn't have anything on his person.

He made this clear to Ally as they stepped across the lawn toward the pretty porch.

"No," said Quinn curtly. "I have nothing."

Quinn raised his hand. A gasp of anxiousness expelled from beyond his puckered lips. He rang the doorbell and faced away from Ally. Quinn imagined she was reaching for her sidearm. Because he could not see her, Quinn predicted this only because she was like Quinn was now: on her toes and ready for anything. Despite the fact that Quinn didn't want Ally touching her gun at all, he didn't stop her.

Once the door was opened, Ally would finally see where she was and how a gun would not serve her well here. She and Quinn had come to a place of solitude and peace. In essence, they were not standing on the doorsteps to someone's house, but rather someone's home—*a real home*.

Quinn did his best to come across as cordial.

Nearly everyone who saw him was either frightened or suspicious. Given his state, as a man standing in military pants and a muscle top, it was a solid assumption. And with a noticeable wound on Quinn's shoulder, there was little he could do to avoid the impact he might have.

Quinn heard the locks turning as another exhale inched its way from his throat.

He straightened himself up and closed his eyes. He mumbled to himself to plead with whomever was coming to the door to please...*please don't scream*. Quinn wanted to hide the truth not because he didn't know what the truth was but because he didn't know how to explain it. In the end, the Custodian was conflicted. He was conflicted and he was ashamed. And, when the ornate door opened, beyond it stood a pretty little girl with rosy cheeks and a pink ribbon tied in her hair.

"Hello." The girl addressed Quinn with a squeaking voice. She was cute as she held the door with her little hand. This was something Quinn most certainly did not expect.

There was a familiarity to her face. It sent shivers down Quinn's arms and he didn't know why or how he was supposed to react. He was never around children, let

alone children as small as this one. He was more frightened staring into this girl's eyes than he was looking into
the barrel of a gun. "Hi."

"Who are you?" asked this innocent, precious girl.

"I'm..." Before Quinn could answer, another voice
peeped out of the hallway.

Quinn followed it as best he could.

Past the hardwood floors was a swirling staircase, and
there, a shadow of a person was just starting to form over
the clean surface. "Bethany, who is it, sweetheart?" The
one asking was a man. He entered from another room.

Whoever this man was, he was tall and dressed in
flannel and had a dishrag draped over his shoulder. He
was a man with thick brown hair and a surprisingly well-
groomed beard. He looked the part of a domesticated
house husband, with everything about him seeming so
dreadfully normal that Quinn was officially uncomfortable and anxious being with him, in this kind of setting.

"Uh, may I help you?" The man was speaking to
Quinn, but Ally had come to the door.

Wanting to make her presence known, Quinn was
now failing at being friendly or normal. Ally felt that
standing closer might help. Truthfully, her being here
didn't help as much as Quinn had hoped. In the end,
Quinn was petrified—frozen. "I, um, I'm here to see—"

"Will, I heard the doorbell ring, who's there, sweetheart?" asked someone else. "It better not be one of those
damn solicitors," this other person snapped. "You know
we don't answer if they come by."

Of all the voices heard, this one sundered Quinn
completely. It was the one he'd been waiting to hear since
he arrived. Ears twitching, eyebrows curving from tension,
his palms were clammy as his heart beat faster. Trained to
never feel fear and to fight anxiety always, even Quinn
could not stop this from taking him.

No, he never felt more afraid than he did right now.

"William?" the other voice returned. This one was female. "I said..." And before this woman could say more, Quinn looked past the man and saw who he was here to find.

In a wheelchair was a pretty blonde woman six years younger than Quinn. In a cashmere sweater, and with sparkling olive skin, Quinn's heart sank deeper as he fought to catch his breath. He completely failed to do so. When the man who was Will and the child who was Bethany both stepped aside, this woman in the wheelchair rolled in.

"Kayla, do you know who this man is?" Will asked.

Kayla.

Quinn opened and closed his hands. He fought the terror currently taking its hold on him, but such was a strenuous task to prevent.

"Kayla?" Hearing the man again, Quinn's head tilted. He was incapable of looking at this woman in any capacity.

"Bethany," The woman in the chair said. Kayla reached out. She took the young girl by the hand. "Come to Mommy."

Quinn read the warning loud and clear. He was, after all, a stranger here in this house. Quinn felt Ally standing next to him. Being his main tool for support, Ally presented herself like she was Quinn's wife. Now by his side, Quinn experienced other feelings of comfort. Nevertheless, the fact that Quinn was not alone made him feel only somewhat better.

"Uh, Kayla, do you know this man?" Will looked at Kayla and then at Kyle Quinn.

No doubt the two were family. Kayla's eyes and Quinn's were precisely the same. Birthed from the same person, they were the same. They were family.

Another Quinn.

"Kayla?"

"I...I do...I do know him." When Kayla admitted she knew the man in her doorway, Quinn's heart rate leveled off.

"You do?" said Will, Kayla's husband.

"His name is Kyle," Kayla said, looking at Quinn only. The two were locked in. There was no one present besides them. "He's," Kayla said, "he's...*my brother*."

CHAPTER 8
A WAR IS COMING

KYLE QUINN DID HAVE A SISTER AND HER NAME WAS Kayla.

Kayla Quinn.

The youngest of the three children, there was Kyle, there was Cane, and there was her. There was Kayla. The only female in the family, despite this, Kayla underwent the same training as her brothers. Shaped to become the same kind of merciless killing machine, Broder raised her to be well versed in weapons, tactics, combat, demolitions, strategy, and death. Kayla was groomed to be as lethal and as unforgiving as her siblings as all the Quinn children were battle-hardened savages instilled with near untold power and abilities.

Kayla and Kyle had not spoken in years because Kayla, unlike her brothers, was not an assassin or a working mercenary. In fact, she was not an operator at all. She did not choose to pursue a path of murder, profit, or one of service, on the contrary, Kayla Quinn was a woman who had clearly abandoned her old life and dealt with her own trauma and demons in a very different way.

And, based on what Quinn was seeing, she was a wife

and she was also a mother. She was a citizen and she was a friend. She had a child whom Quinn had never met and was married to a man who was completely opposite to any man he could have ever known. What the Quinns shared oscillated between hatred and pain and switched between regret and suffering, confusion and brokenheartedness.

They were all part of the same battle to repair their many disparaged spirits.

"Who's he, Mommy?" Quinn listened to this little girl, Bethany, and had not looked away from his sister at all.

Quinn didn't even look at Ally. He didn't because he couldn't. Staring at her brother, Kayla was waiting for him to say something, but he had yet to say anything. Quinn planned on speaking, like so often before, he just didn't know where to begin.

"This...this is your *uncle*," Kayla said, arm around her child. "Uncle Kyle."

"Uncle Kyle?" Bethany beckoned. Her voice was squeaky yet at the same time firm and almost adolescent. She spoke slowly with a drawn-out tone but Quinn could see she was perplexed by her mother's answer.

Bethany wasn't told she had an uncle.

He was not a good man and so, he was not worth mentioning.

He wasn't even worth knowing.

"Yes," Kayla said. "*Your uncle Kyle.*"

"I didn't know you had a brother," commented Will, still standing in the doorway.

"*Brothers*, actually," specified Kayla.

Quinn's shoulders jittered. Did she know about Cane?

"This is my *oldest* brother."

"Okay," said Will. "Well, I'm Will. It's nice to meet you, man."

Will offered his hand, but the Custodian couldn't help but look away. Like a rude boy who didn't know his basic manners, Quinn had manners, but right now, he lacked the courage, the decency, and the pride to follow through. Belittled by shame, burdened by humiliation, and thoughts of profound despair and regret, when Quinn did shake Will's hand, he did so while making little eye contact with the man he hoped knew very little about him.

"You too," Quinn said, almost inaudible.

He shook Will's hand and Ally stepped in to make her own introduction. "Hi," she said. "I'm Ally. I'm Kyle's—"

"Girlfriend," Kayla said for Ally.

Perceptive as Kayla was, it was obvious to Quinn's sister how someone was with her brother. Ally wasn't *exactly* Quinn's girlfriend. The circumstances earned her this title, as well as any others that might follow.

"Yes." So absorbed by his sister's gimlet gaze, Quinn was bombarded by a storm of intrusive thoughts.

He considered if Kayla would cry or if she would yell and scream in her brother's face?

Would she roll forward and slug him?

Would she slam the door in his face or would she, in the end, tell him what she finally thought of him?

Of all the things that might go down, Quinn feared the last outcome most.

"Well, it's nice to meet you too," Kayla said. "I'm Kayla. Kayla Murphy. This is my husband, Will, and my daughter, Bethany. She's five."

"Hello, Bethany," Ally said. She leaned into her maternal instincts as well as her sincerity and was better than Quinn was at doing this stuff, this courtesy stuff. She knelt down to shake the hand of this little, incredibly innocent child and smiled. "I'm Ally."

"Nice to meet you."

"Well," said Will, "would the two of you like to come inside?"

Will was being glib. Going through the motions of a

good host, it would seem, his tone indicated he didn't *really* want to invite Quinn or Ally inside. Still, Quinn believed this Will guy was just playing the *role* of a good husband and Quinn sympathized with such reticence. The visitors to Kayla's and Will's home were anything but normal or expected.

"I would..." said Quinn. He continued to fight through waves of anxiety. Doing this forced him to gag.

"Yes," Kayla said. "Come in." She regurgitated her words like she didn't care for any one of them.

Shortly after, Kayla moved aside to let Quinn pass. How anyone could let someone like Quinn into such a welcoming space only pointed to Kayla's character.

Quinn already knew she was an excellent judge of such things. Whoever this Will was, Quinn believed him to be a good man. And, when in his sister's living space, Quinn heard the door close behind him and he basked in the warmth of his sister's home.

"You didn't tell me you had a sister," Ally said in a fervent whisper.

Snapping at Quinn, she had slipped into full *wife mode*. The Custodian sensed from Ally's cutting voice that she was flabbergasted. Quinn hadn't mentioned there was another member in his family.

"A sister! Really?!" However, Quinn stood by this secrecy.

The right moment to provide Ally with said information hadn't come up as of yet. And Quinn wasn't about to seek it out. There was so much more to discuss than that. Also, if there was one gift Quinn could give Ally, it was the less known about his family, the better.

Quinn walked along the fine carpet and passed intriguing portraits poised on a night table. Every picture captured a moment from Kayla's life. Some revealed her holding Bethany as a newborn child, others of her on a playground with both her husband and her daughter. There was a snapshot of her and William on their wedding day, an event Quinn wasn't invited to and the one next to it was all of them together, as a bright and happy family in matching outfits, holding hands, and smiling.

So perfect.

"Can I get the two of you anything?" Quinn heard Kayla say from the kitchen. He stopped and inspected the photographs.

Now staring at all the harmonious pictures of his sister, William her husband, and Bethany her daughter together, on hayrides, at parks, or having dinner, the old Kayla that Quinn knew had disappeared and she had been replaced by someone living in a world where they could be free of all the things that he had struggled to escape. Quinn grabbed one picture from the table. He admired how Kayla was smiling in it. So happy and yet, Quinn didn't think it was impossible to see it any other way, but it was all so clear.

"Kyle." It was Ally who called out to Quinn, but he was still holding the picture when he saw Ally standing behind him. "The kitchen."

Quinn nodded. He put the picture back and followed Ally into the mentioned kitchen.

This other room was as tasteful as the rest of the home. Quinn looked at the pine cabinets, the marble island, and the fancy tiles, and everything seen was sparkling clean. Although Quinn's own kitchen was nice too, what it lacked was the hominess of Kayla's. The fridge was decorated with kid's drawings and colorful magnets and on the table were kid books as well as a fruit bowl and some flowers.

"You have a lovely home," commended Ally.

Quinn saw William with Bethany. They were both standing with Kayla.

"Thank you," Kayla replied. She prepared coffee and Quinn watched her hands.

Quinn didn't suspect Kayla would do anything. He was a scary man, but when he was with Ally, he was less scary and less intimidating. With much to be shared, Quinn thought about why Kayla had chosen to let him stay here. Quinn was concerned about the thoughts inside her head. He couldn't help but wonder if Kayla had shared any of these thoughts with her husband, William.

He'd met Quinn, yes, but he had yet to meet Kyle Quinn, *the Custodian*.

"Hey," William said. His voice went high as he held Bethany by the hand. "Why don't you go into the living room and play with your toys while Mommy and I speak to our new friends here, okay?"

Quinn glanced at Bethany.

This little girl was his niece. She hadn't taken her eyes off Quinn since he arrived.

Mulling over this great big stranger, Bethany was taking in every aspect of Quinn's appearance so she could make her own assessment of this man. She did as most children do, gauging who her uncle was, and she was attempting to grasp more about his character. As her father told Bethany to go on, Quinn felt only relief. When Quinn learned how he had a niece, his first impulse was to protect her. He refused for her to be present when speaking to Kayla about certain things. All of these topics were not suitable for a child her age.

"Okay," said Bethany.

"Good girl," William said. "You run along now."

Shuffling back, the pitter-pattering of children's galoshes trailed and Quinn lent his ear. On her way into the next room, Bethany stopped to have another look at her uncle. Quinn nodded. He was feeling insecure. He didn't know how he appeared in the eyes of his niece. So, he simply smirked and let her go on her merry way.

Lending the gesture, Bethany scampered and she giggled.

"My apologies," William said to Quinn, "she's always a little silly around new people. She's also perceptive, even for a five-year-old, you know. She doesn't quite know how she comes across to others."

"It's all right," Quinn said. "Fine."

"She's adorable," Ally said.

"Adorable as she might be," Kayla intruded, "she's a handful. She is a Quinn, after all."

Kayla handed her husband a cup of steaming coffee and carried one for herself as well. Wheeling over, Kayla gave her brother his own mug, nearly filled to the brim. Will gave his to Ally.

"That she is," Ally said. Quinn examined his own cup.

"Don't worry," Kayla said. "It's fine."

Quinn nodded.

"Fine?" William said, responding to the comment made by his wife.

"It's nothing," Kayla replied. She waved at Will. "My brother just thinks I did something to his coffee is all. Always on his toes, Kyle Quinn doesn't trust anyone... does he?"

"Can never be too careful," Quinn defended. He stopped looking into his mug and chose to look at his sister only.

"Right," Kayla said.

"Umm, well, should we sit down then?" asked William.

"Sit?" Ally said. "Yes, that's a good idea."

Since they were near a table, all four pulled out a chair and sat around it. Ally was next to Quinn and both of them were across from Kayla and William. Kayla didn't need a chair. Her husband pulled one out for her anyway. He was amazed by how aware and in tune his sister and her husband were with one another. Always, Will was there for Kayla despite the fact that she didn't really need any assistance. She did everything she had to despite her perceived limitations.

"So...to what do we owe this unannounced visit?" William made the inquiry and Quinn rubbed his fingers slowly along the side of his hot mug.

He stared at Kayla, who looked back at her imposing brother. With the two linked by shared trauma, there was so much about the brother-sister relationship William did not know about nor should he. For Quinn, this was all a good thing.

"We were just passing through," Ally said, "and Kyle... well, he wanted to stop by."

"Passing through?" asked William. "And where were y'all passing through from?"

"From D.C.," Ally replied.

"Washington? That's a drive," William said.

"A bit. Yeah."

"Most indeed," William answered. "And may I ask... what was the reason for you coming here?"

"Uh..." Although Ally was attempting to inform William of their intentions, it really wasn't her place to this.

The entire reason for being here was Quinn's idea. It was his extrication and it was his hunt and his pending execution that led to this. It was all him and no one else.

"Work. Work is what brought him here." With a shrewd stare, Kayla expressed to her brother just how much she did not approve of him being here now. Also, she was aware of what he did for a living.

"Work?" William said.

"Work," confirmed Kayla.

So far, Quinn hadn't said a word. And, because he had yet to speak, he did *not* confirm or deny anything that was said.

"I see," William said. "And what do you do if you don't mind me asking?"

When William mentioned this, there was only one way for Quinn to answer. It was a way that was rehearsed because it was not the first time Quinn disclosed his profession to a civilian. Fortunately, the truth and the lie worked very well together. Still, Quinn wasn't exactly lying. "I'm a Custodian."

"A custodian, really?" William, the naïve husband of Quinn's sister, said. He really had no idea what they were talking about. "So...you take care of property and buildings and such?" asked William. "And I take you also clean up the trash every once in a while?"

Hearing this, Quinn couldn't help but grin. Frankly, this was a good way of describing what he did for a living. "Yes, you could say that."

"Hmm," William said. "Interesting. Are you a custodian as well?"

William was speaking to Ally, who opened her mouth to answer but didn't get the chance to do so. Across the table, Kayla sighed loudly and moved like she didn't want any part of this sitcom-style shit now unfolding in the middle of her very own home.

"Enough, Kyle. Enough."

"Kayla," William said. He was concerned for his wife's rudeness.

Being the victim of his sister's dismissiveness, Quinn's expression didn't change. It did not because Kayla had every right to be irked and offended. "He's your brother, and I know you haven't seen him in a long time, but—"

"Don't bother, William," interceded Kayla. "There's

no sense in trying to explain any of this." Kayla's glare was designated for Quinn and no one else. "And frankly, there's no need to go on pretending either."

"Pretending?" asked William, a bit worrisome as he queried. "What do you mean?"

"Custodian, is that what they call you?" Kayla asked, still referring to Quinn.

"Call him, who calls him what?" William continued. Still, he had no idea what was happening.

"Clean up other people's shit, do you?" Kayla snapped. "Yeah, I guess that does make sense, does it? But we both know you're spinning half-truths here, are you not? And, while it might not bother me, I think my husband is owed just a little more, being in his home too and all, wouldn't you agree? You are in his home too, you know."

Ally had fallen silent. Kayla was less upset and more entertained by the change in tone and voice. She wanted to bust Quinn wide open and blow up his entire spot, and since there were few who had the balls to do this, a younger sister certainly fit the profile for someone who could.

"I know."

"Good," Kayla said. "So, tell him the truth about who you really are."

"I could," Quinn said. "I think you want to more than I do, so...why don't *you* be the one to tell him?"

"Are you sure you want *me* to do that?"

"Like you said," Quinn replied, "no more pretending. He's owed a little more."

Quinn glanced at William. He was the one whom Quinn had referenced.

"All right," Kayla said. "My brother Kyle might be called a Custodian, but that's not *what* he really is, see? No, what he really is...*is a killer*. A cold-hearted, warrior-mercenary who's ended more lives than the plague. He's a man without a conscience or limits, supposedly. He's someone who makes his bread and butter off putting people into an early grave. He reduces them to ashes and leaves not a trace. He's a ghost, a specter, a grim reaper. He's a man who safeguards and who cleans up other people's shit and leaves a scene absolutely spotless. In essence, he's a cleaner. He's a Custodian. Did I get that all right?"

As Quinn listened to Kayla's long and detailed explanation about what he did for a living, soon after she finished, the table was left stricken. Though Quinn expected this to occur, he expected this, and fear. Quinn continued to look at Kayla as she sat back with her arms crossed and her chin up, almost with smug intent. Quinn gazed at his sister while William, her husband, looked on perplexed. Later, he answered with a shaky, weak voice. "Is that...is that *true*?"

Quinn could sense that William was nervous because he stammered as he spoke.

"It's..." Although Quinn was about to say more, he wanted to confirm what was said.

He also sought to inform his brother-in-law about how he was not the enemy. And so, there was nothing for William to be afraid of. This was what Quinn *wanted* to do. But, upon trying to explain, he was interrupted by Ally. She decided to respond completely on her own.

"Yes," Ally said, expressing pride as she answered. "It's true."

"Whoa." Struck still, William leaned in before he turned to his wife.

An almost smug smirk began to show on Kayla's once-clean face. She enjoyed exposing her brother. Although, it wasn't an argument she tried to start, it was only to tease. Being the younger and estranged sister of the family,

Quinn could see Kayla was not interested in castigating her brother. What she was looking forward to was exposing him as what he really was.

"Yes, but that's not why he's here now," Ally said. "That's not why we've come. We're here because—"

"We're here to talk," Quinn said.

Diving into her explanation, he hadn't told Ally why they were here to see Quinn's sister.

In fact, Quinn hadn't spoken about what was transpiring or what their plan was now that they had arrived. There was so much missing to their plan, and it was inevitable Quinn's life as a killer would be revealed. And, when this happened, the full truth would be revealed.

Clearly, there was no time better to do this than now.

"Talk?" Kayla asked.

"Talk," Quinn replied. "Talk and listen."

"*Hmm.*"

"Kyle doesn't want to cause any trouble," Ally said. "Believe me, he's done too much of that already."

"I see," added Kayla, unfazed by Ally's statement. "And why should I believe you?"

"Because," Ally said, "we—" Moving into another long exposition, Ally wanted to give another drawn-out justification that would shed light on her and Quinn's whereabouts. But she did none of this now.

When Ally said what she did, Kayla's pitch rose. "I was speaking to my brother."

Now Kayla Quinn was the one being a bully. She was also stubborn and fearless. She was an empowered, gloriously independent individual and no one here would usurp her, and no one would pull the euphemistic wool over her unfooled eyes.

It was no games for Kayla, only truth.

The whole truth.

"Because," Quinn said, biceps bulging as he eased

himself over the table. "Right now, some men are coming to kill me, and I need your help so we can kill them first."

"What?" William couldn't hide his shock or his fear. While riddled by all of these emotions, William's face had practically changed color. "What did he say?"

The stress had risen so much in Kayla's husband that he was standing from his chair too.

Kayla remained unaffected. She continued to stare at Quinn. Her gaze was fixed and unbreakable, same as always. "He said he wants my help," Kayla said. "Kyle never asks anyone for help, but he just did now."

"We both need your help," Ally said.

Quinn nodded. "To do what you do best, what you *did* best," he clarified. "Locate 'em, mark 'em, and then kill 'em."

Quinn watched William flinch at the expletives. Hearing Quinn phrase the order in such an unapologetic way chilled his brother-in-law.

"I see," Kayla replied. "A man who never asks for help, at last, suddenly needs it. The one-man army isn't so one-man anymore, it would seem."

"A lot has changed," Quinn declared. What had changed since they had last spoken?

In a word: *everything*.

"Apparently," Kayla said.

Quinn nodded. Where he and his sister went from here was a big question. It was also a question Quinn didn't know how to answer. At the same time, Quinn was also aware of what could happen now that everything was on the table.

He had told Kayla everything, so now she could either agree to help or she could tell Quinn and Ally to go and fuck themselves and send them packing. Kayla could do this because she refused to put her husband and her daughter in incredible danger.

This was what most people would do.

But Kayla wasn't most people. She was a Quinn. And, when a fight comes and the horns of battle sound, a Quinn answers.

Always, they answer.

"Kayla..." When William addressed his wife, it seemed like he was testing her.

William wanted to see if Kayla was serious about following her brother down this dark and uncertain road. Quinn prepared for Kayla's reaction, whatever it might be, before she could say anything...she had but one more question left for her brother.

"Let's go outside, shall we? We have a lot to talk about." Kayla rolled away from the table and Quinn rose and politely followed his sister out the door.

He went with Kayla like he was her bodyguard, yet it was Kayla leading the way. Together, they went to the side of the house. William stayed behind. "So...there's a murderer in my home?"

"No," Ally said to William, "there's *family* in your home, and you know what family does? They protect their own, and there's no better protector than a goddamn Quinn."

"A Quinn?" William squinted. "Right." He looked at the door, toward Kayla. "In fact, I think she's the best there is."

"Let's hope," Ally said, "because what's on the horizon, why we're here, we're going to need all the help we can get."

"For what?" asked William. "What's on the horizon?"

"War," Ally said. "A war is coming."

———

Truthfully, Quinn was fascinated by the look of Kayla's home, its organization and décor, but particularly when compared to the other houses Quinn had seen. His, which had more security and traps, Kayla's had more blankets, pictures, and lots of places to sit and rest.

A welcoming spot, it was a place where Quinn felt absolutely safe. More than this, Quinn felt good when he was here. Out the door, Kayla wheeled onto the porch that surrounded her house. As a part separated from the front, it was just as homey and just as comfortable as other places.

Following Kayla, Quinn didn't know where he was supposed to sit.

More than this, Quinn had no idea what he was going to say.

"Not quite the welcoming you had hoped for, was it?"

"No," Quinn said to Kayla, "just the one I deserve."

"Cut the crap, Kyle," Kayla said. "You don't need to pretend with me."

"Who's pretending?"

"Oh, I see," Kayla replied. "So what, you're a good man now?"

"Not anything," Quinn stated. "Just trying to sort out a few things, I guess you could say."

"Right, well, in that case, it's nice to see you, I missed you a lot," Kayla said, laying on the dry-wit, the sarcasm. "And I'm very happy that you're here now to disrupt my quiet life and drag me back into whatever shit you're now involved with. Thanks for bringing me back into the life I fought so hard to be free of, free it, free from you."

"From me?" beckoned Quinn. How could his sister ever be free of him?

"Yes," confirmed Kayla. "From you!"

"Okay." Quinn thought more about what was said. If he was being brutally honest with himself, he didn't have a problem with anything his sister had said. All of it was true. Kayla was right.

"Well, I guess all of what you said in there was..."

"Necessary," added Kayla. "Damn right it was, and don't pretend like it wasn't. You come to my home, and I don't throw your ass out. You shouldn't be asking me why."

"And I wasn't going to," Quinn said.

"Good, because there's no sense in you coming back here," Kayla said, "if we're just going to be right back where we started. I take it that you being here," Kayla said and she removed her hands from the wheels, "*wasn't* really part of your plan?"

"No," Quinn confirmed. "It was not."

"Right." Kayla had somehow managed to sound skeptical yet also friendly. Quinn imagined her passive aggressiveness was her way of coping with the current struggle.

All Quinns had their own mechanisms for battling pain. Then, maybe Kayla actually was happy to see Kyle. *Maybe.*

"William is..." said Quinn, changing the subject. "Nice."

"He is," Kayla said, displaying the beginnings of a pleasant smile. "He is nice."

"Yeah." Quinn rubbed his thumb against his index finger.

He had so much to share with his baby sister but also not enough time to do so. As a result, Quinn decided to stay focused on the real reason why he'd chosen to come here. He wanted to tell his sister what he needed to get done and how he needed her to help him do it.

"A doctor, huh?" Quinn asked.

Of all the people Quinn thought were doctors, a man dressed in pressed jeans and whose hair was ruffled was the least likely. Even so, Quinn did mean what he said. He did like William.

"Looks like someone scored big." Quinn tried to sound sincere. He was trying to be genuine mentioning his sister's marriage. He also hadn't kept in mind that William was his family now too, technically.

"Yeah," Kayla said. She snorted to express her derision, yet maintained that same smile as shown before. "What MD is gonna fall for a paraplegic with two murderous brothers and who has mountains of trauma she's been battling through for almost ten years?"

Quinn's words were misconstrued. "Actually, I was talking about *him*."

It would seem the *score* Quinn referred to was Kayla, not William. She was the *catch* in Quinn's metaphor. She was the good one and no one knew this more than Quinn.

"*He* scored big," Quinn said.

"I see," Kayla said. "Thank you. And Ally?"

Kayla eventually took the compliment for what it was, but her appreciation didn't extend beyond the average show of gratitude. There was a mere sign of slight emotion. She looked at Quinn with her lips curled up into her mouth.

"What about her?" Quinn asked.

"Who is she?" Kayla asked.

"She's..." Quinn wanted to say Ally was nobody, but then she was everything but that.

To describe her in such a way, however, would ensure that no more questions would follow. Ally was someone whom Quinn brought here with the sole purpose of using in a war against Priest. The more Quinn considered this as a path, the more he began to see its hidden truth. Ally might actually be the only good news Quinn had to share with his sister.

"*My everything.*"

"Is that so?" Kayla asked.

"It is," Quinn said. "And she's...*she's pregnant*."

A loud gulp squeaked from Kayla's mouth and she was thrust back.

"Pregnant? Did you say pregnant?" Stricken hearing this news, Kayla gawped at her brother.

Quinn nodded.

"Wow. So...you're going to be—"

"A father?" Quinn said. Now he was the one being disruptive. "I am."

"Well, I think that's..."

What? Quinn said in his head. Irresponsible, wrong, dumb, *a waste*?

What does someone like him know about raising kids? While all of these concerns were true, rather than bombarding Quinn with guilt, Kayla opted to say something that greatly impacted her brother. Pulling Quinn's heart strings, it forced him to smile when he thought he never would.

"Wonderful."

"You do?"

"Of course," Kayla said. "Now, you will finally get the chance to see."

"To see?" Quinn asked, unsure what she meant.

"Yes," Kayla said. "To see what really matters."

"Right," Quinn replied. "Look, I'm sorry for coming here. I wanted to because I needed to. There was something pulling me back. There was just so much I needed to say. And, well, there was so much only you would understand. But, before I get into that, I think...maybe it's better if I tell you the bad news first."

"Do you now?" Kayla said.

"Yes."

"Well, then go ahead and say it," Kayla demanded.

This bad news was the kind only a Quinn could carry.

It was also news Quinn preferred to know right away. He had to say it without any pauses or excuses. There needed to be no denying or changing what was. So, when Quinn spat out these words, it was like he was spitting toothpaste from inside his tingling mouth. "Cane is dead."

Nothing was heard after other than silence. When Kayla heard the news, she instantly turned to look away. "I see," she said. "And was it *you?* Were you the one who killed him?"

"No," Quinn barked. "No."

"But you were there?"

"I was."

"Was it Dad?" Kayla asked. "Did dad kill..."

Kayla couldn't say the rest so Quinn answered only by shaking his head.

While it wasn't his father who murdered his own brother, Quinn was somewhat responsible for Cane's demise. Being the one who worked for the very man who was after him now, Priest also arranged for his brother to die at his hands.

This was how it happened. It was the truth.

"But you were *there?*" Kayla asked.

"Yes," Quinn said.

Eyes shut, Kayla's head tilted curiously. Downcast, she was disappointed by the recent news.

"I know it's been a while since we were together," Quinn said, "and I know we didn't leave on the best of terms, and I also know the news of Cane is something you didn't want to hear, but—"

"I want to know something first," Kayla interjected. "I want to know if you were there when he did, when he did die."

"I told you I was," Quinn said.

"So, he didn't die alone, because you were there with him?"

Quinn nodded. "Yes." Fighting back tears with a compressed face, clearly showing restraint, all Quinn could feel now was the weight of his own regret and his own shame. No...Cane did not die alone. Until now, Quinn hadn't considered the weight or the importance of this fact. He didn't until Kayla mentioned it to him.

Did that make Quinn feel better? Slightly, but then that was something.

In fact, it was plenty.

"The man who killed him, he's—"

"The same man who's after you now?" Kayla said.

"Yes."

"And you decided to bring him here," said Quinn's sister, "to my home, to my family?"

"I didn't intend for anything," Quinn added, "and the fight doesn't have to end here, but if I'm going to face what lies ahead, I wanted to at least try."

"Try...what?" Kayla replied.

"If the best sniper I know," Quinn said, "still has some fight left in her, and if she's ready to take one last shot, and show the world it's never too late to come back?"

Kayla sighed. Her head swayed. Shocked by the question, if not also slightly offended by it, Quinn had no idea what she was going to say.

"And that's why you're here? Because you want me to *kill* for you?" Kayla asked.

A tremor snaked through Quinn's tight shoulders. He wasn't exactly shrugging as much as he was dismissing this as the reason behind his sudden arrival. He wanted to see Kayla, not just to use her skills so he could stay alive, but to *see* her. He wanted to see her because Quinn missed his baby sister. In spite of everything that happened, deep down, his love for her remained strong, if also in the form of crippling regret. "No, it's not just—"

"I know," Kayla said. "You wanted to see me too, right?

You wanted to repair as much as you could before the storm gets here, because if you do that, then you'll have less weight to carry should this be your last fight. You wanted to give yourself as much of a happy ending as you deserve, before it's too late."

"No, not...that...I mean..." Quinn stammered. His words were hardened by determination and urgency, but the sentences were even harder.

"Who are you, Kyle?"

Quinn squinted at his sister. He asked himself, *what the hell did she just ask him?*

"What?" Quinn responded.

"I asked you a question," Kayla said. "I want to know... who you are."

"I'm your brother."

"That you are," Kayla answered, "but that wasn't up to you," she elaborated. "See, you were *born* my brother, and I know that's why you think you're here, but it's not. Now, I'm going to ask you again. Who are you? Who are you, *really*...Kyle?"

Quinn didn't know what to say. He didn't know who he was, though he thought he did, now he was not so sure. So, he asked himself the same question that Kayla just did.

Who am I?

Quinn was many things. He was a soldier, a mercenary, a fighter, a killer, a world-ender, a meat-eater, and the goddamn Grim Reaper. But, as he thought of this question, still, he weighed his answers. When he did this, his response had deepened.

He began to see this was what he did but not who he was. "I'm..."

"You're someone who's done some very bad things," Kayla said.

Quinn thought this was her attempt to make him feel worse. Kayla was turning the knife already plunged deep into Quinn's heart. Doing this, however, Quinn thought of all the things he had done. He knew them all well because, right now, he was staring at the worst one of all.

Legs. He blinked and looked at Kayla again. *His sister's legs.*

"You're someone who's hurt," continued Kayla. "Killed, and destroyed, and left nothing but chaos, death, and despair in their wake. You've murdered and you've eradicated. You've pillaged and there's no telling just how many have been affected by your actions. Many people have been hurt because of the things you've done. So many have shed tears because of you. No, Kyle, you are someone who has caused immense pain and so much sadness."

Kayla's response was a blatant statement of obvious facts. If this was her attempt to make Quinn feel bad, it was working, very well. Most of the people she mentioned were people who, in Quinn's mind, deserved to die. They were those who deserved to be taken from this Earth because they were bad, evil, or any other trite, dumb classification he could use to justify their execution. But, as Quinn accepted when he first embarked on this path to new retribution, it didn't matter.

Pain was pain, suffering was suffering, and death was death.

He was still, as his sister noted, *a bad man.*

"Is that all?" said Quinn. "Is that all you have to say?"

"Nope," Kayla said. "There's more."

Quinn looked down. How could there possibly be more? Then again, there was nothing Quinn could do to make her stop talking. And so, he declined to try. If Quinn examined his sister's legs again, then his heart would sink even lower. But then, it couldn't go any lower. He had fallen so much these last few minutes, and he was now down on his fucking knees. And while this was painful, it was also necessary.

The truth always was.

"You've done all those things," Kayla said. Staring at her brother from the wooden banister that guarded the sturdy porch around her magnificent home, the sun was low now and getting lower with each passing second. "But you know what?" Kayla rolled forward. "That's not *all* you have to be."

Quinn's eyebrows furrowed and his ears twitched with a boyish embarrassment. What Kayla said was unexpected.

It was also, at the same time, kind.

"What?" Quinn asked.

"What do you want to do, Kyle?" Kayla snapped back at her brother. "Do you want to continue to live your life, going from city to city, place to place, offing bad people, and ransacking people's hideouts and bases? Do you want to do this while all the while you're gifted with the promise that what you're doing is for a good reason? Do you want to continue to sink deeper into your own pain and your own despair? Do you want to keep indulging in the outlets that you think will take away your regret? I know how you feel about dad. I know how you feel, because it's how I felt when I too let what he did eat away at me for most of my life. I thought of him and then I thought of you..."

Kayla's hands, now on her thighs, Quinn wasn't sure if this was intentional, if she wanted to draw attention to her legs or not, but while uncertain, he didn't care what the reason was. Quinn listened to Kayla. No one ever had ever spoken to him like this, no one except for Ally, but then she didn't know Quinn as well as Kayla did.

Kayla was family. She was a Quinn!

"I thought of you," Kayla said, "and then one day, I

decided that to think of you is to give you power you don't deserve. To think of the people who've wronged us, hurt us, is to give all of them power they don't deserve. And, while so much was taken from me, and so much pain was caused, no...I finally said to myself. No, I'm not going to let you, or anyone else, have it anymore. And, it was only when I accepted that that I was able to do something I never thought I could."

"And what's that?" Quinn's voice cracked. He could barely say these words as they clawed at the back of his tender throat. His knees felt weak. All other body parts that were once only sore increased to the point where they burned brutally.

"I forgave you," Kayla pronounced every word slowly as to emphasize their clarity. In doing so, she had gifted her brother with an endearing hopefulness he had only felt once before. It was when Quinn was with Ally, back in the car. It happened when she told Quinn he was going to be a father.

"I forgave *you*," Kayla declared. "And I forgave our father, and now that I have, at last, I can finally live. I can be who I need to be. I can *win*."

"No one is ever going to forgive me for the things I've done," Quinn said. "There's just too many who've been buried." A tear pushed its way out from beneath Quinn's left eye. He didn't intend for this to happen, it just did. "All of them filled with the bodies of the faces I'll never forget," Quinn said. "Forgiveness is not what keeps men like me alive, because it's not something men like me will ever get."

"No, it's not," Kayla said, "but then it isn't about your life anymore, is it?"

At the time, Quinn was unsure what Kayla meant. Then, he remembered.

"You're going to be a father, and hopefully a husband

too, and so, you're going to have to decide the life you want to live so you can have the death you want to have. Do you want to be buried as a gifted, capable killer?"

Quinn thought for the longest time he was going be buried only as a Custodian and nothing else.

He was to die as a deadly man who did deadly things and who had left a dangerous mark on the world. Not once did Quinn think he might have a wife or children coming to visit his grave. And yet, Quinn saw where he was and who he was with. His sister had endured, but she had also survived. Here she was, a mother, a wife, a citizen, and she was happy; happy and alive.

"I want you to have a good life."

"I don't know if that's possible for me," Quinn said. His chest ached.

"Why not?" begged Kayla. "Why not?"

By asking this, Kayla said the only thing that Quinn wanted—needed—to hear. This didn't just apply now, but always. *Forever*.

"You're not dad. You are *not* our father."

It was in this moment that Quinn experienced epic yet satisfying feelings of pure, unabashed relief. In that moment, he was absolved of what once was his greatest fear, that he would never be forgiven and he would turn into the person he hated most.

Never did Quinn want to be like his father.

He thought that transforming into him was an unavoidable outcome brought upon by his choices and his rage. Quinn believed it was completely inevitable and he feared this transformation most of all.

"Don't just be a man with a gun," Kayla said. "Be a man who has something to say, something to instill, to live for and to protect. Be someone your child would someday be proud of, *a real father*."

"A real father?" said Quinn. These words were the most difficult for him.

"Give him what you didn't have. Use it to become something more. Fight not with our hands or with guns but with hearts, spirits, minds. It is then, and only then, that a person becomes better. If we do that, then he, dad, and all the others like him...they will not win. They don't exist in the places they're not allowed to. They're buried, put to rest, and all you have to do is just be strong enough to say goodbye and end the cycle, on your terms and only on your terms."

Quinn's eyesight, suddenly, felt limited. His shoulders were the only part of him that felt light. He had carried this weight for too long. Now, it all felt like a pair of delicate hands had reached out and lifted what was weighing on Quinn for most of his life. Then, it was tossed aside and removed from existence.

It was gone. Forever relinquished and destroyed.

"Break the cycle," Quinn said.

"Break it," Kayla said. "Break it right here, right now."

Quinn mediated on this expectation.

The whole notion of breaking a cycle of violence and abuse felt enthralling. Quinn swore he would not turn into his father, even as a child, he'd made the same declaration.

Years later, now...he was more similar than he wanted or had accepted.

Today, Quinn understood why.

Should he want to end his own cycle of pain, then one day, the killing must stop.

The death must die.

"I'm sorry. It's because of me you're in that chair."

"Don't do that to yourself," Kayla replied. She waved her hand to dismiss Quinn's need to deliver a heartfelt apology. "You can't live in the past, my brother. Don't think about what you did back then. You were broken the same as I was, and it's not about what your choices were. No, it's about what you'll *choose* to do here and now. Are you going to let your beginnings burden you or are you going to kick them aside and fight for yourself, for tomorrow?"

It was then that Quinn knew what he was supposed to do. He knew it soon as he pulled up along Kayla's driveway and laid eyes on his baby sister.

"Fight," Quinn said. "Always...fight."

And so, the time for discussion had come to an end.

Kayla agreed to join Quinn against the forces now approaching. Both were done talking and the two siblings stepped up a curving ramp that led to the driveway and into the garage.

Quinn had talked with Ally beforehand but only briefly. He told her about what happened and how they could count on his sister being "eagle eyes" in order to defend against Priest's forthcoming attack. They needed to beat Ronin, KEYS, and whoever else was coming.

Kayla pressed a button to open the garage and among the rumbling of mechanisms and the sliding of chains, Quinn and Kayla were side by side, watching as the door began to fold upward. It was a spacious garage and did not smell of gasoline, soil, or mold of any kind.

No, it was an appealing scent, like Evergreen trees and freshly cut pine.

He liked it a lot.

Quinn passed a Dodge Caravan as well as a navy Camry. He followed Kayla as she cut between these two vehicles. She was going to somewhere at the back.

"Big space," Quinn said.

"Yeah, well," Kayla said, "one of the perks, I guess you could say, of living so far out and away. You get more bang for your buck 'round here."

"So it would seem." Quinn reached out to assist his sister.

The trunk Kayla had recovered from her workbench looked too heavy for her to carry. It barely moved as she pulled its rickety handle. Quinn believed it was best lifted with two hands instead of one. Quinn extended his arm and helped Kayla to bring the box down. He stared at this robust container.

"It's been a while since I've used what's inside, but..." Kayla said.

"By inside," Quinn said, "you obviously mean..."

Kayla snapped the locks in a unison flick. Quinn loved the sound of a case being opened.

"Of course, inside is my beauty, my rifle, *my gun*." Kayla lifted the lid and Quinn took a peek.

"Whoa," Quinn said, entranced by the chest's contents.

Quinn expected a Remington, a Colt, or some other sniper rifle he was well versed in. From what he could recall, Kayla was a Remington gal through and through. This was *not* what Quinn was seeing.

"Yeah," Kayla said, "it's new and improved. Oh, and don't tell William about any of this. He hasn't seen it in a long time."

"I won't," Quinn said, "but it's just...not what I expected."

"Not what anyone expects," answered Kayla, "and that's the point."

"How'd you get it?"

"What," Kayla replied, "you think just because I put the past behind me that I don't like playing with guns anymore? Bad shit doesn't equal bad ownership. Remember that."

Quinn said nothing. Kayla had her ways of phrasing things in a really cool way. Sometimes, she reminded

Quinn of Ally. "So, is this your particular brand of poison?" Quinn asked.

"*Mm-hmm,*" Kayla said, hand on the rifle. "I had a past fondness for that old-school shit, but now, I figured I treat myself to something a bit different."

"And this is what you landed on?" Quinn asked.

"Yep," Kayla said, "the CheyTac M200 is my baby now."

"Good choice," Quinn said.

"Yessir."

Quinn inspected the gun.

Its barrel was long and the weapon housed within its own compartment, exactly how Quinn transported his own guns and toys. Quinn and Kayla were taught to disassemble and reassemble firearms by the exact same man. And, what Quinn saw was a bolt-action, anti-materiel rifle. It used a seven-round single magazine, and the CheyTac was also known to be accurate as hell. It could see a target from twenty-five hundred yards and was an exceptional firearm, though not too heavy, it was equipped with a collapsible buttstock and came with its own stand. As Quinn examined the gun, he ran his hands along it and leered.

"Not bad, huh?" Kayla asked.

"Not bad at all," Quinn confirmed. "You got a nest?" A nest was a place for a sniper to hide out and shoot for far away.

"I was going to camouflage in the field not far from here," Kayla said to Quinn. "Should make for a nice spot."

"And William?" Quinn asked. "Have you figured out what you're going to say?"

"Yeah," Kayla said, still staring at the rifle stored in its chest. "I told him bad men are coming to kill us and we need to kill them first." Quinn looked at his sister, blankly. That was pretty much it. "So, he's going to take Bethany to the hospital where he works and wait there until it's all done."

"And that was it? That was all you said?"

"William's a good man," Kayla said. "He trusts me. Besides, he knows who he married and how my past was something that paved the way for my future."

Quinn's heart skipped a beat. If William knew about Kayla's past, then he knew what Quinn had done to her. How William was able to look Quinn in the eye spoke to his character. It further confirmed how good a man William really was.

Maybe William was more than good. Maybe he was great.

Quinn had not yet considered the weight of what lay ahead of him, his sister, or Ally. He was under the impression he was going to face Ronin and Priest. Priest was not a formidable fighter. But, with Hyper-X and KEYS engaged in his invasion, no doubt Priest had a few tricks up his sleeves. Also, Quinn didn't know where his father was at this point. Now that Priest knew Quinn's location, he was going to find him here, with his family. And, if there's one thing Quinn's former contractor knew how to do, it was how to exploit another person's weakness.

And what was likely waiting for Quinn was not one man, or two, or even three.

No, the threat was to be much, *much* greater.

It would be worse than anything Quinn could possibly imagine.

"Are you sure you want to do this?" Quinn Kayla asked.

"Yes," Kayla said, with not a single doubt in her mind.

"But this...this isn't..." *Your fight.* Quinn wanted to say this but chose not to.

"Yes, it is," Kayla said. "It'll *always* be. Since the day we were born and until the day we die."

"No one's dying today," Quinn said. "But I'm glad you're with me."

Kayla nodded. She agreed. "We have to finish this. We have to."

"Yes," Quinn said. "Stop Hyper-X, stop the spread, stop Priest. End the cycle."

When Quinn looked up at the sky, he could feel the winds starting to change. Quinn raised his hand and wiggled his fingers. How many had he killed with these things? Honestly, Quinn lost count. He thought about how his hands might one day be used for something else, maybe for building and not destroying.

"We should get inside," Kayla said. "Sounds like a storm's coming."

"In more ways than one," acknowledged Quinn. "In more ways than one."

————

Back inside Quinn's sister's house, Quinn had unpacked his things into one of Kayla's guestrooms. A home for a family of three, it was a robust manor, with plenty of spare rooms and each one was equipped with its own amenities. There were places for storage and lots of unused space. Quinn walked up the stairs with his MPX carbine, his Benelli, his Triumph Master Glock, his OTF, and his tonfa all stored in a heavy case. Everything Quinn owned was present and accounted for. In the room, Quinn was greeted by the enriching scent of a wallflower from a nearby outlet.

He breathed it in and loved every second of it.

The sheets in the room were colorful. The walls were white and the room was illuminated by a lamp and a chandelier. Quinn enjoyed the décor. All of it could not be a worse match for what he was holding now, however.

Quinn placed the rifle and his shotgun down first, then grasped his Triumph Glock.

Quinn removed the gun's mag and checked the rounds.

The chest plate built within Quinn's Phalanx armor, as well as his Corinthian, were all placed in the center of the bed too. Quinn checked his reflection in the armoire mirror. He was starting to feel like this was a holiday visit. Maybe someday it would be.

He unpacked, disassembled, and reloaded. Doing all of this, a chortle squeaked from near the door. Quinn peered over and spotted a girl. His niece, Bethany, was standing there behind him, watching her uncle with eyes opened wide. Quinn stood before a child and a massive arsenal and then he was hit with a discomforting thought.

A kid shouldn't have to see such things.

Quinn pulled a blanket over his gear and hid his weapons . He was about to jump into the shower. The bathroom wasn't far. All Quinn had to do was pass through the door and walk down the hall. Bethany was standing so close Quinn couldn't go. She ogled the man who, to a child, was larger than life.

"Uh, hi," Quinn said. Bethany clutched her teddy bear and stayed in Quinn's room.

A precocious child, although only five, she acted like she was closer to eight, maybe even nine. Bethany curled around the bed, stepped up to the mattress, and raised her hand in a celebratory hoot. "You can't catch me! You can't catch me!" Bethany ran around the bedroom.

Every one of Quinn's guns were stripped down. None were loaded.

"I, uh..." Quinn didn't know what to make of the interaction. Bethany was his niece and he was her uncle. Quinn supposed it would be the duty of any uncle to participate in whatever game their niece or nephew was playing. Maybe Quinn could run. He could try and play along. This was what Bethany wanted him to do, and so, he needed to be generous. Good.

Quinn wasn't comfortable.

A war was coming and Quinn needed to focus. When thinking about the approaching battle, suddenly Quinn realized that there wasn't much to focus on. He was aware of what needed to be done and he was prepared. Quinn remembered Hyper-X. He remembered how it made people numb to their pain. The compound also gifted Quinn with a speedy recovery as well as the ability to withstand much suffering and still get the job done. It helped Quinn to fight after so many others would either quit, burn out, or die. Quinn's time would be better spent with something worth protecting and preserving. He could have precious time with someone he loved.

"Chase me! Chase me!" Bethany wasn't making a request but a demand. She circled Quinn the third time and he jumped. He was careful whenever he was around her, very careful.

"You want me to...to chase you?" Quinn asked. He didn't know how to play along. He could easily catch his niece, but Quinn was beginning to understand how this was not the purpose of the game.

"Yes! Yes! Yes!" Bethany continued to encircle and Quinn watched his niece run about like a wild cat.

Quinn studied the young child's appearance. Lively and free, rejoiceful, pleasant, and overwhelmed with joy, Bethany hurried as far and as fast as she could get. She scurried, and it was then Quinn decided what he was going to do. Chasing his niece, Quinn followed her as she cut across the room. "Okay," Quinn said. "Play."

"Yes!" exclaimed Bethany. "Follow me! Follow me!"

"All right," Quinn said. "I'm following. I'm following."

Quinn kept his voice down. He did possess certain qualities most kids might find scary.

A raised voice was not one of them. Quinn was actually hard-pressed to find a single moment whereby he was behaving the way he was now. Moving at one-tenth his regular speed, Quinn indulged in his niece's playfulness. He pretended like Bethany was too fast for him. When he played with her, he laughed and made silly faces. None of this was hardly the work of a cold-blooded killer. Right now, Quinn was nothing more than a fool. That's all. Just a fool. The act itself was so beautifully liberating that Quinn wanted to enjoy it for as long as he could. Bethany spread her arms and made herself into an airplane, then pleaded with her uncle for him to lift her up and carry her around the room. "Higher! Higher and faster!"

Quinn obeyed his niece's command. "All right. All right."

Bethany, who was roughly sixty-five pounds, was a weight equal to what Quinn would strap to his waist whenever he did pull-ups. Even still, Bethany felt lighter than a laundry basket. He held Bethany high up. Quinn showed a side that, until now, he didn't know existed. To know he was capable of real warmth and care, there was a lack of an inhibition that lingered deep within, and Quinn could access all of this whenever he wanted.

If he was to succeed in this fight against Priest, then this feeling of being light and free was a reminder of how he *could* be someday. And this, in some capacity, was what awaited Quinn at the end of it all.

This could be Quinn's new, possible future.

"Kyle!" Ally called to Quinn from the floor below. She was barely heard over Bethany's giggles. Quinn continued to lift his niece up and down. Spinning Bethany like she was light as a feather, Quinn imagined that Ally had something important to tell him, as of now, nothing was more important than this.

"Higher!" screamed Bethany.

Quinn let out a shrieking *weee* as he continued to play along.

Bethany blushed. Quinn was called a third time and he stopped and looked at the door. Ally was there, but it was not where his focus was supposed to be. Still enthralled Bethany's infectious energy, Quinn watched Ally smile. She didn't want to stop what was happening now.

She enjoyed seeing the man she loved so affectionate and free.

More than this, Ally was enamored with the man Quinn might turn into one day. He would make a good dad because, deep down, Quinn was a good man.

"More! More! More!"

"Maybe later," Quinn said. He lowered Bethany back down to the floor.

"Nah," Ally said. "You're fine. Stay here, play a little longer."

Quinn rotated to look at Ally. Still smiling, she was actually glowing. After telling Quinn to stay, he let these feelings of happiness and joy deepen. Then, he picked Bethany back up and continued to fly her around the room.

Wonderful.

———

Half an hour later, dinner was served. Quinn walked down the stairs with Bethany and joined Ally, Kayla, and William at the long table. So far, Quinn had no idea when Priest would be arriving. Therefore, the moments in between were precious and sacred. Quinn refused to waste a second. He expected the food to be well prepared and tasty. Based on what he could smell, and it had been some time since he had a homecooked meal, it was meatloaf and succulent mashed potatoes and Quinn saw a bowl of Caesar salad in the center of the placing. All of Quinn's favorite people were now arranged around him. Quinn slid his hand across his lap and placed it on Ally's knee.

Touching her under the table, Quinn held Ally before indulging in the delectable food presented to them. Quinn cut through the loaf of tender meat and scooped up a dollop of steaming mashed potatoes. He shoveled everything into his mouth but did his best to mind his manners. Quinn tried not to eat as quickly as he did back home. Seeing William, Quinn noticed his eyes were glazed with tears and his face was red. And, when Quinn saw his sister's husband like this, William's thoughts became clear. He understood his wife was about to enter a dangerous situation she might not return from.

"Hey, hey," Kayla said. She could see her husband was in distress. "I'm the eyes in the sky, remember? Nowhere near the action. Completely out of the fight..."

"Right," William said. "It's just..." He dried his eyes with a napkin.

There was no such thing as anyone out of a fight. This was something only Quinn knew. What Kayla told him was a blatant lie. She told him this because it's what he wanted to hear. But as she lied, Quinn understood why.

Love is what holds a family together, but it's what also propels it to go on and to keep going. It's what is responsible for not only forcing people to do crazy things but also the bravest. And the Quinns were nothing if not brave. Quinn had come to embrace what he's fighting for and now who he was fighting for.

They finished their meal and Bethany skedaddled up the stairs.

She raced up the stairs while Quinn watched his niece disappear.

"She'll have to pack, obviously," Kayla said. She was by the sink washing dishes.

"Yes," Quinn heard William say. "I'm pretending like we're going on one of our special camping trips," he said. Suddenly, there was hope gleaming in his eyes as William looked ahead with fair sensitivity and relative happiness.

"Good idea," Kayla replied. Her eyes stayed locked on her husband.

"She'll need help," William said. "We might be at the hospital a long time, but..."

"I'll help her," Quinn answered from out of nowhere.

By doing this, he gained the attention of his sister as well as his brother-in-law. "You?"

Quinn nodded. "Yes," Quinn said. "I'll help."

"Just...make it quick," William said. As Quinn was about to nod again, the idea of time was the one that rang truest. Time was never on Quinn's side. Oddly, today, it seemed like it might be.

Priest, taking his time behind the scenes, wherever he was, was now approaching. His pursuit was not as intense as before. There was much planning being taken into this final attack. Quinn had certainly taken advantage of this day.

"Right," Quinn said. "Of course."

He nodded at William and at Kayla. What they were extending to Quinn now was a privilege. They were gifting him with time—time to spend with his niece and time to spend with them. For Quinn, being the uncle, he should enjoy Bethany's company.

It could be the last time he ever did.

Into her bedroom, Quinn saw Bethany in a space. It

looked like someone had tossed a can of pink paint on every wall.

"Bethany, your father would like you to pack a bag as quick as you can."

Bethany, sitting on her canopy bed with a doll in her hand, bounced up and down, turned her head, and jeered. She then loaded everything into her big bag and pointed after telling her uncle something even he didn't think to hear. It was also something, deep down, Quinn didn't want to.

"You're awesome. You're my hero." Quinn halted. He froze after the compliment.

How this girl was able to say such a simple word sent chills through her uncle's body and forced him to cease all movements and ask, did Bethany even know what a hero was?

In all likelihood, she didn't. She didn't because she couldn't. Most likely, Bethany only said the word because she was a smart little girl, and this word had a different meaning for someone like her. If Quinn's niece knew what a hero *really* was, then she would know her uncle was far from one.

"No, I'm afraid...I'm not that," Quinn said humbly, almost embarrassed hearing the word.

"Yes, you are!" Bethany shouted. "You save people! You saved Mommy!"

A shadow began to form outside Bethany's door and Quinn knew he was no longer alone.

"I did *not* save your mom, kid. I've..." Quinn struggled to determine how he was going to explain this next part to a child. Then, Bethany was not just a child, not to Quinn. And, as the shadow by the door continued to grow, so did the person who it belonged to.

"Done terrible things," Quinn went on. As simply as he could say this, Quinn would be careful about he phrased the rest. The statement was the central focus of his long and overdue confession.

"Terr-*ib*-le?" pronounced Bethany.

"Yes. *Terrible*." Quinn considered this. For the longest time, this was Quinn's mentality. It was the philosophy that shed further light on the flaws of his own morality. It enabled Quinn to live with all the lives he'd taken. It was only recently he decided that this was not enough.

So, when Quinn shared this with his sister, he knew he never would be enough.

"I wasn't there for her when she needed me to be," Quinn said. "I failed her, and I hurt her."

"You...*hurt* her?"

"More than that," Quinn admitted to Bethany. "I took something from her."

More chills lambasted Quinn because what he said singed his nerves and forced a bad taste in the Custodian's mouth. He could taste the meatloaf and the potatoes in an upchucked bile; a potent mix of sour, grimy morsels. Whatever urine lingered in Quinn's bladder squirmed to the precipice of his tract, and his once singular tears multiplied into many.

He couldn't stop crying. "Did your mom ever tell you how she ended up in that chair? Don't."

Quinn, who had already said more than he should, finally wanted to tell her the truth. The next part of Quinn's confession was too difficult for anyone to articulate. He couldn't say it to a child, even one as bright as Bethany. The need to speak remained. When Bethany asked Quinn about the *thing* he'd taken, the Custodian reached for a doll on the bed.

And, when he brought it to his face, Quinn gripped the toy by the legs. Then, he folded them back and tucked them until they closed in around the doll's waist. Quinn did this until the limbs were gone and there was nothing for the doll to stand on.

"Like I said," Quinn said to Bethany, his head was shaking and he was fighting back tears. "I'm not a hero. I'm not even close to a hero. I'm the bad guy, kid. I'm the *worst* guy."

Quinn let go of the doll and dropped it onto the bed.

With Bethany's bags packed, Quinn grabbed the strap and hoisted it up. William stood hunched by the door. The look in his eyes was almost an exact replica of Quinn's. No words were exchanged and no act was taken. The Custodian nodded, stepped to William, and handed him Bethany's loaded bag.

What's done was done and what needed to be said... finally was.

"Thank you," William said, referring to the bag.

Quinn's impulse was to say *you're welcome* and *no problem*, but he did nothing. Quinn owed more apologies to this one man than any other, and the very last response Quinn should give William was *you're welcome*.

"We'll be leaving soon," William said.

"Yes," Quinn said. "Good."

William's head moved and his stare shifted past Quinn and to his daughter. William moved while Quinn stayed back. He dried his eyes with his sleeve and motioned down the hallway. All was said and all was done, and now, Quinn had the time he needed to prepare.

A storm was still on its way.

———

When the time to say goodbye arrived, Kayla kissed Bethany and William. Ally and Quinn stood on the veranda, with no tears and no regrets. Seeing a husband taking a daughter to work while the mother stayed, this was not the most traditional kind of departure, a man leaving his wife to fight, but then William was everything but a traditional man. Hauling everything into the Camry, William kissed Kayla once more before heading to the driver's side. William waved to Kyle and Ally.

Ally was the first to wave back. Quinn wasn't much for the gesture.

He nodded and smirked.

In his Phalanx armor, Quinn's body was covered, but he also had his jacket on too. Holding his Corinthian helmet/mask, Quinn's guns remained inside his sister's house. Quinn bid farewell to all and watched the Camry pull out of the driveway. Rolling back, Quinn stared at Bethany.

In the backseat, Bethany held her doll.

Quinn reflected on all the times he shared with her as her uncle.

They were all great, all right.

"He'll be back when I tell him to come back," Kayla said, rolling up the ramp.

She was on her way back to the veranda to Quinn and Ally.

"Of course," Ally said. "I don't know about local PD," she said. "My contacts here are limited. This isn't my scene. Might be able to call the station chief, but—"

"Knowing Priest," Quinn said, "he's probably taken care of anything that will stand in his way of getting to me. All that's left to stop him...will be us."

"So, it would seem," Kayla said.

Quinn looked at his sister as she continued to wave at her husband and daughter. Quinn thought about what he really wanted to say to Kayla. He wanted to tell her about what he shared not long ago, the truth about what happened and why he would never ever live it down.

"There's something I need to say to you," Quinn said.

He watched as Kayla's hand lowered and her expression melted from happy to mopey and dull. "Back when I was with William, I had to tell him. I had to because I thought I wouldn't get another chance, so I—"

"You told him it was you who put me in this chair," Kayla interjected. Taking the words right out of Quinn's fucking mouth, he quivered as he looked at Ally. Eyes wide, in shock, it was a struggle for Quinn to imagine how Ally—or anyone—could not be.

"I did."

"Figured you would," Kayla replied.

"I'm sorry, but I had to."

"I get it," Kayla said. "But it doesn't matter. He knows."

Kayla wheeled back around. Focused, she was now facing her brother as well as his future wife. "And if you're done with your moment of pity," Kayla said, denying sympathy or regret from Quinn. "I think it's time we head inside and get ready, yeah? Are you coming or not, Kyle?"

Quinn found himself feeling exhilarated and, at the same time, humbled. He admired his sister's fortitude, her assertiveness, and her lack of sorrow or hate for herself and for Quinn. And, for a moment, she sounded exactly as Quinn wanted her to: real, ready, and strong.

"I am."

"Good," Kayla said. She rolled past her brother, almost like she was running him over, but in a good way. "Because I was born ready."

Kayla continued to grin as she made her way into the house. Quinn chuckled. Then, he joined his sister and Ally as the sounds of thunder clacked and a daunting shadow began to consume the sky.

The storm was here, at last.

CHAPTER 9
A BEAST IN THE SKY

THE BULL WAS A PROTOTYPE CARRIER AND SO, ITS ability to traverse great distances was challenging and beyond its design parameters given how new a machine it was. As well, it was also engineered to be a stealth transport hidden when sailing through the atmosphere. Up so high, it was a giant floating temple containing not only an army of militants but also an emperor, a general, and a champion. It was shaped as the skull of a ferocious beast with its eyes being the windows and its face the door. Staring at the world below, Priest—prepared to arrive at his location—smirked like a cretinous overlord. It had taken too long to find Quinn but the Custodian's whereabouts, however, were not determined by any surveillance technology possessed by the US government.

Instead, it was given to Priest by the man standing with him now.

"When we touch down, the priority will be Quinn," Priest said to Broder. Quinn's infamous father stood in fatigues and was holding a Glock 17. "We find him and execute him, sight on scene."

To this, Broder responded. "It will be done."

"Good," Priest said.

"So the pawns move while you sit safe on your throne? Sounds about right." Priest turned to glare at Ronin, the last Custodian still alive in this game.

After the incident at the park, Ronin contacted Priest and Priest told Ronin where to go. The directions were simple. *Look up.*

Although the other Custodian did not fear Priest, insulting him was not an act of antagonism for Ronin. It was something done purely from observation and recollection. Priest had never been in a fight. It was not his job to crawl through shit. Until tonight, Priest thought he wouldn't have to.

But things change.

"Don't be coy," Priest said to Ronin. "Given what's been happening, nothing's off the table. There might be a few surprises that might even impress someone such as yourself."

"I hope so," Ronin said. "I really do."

Priest moved to another section of the Bull, to the ship's center, to a sprawling field of turf, strobe lights, and to a serried row of ready-to-go soldiers each one vacant of expression and individualism.

They were uniform—with one goal and one purpose: *seek and destroy.*

"The real question is...are *they* prepared too?" Ronin asked. "Will *they* deliver?"

As Ronin walked away from Priest and the conversation, he delivered the cold shoulder and was robbed of all his endearing qualities.

"Better get ready," Priest said to Ronin. "We'll be arriving soon."

———

Standing on the porch in his armor, fully stocked with all ammunition and blades, Quinn's Corinthian was folded back and he wielded only his assault rifle. Staring at the clouds, Quinn listened to the menacing moans bellowing from the now approaching storm.

"Anything?" a muffled voice hissed in Quinn's right ear.

Hearing this inside his Corinthian, Ally and Kayla had radios looped around their ears so they could communicate with Quinn. As of now, both women were situated along Kayla's vast and expansive property: Kayla in the field and Ally hunkering under the veranda.

"Negative," Quinn said, hand pressed to his Corinthian. "You?"

On the porch, Quinn gazed at Ally. He was standing behind a pillar and armed with a SIG.

"Clear for now. Kayla?" Quinn radioed his sister, who was almost fifty yards in the other direction. She was a badass sniper decked out in full camo. Also hiding under a blanket of similar color, the barrel of Kayla's CheyTac M200 rifle poked out like a provoked snake.

"All clear here. Nothing yet."

"All right," Quinn said. "Stay frosty. Clouds are gonna start movin' real soon."

"Copy that."

The shadows thickened, the trees rustled and swayed in a foreboding rock as the ground began to quake. From above, the face of a mechanical beast emerged from behind a broken cloud formation. Quinn squeezed his gun real tight.

"Are you seeing this?" Ally inquired. Quinn stepped.

From here, he could see almost the entire vessel—the great carrier held up in the sky. Unlike more conventional aircraft, this gargantuan beast of a machine appeared circular, more unique.

"We got company," Kayla said.

"Yeah," Quinn said. He stepped off the porch. With no response from Ally, Quinn trekked.

The ship was bullish and looked very similar to the animal itself.

As it began its descent toward the field, Quinn marched.

The ship's engines hissed and its propulsion systems unleashed a monotonous groan. Obviously a prototype, Quinn figured this one ship was something the government built the same as they had manufactured the elite compound-performance enhancing drug known as Hyper-X. For a moment, Quinn actually thought he was staring into the very ship used by the Kryptonians in the film *Man Of Steel*. Though this was only a stretching comparison, as it opened, the jaw of the Bull unfolded to reveal a steel, corrugated ramp. Walking along the metal decline, a man in white garb inched himself along. Not dressed in his usual attire, Priest stood proudly in new clothes and ogled Quinn like he was happy to see him.

"Howdy there, Quinn," greeted Priest with a poor, cowboy-like charm.

Quinn nodded and glared. "Nice ride you got there."

"You like it, huh?" Priest replied. "Yeah, it's just something we're testing out, you know, for quick deployment and extraction. Now that our plans have changed, we will need all the help we can get."

"I second that," Quinn said.

"Of course you do," Priest said.

"Took you long time to find me," Quinn said. "Thing's big, so I'm guessing it ain't fast."

"No, it's not the fastest," Priest said. "But it's not always about being fast or first, Quinn. Sometimes, actually, most of the time, it's just about having more than the other guy. And I know that you know...I always got more."

"Guess that means you didn't come alone, did you?" Quinn asked Priest.

"Well, I *would* have if there were any hopes of us doing this thing quietly, and I doubt there's any chance of that happening, so, I'm sure you can understand why I decided to come, as you said, prepared."

"Maybe," Quinn said, "but then, have you ever known me to *not* come prepared?"

Priest sneered at Quinn's smart-ass comment. "Nope," Priest said. "But then, you wouldn't describe *me* as someone who goes anywhere alone or as someone who doesn't always have a few tricks up his sleeve, am I right? I'm a man who relies on good old-fashioned ass-coverin' to ensure maximum power and total destruction."

"Yeah, well," Quinn said, "we'll just be seein' about that."

Taking a deep breath, still, Quinn wasn't done talking. "So...why didn't you just shoot me down from the sky then?" Quinn asked his former lord. "Seems like the easier, maybe even the better choice at this point."

"Well, you know how I feel about killing people from far away," Priest said. "You know I believe that when you take a man's life, even if you're not the one doing it, you should still send people there who are willing to see it with their own eyes. You should still be close enough to see the light leave their eyes as you watch 'em fucking die."

"I guess you couldn't resist the opportunity to do that here."

"It's been a while for me, so yeah...I want to do it again, but then why are you taking all of this so personally, Quinn?" Priest continued. "The code is the code and it needs to be protected. Besides, you're a loose cannon, a serious liability. You know things, things that no one should know. And, because you went lookin' where you weren't supposed to, I have no choice but to take action and get this done. And I will, Quinn, because that's what I do. I always...get it done."

"Maybe." Quinn, being purposefully dubious, didn't believe Priest would get anything done. He would try, but he would not.

"You know the game," Priest said. "You always have. In the face of a wrong call, you have to shatter it, strike it down, clean it, pull it apart, and then watch it die. It's how it's always been, Quinn, and it's how it needs to stay."

Quinn scratched his head, almost contemplating the extreme logic.

In the space between Priest's arm, he saw silhouettes beginning to take shape from within the pervading darkness. They moved like lights flickering on a black shore. Priest was not alone because he never was alone, but Quinn did not see his father. He did not see him or Ronin.

So far, all Quinn could see was Priest.

"How long do you think this fight will go on for, Quinn?" Priest asked, smiling. No answer came from the Custodian. He didn't want a trite exchange made of pitiless and poor words. This was, in the end, another attempt from Priest to delay. He also sought to convince Quinn of the flaws in his new moral compass, how his path to new retribution was a complete and utter failure.

Quinn was used to all this by now. He didn't care for anything that was going to be said.

All of it was futile. Quinn's mind was already made.

"How long do you think it will be before someone else takes my place, hmm?" Priest barked. "And then they come...*for you?*"

Quinn didn't answer. He had already considered this possibility.

Yes, Quinn knew things, and yes, they were things that most people should never know or understand, just as Priest said. Quinn was no spy and he was no spook. He was not like Priest. He *did* hurt people. He did kill. For the longest time, the only man who ensured Quinn did not face consequences was the same man standing before him now.

But where could Quinn go?

What were his options once he was done with this so-called life?

Tonight, Quinn thought only about survival and victory. This made tomorrow a mystery so dark and terrifying it might stay with Quinn for the rest of his life.

"You might have changed, Quinn," Priest said, "but the game hasn't. And no matter how much you want it to be different, it never will be. Sooner or later, someone will find you. They will find your family, and they won't care if you're better or worse or the same, they'll still want you dead."

Silent, Quinn had no words.

"Don't you see, Quinn? Even if you win," Priest continued, "*you lose.* There's no way out, no way back, not for people like us. We're both monsters, see? We're both the eradicators of our own worlds. We're the killers and the terrorizers and we don't belong in the world as it is, and that's why I'm going to give you one last chance, one last opportunity to change your mind. Come with me. Let's go back together."

Quinn scanned Priest while the shadows beyond shifted again. Two new faces suddenly appeared in the opaque space. Priest was...not alone.

"One last opportunity?" Quinn begged.

"Yes," Priest said. "Pack up, come onboard, and join me in our fight for a better future. Be what you were always meant to be, Quinn. Be a real soldier, a real assassin...*a real patriot.*"

Eyes shut, Quinn considered the eeriness of Priest's candid offer. He was seeing his audaciousness and how twisted the man's way of thinking was. Then, opening his eyes—literally and figuratively—Quinn gazed at this would-be genie standing in front of him.

Was Priest prepared to grant Quinn his final wish?

Oddly enough, Quinn had one. It was not a fantasy or a dream. It was real. It was honest and true.

"Not an assassin," Quinn said, and he lifted his carbine. "And I ain't a Custodian either."

"Oh no?" said Priest. "What are you then?"

Quinn smirked. He thought his answer was obvious. Then, he understood what he was thinking no one would ever accept, certainly not Priest. "I am..." Quinn hesitated to say the next words. If he did, then he would be revealing what was his greatest and most valued secret.

"Now...I'm a husband and...a father."

"What?" Priest said, baffled by Quinn's reply.

But now with his gun up, Quinn didn't hesitate. He shot Priest, who huffed as the bullets ricocheted off his protected body. Backing away, Priest glowered after being shot at.

"Big mistake there, Quinn. Big *fucking* mistake." Priest forewarned the Custodian as the shadowy haze lifted to reveal more men. Marching in unison, wielding MP5s, their eyes appeared redder than the blood pumping through their veins. Quinn activated his Corinthian and the mask enveloped his face. Quinn gazed at this new breed of enhanced Custodians and then raised his rifle. Nearing the pinnacle of an eventual slaughter, like all the previous fights, this one was an amalgamation of all the others. It was to be Quinn's best fight yet—his last and final moment to be what he was born to be.

"All right, boys..." Quinn addressed the killers of KEYS, now TAURUS, in his sister's backyard where he marked all his targets. "*Let's play.*"

———

Click, click...BOOM!

Three rapid shots spit from Quinn's gun and he was off to killing.

Indulging in the explosive firefight, Quinn felt as though he was in a gun range with infinite time and infinite ammunition. He likened the fight to diving into a pool after running a marathon and was in turn completely infatuated and ready for more.

Pile it higher and deeper, thought Quinn. Higher and deeper.

First soldier out, the others dispersed in concentrated groupings shortly after.

As everyone fired, Quinn enjoyed the solid protection provided by his Phalanx but pulled back to dodge and not to run. Stock tight in his shoulder, the MPX clung to Quinn's fortified body as the gun soon became one with the trucking assassin—an extension of Quinn's now fully equipped self.

"Eyes up!" Quinn yelled. More approached and Quinn fired. Hitting two more in the chest, another in the throat, back in the field, Kayla Quinn lined up her shots. She executed.

"I see you, you bastards."

The TAURUS infantry stomped from inside the Bull and this swarm of marching henchmen were nothing more than expendable foot soldiers trained to never quit and never back down.

Quinn curved in a tight circle and marked more of his targets. Soon, he was collecting headshots like a photographer. No misfires, and not a single one Quinn did not hit, his targeting might be precise and perfected, but it was not easy. Although striking each one in killshot sections, none were falling like they were supposed to. Protected by armor, they were safe in ways similar to Quinn. The bullets were not penetrating, and so these men were *not* dying.

Later, Quinn heard a booming sound from Kayla's rifle and watched as she struck two TAURUS foot soldiers in an attempt to *bottleneck* the opening of Priest's ship, the Bull. Kayla's strategy was right because it would force the men to spread and would allow for Quinn to move in. Penetrating the brigade, Kayla gave her brother the space he needed to get closer to Priest's position. Quinn could still see his nemesis standing there, chin up and smug. "Go! Go!" Priest roared from the Bull. He ordered the TAURUS to take the property. Quinn ducked and fired at the men making their way into this vicinity. He emptied his MPX and ejected the clip, reached down to his belt, and grabbed a fresh mag.

"Damn, these bastards are tough!" Quinn heard Kayla through the mic just as he smoked a third fucker in the face. Still not going down, the man's helmet popped off his exploding skull and Quinn guessed his age.

Looking no older than twenty, Quinn's head shook, disappointed.

Too young to die.

"What the fuck are these assholes on?" Quinn heard Kayla say. She shot two more and pierced another through the chest. Blood splashed Quinn's back and doused his body armor.

"Hyper-X," Quinn informed.

"What?!" snapped Kayla.

Quinn remembered how his sister was unfamiliar with the compound. He didn't have time to explain. Quinn, Ally, and Kayla were handling the invasion as best they could. In the end, it was one against fifty and two against twenty-five. And, though armored and durable, what Quinn was doing was *not* working.

He dropped his SIG MPX, withdrew his Glock, and went to work.

"We need more guns!" Kayla shouted. Quinn flinched.

"Right," he said to Kayla. She shot too.

Quinn grinned, peered over his shoulder. "That's your cue."

"Right." Quinn heard another voice say in the mic, now scratching his ear. After notifying Ally, Quinn shot another TAURUS through the neck and then snuck in underneath for a quick flip. Quinn grappled the invader and lifted him up from the ground and shot him through the temple.

Ally sprinted and wielded her gun with one hand as she stormed out of the bushes and joined Quinn in this bloody battle.

"No problem!" Quinn heard Ally shout and could feel her lungs deflating like balloons.

Quinn watched Ally roll across the grimy lawn. Shooting three rounds into three separate TAURUS, Quinn wasn't going to lie, witnessing Ally in action like this was very steering. Quinn and Ally were side-by-side: symmetrical and firing from every direction and dividing the army as it began to close in.

"You good?" said Quinn, shooting another TAURUS in the skull.

What number kill this was? Quinn could only guess. Maybe close to twenty, it was almost half of the assembly, but then he couldn't discern which ones went down and which ones would *stay* down.

"Fine!" Another two fell but this was because of Kayla and the entire yard was now a graveyard littered with unburied bodies.

"Good!" Quinn answered. He delivered a jumping back kick.

All these men were tough but what they lacked were skills, tactics, and efficiency. They were just pawns, *remotes*—no voice and completely expendable—and at times, Quinn felt as though he was in a face-off with an army of zombies. But, much like those monsters, Quinn could not do enough to stop the swarm.

"Spread out!" Quinn yelled.

He leaped and capped a third. Blowing another TAURUS in a messy burst of blood and bone marrow, Quinn kicked an additional foot soldier before shooting him square in the face. Seeing so many fall and die, Quinn looked up as Ally shrieked.

"Ah!" Ally's shouts were fierce. She fired five rounds and Quinn saw her and he heard her. Then Quinn's Corinthian unfolded and he followed the numbing sounds of his love's pain-induced voice.

"Ally!" Quinn rolled along his shoulder, reached up, and shot a new TAURUS. Quinn followed Ally across the field as he unloaded more rounds into more disoriented men. "You good?" Quinn asked Ally just as a new TAURUS approached from near Quinn's left shoulder.

Quinn turned and fired.

Ally inspected her body for wounds. "Fine!" she yelled back. She sprang to attention like a student at the sound of a dismissal bell.

"You sure?" Quinn asked.

Ally executed another TAURUS sneaking up behind her and Quinn extended his hand past the side of her face and fired.

"Yeah! Come on!"

Returning to standing side-to-side, Quinn and Ally had enough firepower to halt the invasion, yet these TAURUS men had little success with range and targeting, much of which was due to Quinn's armor as well as Kayla being the eyes in the sky. In truth, Kayla was more like the eyes in the field and possessed skills far better than these fools here to take her and her brother down.

Quinn hadn't been hit bad. So far as he could count, he'd been pegged over five times, give or take. The bullets deflected off Quinn's armor and not a single one managed to get through.

This was the case...for now.

And, as Quinn grimly gazed at his surroundings, the slaughter continued to build. In the Bull, Priest, Ronin, and Broder all watched as their plan to remove Kyle Quinn was thwarted.

This was not how they wanted it to go, not at all.

———

"Jesus Christ!" yelled Priest, his complexion red due to the frustration boiling inside of him like a tea kettle.

Acting like a pissed-off king, Priest was more than aggravated. He was consumed by his rage and his hate. Not getting what he wanted, Priest could only throw a tantrum and give orders at the same time.

"Are you just going to stand there and watch this happen?! Get out there! Now!"

Generally, Priest did not speak to his men with such anger. Ronin had never heard or seen Priest so loud. He took a step back and Broder took a significant step forward. "They have a *fielder*."

"A what?" Priest didn't know what Broder was referring to. A fielder was a term someone like Priest was not familiar with. What Priest desired was what he had upon arrival.

He wanted Quinn dead, but so far, the Custodian was still, very much, alive.

"*A sniper*," said Broder. "And I know exactly who it is."

"Do you now?" Priest made his inquiry as cutting and condescending as he could. Priest had no qualms regarding insult or rudeness. "Well, then, perhaps you should go and find out exactly who's been offing my men? Go and kill them now, before they kill more! Now does that sound like a suitable plan to you?!"

Broder cocked his Remington and marched toward the forest surrounding his daughter's property. "Yes. Yes, it does."

———————

"Kayla," Quinn said. Hand up to touch his Corinthian, and glaring at more of the approaching men, Quinn was focused on one in particular. "You got company."

Quinn saw his father disappear among the swarm of TAURUS.

Quinn couldn't comprehend how his father might attack Quinn's sister, who was his daughter. Usually, Quinn's father's strategy involved camouflage and misdirection, with him sneaking up on people and taking them out before they knew what was happening.

All of this was bad.

Kayla's kill box was the field. She was supposed to shoot multiple targets, not just one, which Broder Quinn was. He was only one target. Nevertheless, with the battle booming, Quinn's sister would encounter the man who was coming to hurt her. Quinn knew firsthand how this would be a difficult fight that so few could win.

Kayla wouldn't stand a chance.

"I have to stop him!" Quinn shouted at Ally. "Have to go!"

"Go!" shouted Ally. "Got this!"

Quinn popped another TAURUS and this time, fired multiple rounds in their midsection. Head shaking,

Quinn's path cleared and he stared dead ahead at his notorious rival. Now, as Ronin appeared, he looked at Quinn all fearless and unshaken. When Quinn returned, Ronin unsheathed his ninjato. "Your plan to draw us out was a good one," commended Ronin, "if not also...*entirely counterproductive.*"

"You think?" Quinn refused to make eye contact.

Ronin, prowling as a lion, made stillness more intimidating than movement.

Quinn was not interested in talking, nor did he want to hear the sound of Ronin's voice. What he wanted was to take Ronin's swords and shatter them with his tonfa. Then, Quinn would stand over Ronin's cold body, cut open his throat, and watch as he choked on his own blood. He'd do this before the night's end. The sun was just starting to set.

"I do," Ronin said. "Bringing in others...how...*Kyle Quinn of you.*"

"A good family sticks together," Quinn replied. "I don't think you could ever understand that."

"And I still don't," Ronin said. "I just know how terrible you're going to feel once you realize that it's you who is going to be held responsible for their deaths. It will be you who will beg as I walk over your family's cold corpses and smile. Only then will you see that the lives of your loved ones could have been spared and it was your arrogance that got them killed, killed because you could not protect them."

There was no grace Quinn could extend to Ronin. The mutual respect among them was now gone and the time for fist and sword was all that was left.

"I can't tell you how boring you are right now," Quinn gave Ronin the harshest glare he could. Ronin was not moving. Still in a fighting stance, he held one ninjato down by his chest while the other stayed tight by his side.

"How useless you can be," Quinn finished his statement. "Now...are you going to just stand there...or are we going to fucking *fight*?"

Ronin grinned. Rarely did he ever show pleasure or satisfaction. The fight, now taken in a new direction, had come.

Here, it was spartan versus ninja.

Legend versus myth.

Custodian versus Custodian.

Man versus *better* man.

Quinn tossed his Glock aside. It no longer served a purpose. And, with his primary weapon gone, Quinn's hands slipped behind his back, and he gradually removed his tonfa. Spinning the weapons, Quinn set them on his forearms.

This was exactly how Quinn wanted this fight to go.

And, as Ronin wielded his swords, in a flash, he and Quinn leaped at each other—two wolves fighting for alpha superiority. Careful upon approach, for that, Quinn could not be more grateful. Ronin jabbed and kicked, yet it was Quinn who landed the first blow.

"Ah!" exclaimed Ronin—stunned by Quinn's picture-perfect roundhouse.

Then, in a series of sideswipes and a myriad of strikes, nothing could touch Quinn's notorious rival. Ronin was an apparition—there one minute and gone the next. Quinn's aggression had served him well, but this fight called for something more versatile and profound. Ronin reoriented and Quinn decided to push. And then, with a clean flip, Quinn dove over his opponent and back-kicked Ronin in midair and knocked the ninja down. Relying on his strength, Quinn delivered five vicious blows—each one was more brutal. In a cascade of recollections, Quinn conjured all his best attacks from his life of many kills and winning fights. He could see all of them in a great montage of training, discipline, dedication, and coaching, and as Quinn lowered his tonfa, he flicked it up to his wrist.

Ronin, who stabbed only to have his blades caught by the clutches of a baton, he was pushed back and then forward just seconds before Quinn shattered his rival's notorious weapons. Then, in another spin, Quinn opened his stance, and hammered the tonfa into Ronin's chest—its blades ejected and inverted. The Custodian screamed in a ferocious roar akin to a brooding lion. In another cyclone of perfunctory moves and techniques, Quinn jammed the weapon straight into Ronin's heart, killing him.

At last, he brought an end to the final Custodian.

At last, Quinn finally knew who was the better fighter and it was not Ronin.

"Gah." Blood spilled out of Ronin's gawping mouth.

The defeated warrior fell slowly to his knees and Quinn stared, shivered, and then fell too. Ronin's breathing turned to an asthmatic wheeze before he finally ceased to breathe at all. Quinn chose to let his enemy—the only man who could hold him in a fight—die in peace.

Now weak and broken, Quinn chose the path of honor and not the one walked by so many others.

Ronin had fought well. He risked much, and now that he was at the end of his long road paced with fire and ash, Ronin earned a good death. And so, this was Quinn's gift to his rival. He chose to stay with Ronin until his eyes closed and he lay cruciform among flakes of grass.

He was a man done and gone to a better place, which was anywhere but here.

————

When Quinn was done wiping his face clean of blood, he looked around at his sister's property. Amid all the massacred and slain, Quinn spotted Ally covered behind a concrete divider located in the garden section of Kayla's massive yard.

Quinn watched as Ally picked up an MP5 rifle discarded by one of the dead. All the KEYS' "Custodians" were gone, yet the most crucial of invaders continued to stand and observe the land below. Quinn eyed Priest as he hid in the Bull.

"Looks like we got 'em all," Ally said to Quinn.

"All...but one," Quinn replied. He jerked his chin to gesture to Priest.

"Quinn, where are you..." Priest uttered these words as Quinn raced up the ramp.

The only weapon he had on him was his tonfa.

Quinn marched through the arched entranceway and explored the inside of this gothic craft. Ensconced in darkness, Quinn was again in the company of silence and negative energy. He studied the construct and then realized he was standing inside of something that represented the pinnacle of American military ingenuity. He was inside a futurist's wet dream of what might someday carry soldiers into battle.

As he crept, Quinn moved to a light glowing in the center of this great house.

For a moment, he thought he was alone. Then, Quinn heard a whistling before coming across a cluster of flashing gizmos and gadgets. Not far ahead was a swiveling contour throne so outlandish it could pass for a prop in a science fiction film. Quinn expected nothing less from a man like Priest. While Quinn did think he was by himself, he wasn't. Two seconds later, he turned and felt someone standing there.

"What are you doing here?"

Quinn flinched. It was Ally. Her eyes were pasty, presumably from exhaustion and fatigue. Her hair was left in clumps of frizzy strands which clung to her now sweaty skin.

"What do you mean? You think after everything we've done side-by-side that I'd let you finish this all by yourself? I want this thing over as much as you."

Quinn wanted to shake his head so he could outrightly deny the truth of that statement. No one could possibly want this over more than Quinn did. Ally was already here and the Bull was already up.

Bowing his head, Quinn sighed. "All right," he said. "Come on. I think I can smell him."

Ally followed Quinn as the Custodian walked through the monolithic structure. Accompanied by a non-linear framework, the ship's walls were high and accentuated by steel entablatures. In addition, there was an elliptical amphitheater engulfing a tall throne within the lair's concave center.

Quinn walked toward the grand throne. Behind it appeared two distinct windows—the Bull's eyes. And in front, standing at attention, was Priest. Quinn steadied up to his former master and could hear Ally following closely behind him. Then, raising his hand, Quinn ordered her to stop. This next part of the fight was between him and Priest.

No one else.

"Beautiful, isn't it?" Priest's need to segue into a daunting speech was a tactic he used too often. He did this when he was about to be pushed into a wall or forced to fight. Here, he would likely have to do both.

"From here," Priest said, "you can see everything below, can't you? You see what lies beneath and what lies ahead. And yet, they, the ones who stand below us," Priest said, "all the people you see down there...none of them have any idea about what it is that hovers over them, do they? They can't see who's watching or who fights to keep them safe. Always, they assume protection and safety are things granted with ease and without pain. They think there's no struggle or deception or great sacrifice needed in order to make their homes what they are today. Safe and secure, protected and loved. It's just...welcome, enjoy what you have while so many other people have to die to keep everything you adore stays yours forever."

Quinn began to encroach Priest's territory and he twirled his tonfa once again.

"No one has any idea what it truly takes to preserve and to serve." Futile as it was, Priest continued with his long and drawn-out exposition. "Everywhere, men and women die to make our country better. We sacrifice and we endure, even though we know we could all be doing so much more. And that's all I ever wanted, Quinn," Priest said. "I just wanted more."

"All you wanted was more blood," corrected Quinn. "And sacrifices from people who were not you. It always had to be someone else, right, Priest? *Always someone better*."

In a gradual turn of amused arrogance, Priest rotated to peek over his shoulder as his signature, maniacal grin began to show. "You don't think I've made sacrifices and lost things...just as you have?"

"You have," Quinn said to Priest, "but what I know now is...*real* sacrifice and *real* loss only happens when you're willing to surrender the only parts of yourself that matter, the parts that make you human. You do that so you can make other people happy. Sacrifice happens only when you let go of the things that can break you. And for me, the person who took the most ...always has been been you. You were the one with the key to people's secrets, their lives. You knew how to see into people's souls, and whenever you wanted to, you could reach inside and take what you wanted, because that's what you do, Priest. It's what you've always done. You're a breaker *and* you're a *taker*."

Quinn spoke in a higher tone now and emitted an almost childlike pitch. He called Priest what most would find to be an offensive and sinister title, *a taker*. Referred to this now, Priest was actually called a taker by a person who knew him better than most.

Priest sneered.

"Maybe," he said. "And maybe...there's just one more thing left for me to take."

Quinn responded to Priest with a furious gawk. Knowing what this *something* was, Priest continued to turn. From below his waist, he revealed his weapon . And, what Quinn saw, like so much else, he found unfathomable.

Quinn held his tonfa but Priest had removed his own, *his own tonfa*!

Unlike Quinn's, which was black, Priest's tonfa was white. It was made from what Quinn thought was oak. Elegant and smooth, the color coincided with Priest's outfit. He too was dressed in white. All of these details were things that, until now, Quinn hadn't noticed because of the dim lighting that consumed the Bull's rather spooky interior.

"What?" asked Priest. "You didn't think you were the *only* one who knew how to play these trumpets, did you?"

"No," Quinn replied. "I knew you're a tricky one, a slippery one. And so, what I see now is—"

"*Very* slippery," Priest finished. "Perhaps," Priest said, "but then you should also trust me when I say...you haven't seen anything yet."

Though not a minor threat, Quinn refused to hear anything more.

Holding his tonfa in both his hands, Quinn and Priest circled in the center of the coliseum. In the pit, they stood before the throne and the windows. And, as Quinn stared at the face of his greatest adversary, he knew his nemesis would not stop waiting for him.

This was to be Quinn's finest hour. His destiny. "Time to finish this. It ends here."

Lending a glorious invitation toward certain death, Priest had one reply.

"Bring it."

CHAPTER 10
NEMESIS FALLEN

Although she could not see him, she knew he wasn't far away.

The field was cleared and Kayla Quinn had done her job.

She'd done it well.

Now, it was time for her to return home or at least to make her way *back* home. Kayla wanted to try and get there before the day's end. How was she going to gather the dead and explain all the corpses that now decorated her illustrious property?

No idea.

Once Kayla saw Quinn board the Bull, she unloaded her CheyTac, disassembled the rifle down to its bones, and placed it back into its case. Once on her stomach, Kayla rolled over while next to her was the wheelchair as well as a clear path from her post.

What Kayla saw just seconds before she took apart her gun was him.

She saw him—her father was now walking toward her. Wheeling along, Kayla leaned into the path and felt her wheels grinding against the sandy surface. Soon as she moved, a branch cracked inches above her right shoulder. Broken into two pieces, Kayla gazed into the face of a man she only barely remembered. Now that she could see him, Kayla felt like she had encountered him at a time much sooner.

"Kayla." Broder Quinn managed to sound so surprisingly tepid it was actually quite calm. Completely out of character for a man like him, in fact, to Kayla's ears, it sounded like her dad was trying to come across as paternal: warm, tender, and kind.

Perhaps Broder was even pleased to see his daughter now.

And yet, Kayla didn't know if he was being sincere or whether this was a tactic done to bring her guard down. Choosing to see him not as a monster but as a man, it was exactly as she saw her brother. *They were the same.*

"Dad."

All Broder Quinn could do hearing the word spoken by his own daughter was to give whatever smile he could without shedding a tear. And Kayla could see from her father's long gaze, his infrequent glances, he was absorbing every facet of his daughter's appearance. Taking all of it in because to admit what happened to her required time and strength, doing this now...took every increment of Broder Quinn's remaining strength.

"I knew you were the one up in the nest, picking off strays," he said. "Nicely done, by the way."

"Thanks," Kayla said.

"See you haven't lost your touch," added Broder. "Have you been practicing?"

It was a quasi-joke that Kayla didn't laugh at, though she did find it amusing.

"I was always a good shot," Kayla said, chest out, chin up, and acting strong in the presence of her old man. "Why stop doing what you're good at?"

Shaking his head, Broder disagreed. "That's not *all* you're good at."

"Right," Kayla said. "Indeed."

Looking back, Kayla Quinn waited for her dad to tell her why he was here and what he wanted. As of now, he hadn't provided either. "Here to finish what you started," Kayla said, "to follow the orders of another madman or, for once, are you going to be what our mom thought you were...*a long time ago?*"

Kayla reflected on this next part thoroughly.

With as much concentration as she could lend here and now, she knew her mom thought her dad was a better man than he was. He had to be if she married him, but before Kayla could speak to this, she hoped to see some changes to her father's gruff appearance.

Truthfully, Kayla saw nothing, nothing except one thing. "A father."

"A father," repeated Broder Quinn. "Is that what you think I still am?"

"It's what you've *always* been," affirmed Kayla. "All you have to do is step aside and let me pass. Let me go."

"I would," said Broder, "but if I do that...what would that prove? You'd still hate me anyway. You'd still want me dead, and maybe you'd even shoot me in the back of the head. You would do this because you can do it, see? Because deep down...you want to do it."

"Is that what you really think?" Kayla said. "Is that something you think your own children would do to their father?"

"It's what Kyle wanted, what Cane wanted, so..."

"Yeah, and it's not what I want," Kayla fully expressed. "It's something I've never wanted. I let that part of myself go a long time ago. It's gone, and it's never coming back."

"And yet...you still *kill*," said Broder. "That part of you, well, it can't be that dead."

"I said I let it *go*," Kayla said. "I didn't say I let it *die*."

Broder was despondent. He sighed but then his downcast demeanor revealed a slight smirk later on. "You're the most like your mother, you know that?"

"So honor her then," Kayla said. "And for once, act on the better part of yourself, the part you forgot but I—*we*—never did."

Kayla observed her father the same way he was once observing her. Broder Quinn was a frail old man now. And, through this old man's broken gaze, what Kayla saw was a tired, exhausted, busted remnant of what *used* to be a human being. He might be broken, but he was not gone. Still, there was something there, small but present, so small it was, at the same time, almost beautiful.

"Now..." Kayla said, and she began rolling. "Are you going to let me through? Are you going to let me...go?"

Go.

This was a word Kayla Quinn selected herself. It was to remind her father of the simple truth about how the past *is* the past. She wanted her dad to abandon the darker parts of his soul, if he still had one. She wanted him to do what was right.

Like a dog who lost its master, and who was mad from years of torment, Papa Quinn was evil but not as evil as those he served. One day, Broder would answer for his corruption and his terror but it would not be here or now. Now, Broder had chosen to step aside and he chose to let his daughter go home. And, the Benelli that Quinn granted his sister with remained secured under her chair, and was unfired.

Safe as it was, Kayla was too.

Kayla embraced her dad's decision. Everything can be saved, Kayla reminded herself.

For her father, a conscience was present, and so was God.

He walked home with his daughter, by her side and hand on her shoulder.

There.

In the Bull's coliseum, Priest and Quinn were two gladiators fighting in the joy of combat and the deep-seated love of prolific carnage. One in white, the other one in black, together, they were the other's exact opposite.

Despite this, neither was prepared for what was about to happen.

Quinn seized his tonfa against his forearms and knew exactly how to wield the beautiful weapons. Still fascinated with Priest's decision to acquire the very same fighting tool, Quinn stampeded toward his former master and twirled his baton back around.

Now holding it in the natural position, and then switching to the special way of wielding the weapon, Quinn reversed the tonfa, and smacked Priest in an epic tornado of endless whacks. The grinning maniac stood and took each one clean like a champion.

"What?" barked Priest. "You didn't think I would risk a fight against you without having my own protection, did you?"

"Yes," Quinn replied. He thought of the only man capable of teaching Priest how to develop the deadly skills needed in order to fight. "He taught you well."

"Yes," Priest said. He flipped his tonfa back and then struck at Quinn.

Quinn blocked, parried the blow, and oriented himself again. Locked in an ultraviolent game of trading and showing, one would deliver and then the other would either sway or deflect. Quinn deployed an array of push kicks, straight punches, wrist locks, and elbows. He dished out hard knees, flips, tosses and throws. He channeled everything from judo, aikido, jiu-jitsu, Shotokan, Jeet Kune Do, and anything else he learned throughout his life.

Quinn had it all. *He was a tornado of martial arts prowess and perfection!*

"He taught me all I needed to beat you," Priest said.

"You won't beat me," Quinn said.

"Oh no, and why is that?" Priest asked.

"Because you're not a fighter, Priest. You're a robber and a fool."

Locked up, both Quinn's and Priest's tonfas were connected. One inserted was inside the other and so, neither man could move. Both were trapped. More than this, both Quinn and Priest were ensnared by their own brand of hatred and despair.

"Is that what you think?"

Fury burned in Quinn's set eyes and he coiled his lips. "Is there any other way to see it?"

The answer was obvious. Before Priest could speak, Quinn headbutted his chin and pounded Priest's ghoulish mug as the devilish fucker stared back with his Grinchy smile. "You can't hurt me, Quinn," Priest said. "You can't hurt me, and you won't kill me because now...now I have what you have, I am...*what you are.*"

At first, Quinn was puzzled by the statement.

The more he thought, the more he began to see its greater truth. It was then Quinn began to understand. Quinn recalled when he encountered Cane, remembered when he entered that hidden lab and discovered who he really was. Recalling how he unlocked Priest's plan to recreate a new breed of Custodians, it was a time whereby he had obtained Quinn's blood, and now...Priest possessed that exact same change. Whether or not he had ingested or injected himself with Quinn's own blood, this did not matter. Hyper-X was inside a man who was trying to kill Quinn but it was, at the same time, helping him to become stronger, better, more dangerous.

Would it make Priest better than Quinn? *Possibly*.

More enhanced? *Perhaps*.

Making someone immune to pain and suffering was the substance's true purpose. It was also Priest's sole intention for taking it in the first place. And, it was all he needed to stand toe to toe with Quinn. Priest was not better. He was not better because he was cheating.

And, as Quinn rained down on Priest, he punched until his fists sounded like a towel clacking against a stone. Still, the Custodian persisted. He hit harder and faster and Quinn attacked Priest full force and all he wanted was to throttle his lord's neck and snap it like a twig. But with every blow delivered, Quinn found himself descending deeper and deeper into a realm of pain he loathed. He was feral and he was screaming. Kneeling over his bludgeoned former master, Quinn clattered his once employer's wrecked jaw.

Quinn had beaten Priest's face into oblivion. Treating it as if it were a sick gag, Priest just kept smiling and laughing, laughing and smiling. He loved every second of it and all he wanted was more.

"Kyle!"

Unleashing more of his repressed pain, Quinn was lost in a typhoon of his own viciousness and fury.

After each blow, Quinn saw a new face.

He saw his father's and then he punched.

He saw his own and then he punched.

He saw Suloco, Briggs, Onix, Ronin, Ramos Mandilo, Alistair and Sirius Tenet, and then he punched, punched, and *punched*. And, with Quinn's fist set for yet another blow, he looked at the horrid mosaic of absolute savagery created by his hand alone. Beaten to a pulp, Priest face was a heap of mushed dough and he was decimated by a succession of bashing fists, and with no show of mercy at all, Quinn continued to hear Ally's screams as his hand slammed again and again into his beaten enemy.

"Kyle!" Lunging at Quinn, Ally grabbed his quaking fist. She held on as she held her stomach. Covered in sweat and tears, Quinn was a child who'd been pushed too far.

"No!" Quinn yelled. Clutching Priest by the collar, he gripped the wet bundle of tough material until his knuckles turned white. "He has to pay!"

"I know!" Ally screamed back, now nestled next to Quinn. "I know!"

"He has to pay!"

"He has!" proclaimed Ally. With a heavy breath, she guided Quinn's fist away from Priest's cratered mug and whispered. "He has. *He has*."

Ally addressed Quinn while she cupped the Custodian's shivering hands. It was only then Quinn's rage began to subside, that he settled to finally...rest.

He breathed.

"He has," Ally said this for the last time and then Quinn encountered the part of himself he never wanted to see ever again. He didn't want to be a killer without purpose—a vessel for rage, hatred, and destruction. Quinn, who was someone who only knew how to destroy and how finish a mission, this was now all a part of his past, and not his future.

"You don't have to be like him," Ally said. "You don't have to be *anything* like him."

Quinn's hand flowed from Priest, a man who lay crumbled and annihilated. After looking at the mural painted with hate and wrath, waves of gratification coursed through the Custodian's apathetic mind.

Enlivened by this feeling, Quinn recalled the words of his sister.

"End the cycle. Break free from the pain."

Quinn had broken Priest but it was not the kind of breaking Kayla had once referred to.

No, instead, it was justice—*justice exacted by his hand*. Better than an Eradicate or an Eviscerate order. It was better than Quinn's choice of Extrication. Quinn knew this was true even as he shivered, even as he felt Ally holding onto his hand.

"He's had enough," she said. "He's done."

The tremors in Quinn's hands stopped and he was up while Ally touched his shoulder. Quinn glared. "Get up, Priest. Get up..."

Priest chuckled.

He gobbled back more blood and leaned onto his now busted arm. With little strength left, Priest stood. Quinn wanted nothing more than to keep beating Priest into the ground. But, at last, Quinn accepted the will of the woman he loved.

"I'm going home," Quinn said to Priest. "I'm going home to my wife and to my life..."

"Your life?!" Priest exclaimed through curled lips. His crooked face bent even more as he splurged out his muddled words. "Is that what you think you have now?!" Laughing on, Quinn glowered at the hysterical madman.

"No," Quinn said. He denied Priest the chance to go on as he did before. "No more talking. No more convincing. I've beaten you. You lost and I won. That means I get to walk away. I get to go home."

"Maybe..." said Priest, "but then you broke the first rule of stepping into a new place, into a world you can't control."

"And that is?" Quinn gazed at Priest.

"Learn how to pull off a...successful...*landing*..." Priest said all of this with a grin.

Although perplexed, both Quinn and Ally had no idea how to land this gargantuan aircraft. Priest, still in the theater, leaned on his knees and lifted his arm. Laughing like a maniac, Priest wielded a remote he had pulled from out of nowhere. With this device in hand, Priest pressed a red button in its center.

"*Auto-destruction in ten*..." A notification rang out from speakers positioned throughout the Bull.

"Destruction?" snapped Ally. "What?"

"Son of a bitch," Quinn said. He continued to hear Priest's incessant, condescending laughs and he stepped aside and away. "He's taking us down..."

"Down?" asked Ally. "Down *where*?"

Sprinting to the windows, Quinn looked down. Though they were away from his sister's property, they were still not far enough. Sailing above a suburb comprised of semi-section houses, Quinn was already starting to feel the drop.

"Get back..." Quinn stomped in the opposite direction, now making a move for the controls so he could try and pilot this falling aircraft. If not, then Quinn would need to take cover somewhere, but Quinn was really searching for a safe place for when the vessel did eventually find a way to land.

Back on his feet, Priest aimed his Desert Eagle and completed another trick for Quinn and for Ally.

"Ally," Quinn said, pushing her behind him. "Do not move."

Priest, conceitedly licking his lips, he was looking like a human car accident, and the fact that he was armed meant little to Quinn. There were no more bullets left in his gun.

Maybe.

"You played your hand well, Quinn," Priest said. "You played it well, just as you always do. But, like you should know by now, I always cover my ass. For me...there's always a way out."

"Put the gun down, Priest. *It's over*."

"Nothing's over...till it's over." Showing his classic clownish grin as if it were the last time he ever would, even near death, nothing had changed for this horror of a human being. "And, as you can see. I'm still here," Priest said. "I'm still...fucking breathing!"

"Priest..." Quinn uttered Priest's name and phrased it like a warning. "Don't..."

"You can't win," Priest barked. "I keep telling you this, and yet, you still can't seem to get it through your thick fucking skull! You can't win, because people like me...we always win! *We* are winners! No matter what you do, no matter where you go, me—someone like me—they'll always find a way to beat you! And when they do, they'll take everything from you! Whatever you have, whatever you love, I'm going to have it, Quinn! I will..."

"And they," Quinn said, speaking for himself. "Whoever they are, *can* come for me..."

Eyes on Priest, Quinn would have the final word. When he spoke, he ejected the blades from his tonfa and turned around very slowly. "They can...come...for *me*." Quinn made this declaration while standing next to Ally so he could protect her from Priest's gun. "They just can't have them," Quinn said. "Never *them*."

The *them* Quinn was referring to was Ally and his unborn child. And when Quinn said this, Priest did what he had before.

He laughed.

"Well, they don't have what I have, now do they?" Priest lifted his hand and showed Quinn the remote—the very tool he had used to place the Bull on its current crash course toward obliteration and doom. "Without this," Priest continued, clutching the last tool he would ever hold. "You have nothing. The same as you always have."

"Now that's where you're wrong," Quinn quickly debunked. "I *don't* have nothing, not anymore. Actually, I have exactly what I need...to bring you down."

"Oh, and what? You're going to let me walk away *twice*, are you?"

"No," Quinn said. "You just don't have what you think you do."

"I got your gun," Priest said, aggravated.

"You do," Quinn said, glancing at the window. "But what you don't have...is a *shot*."

"What?"

Quinn gallantly pushed Ally aside and shouted. "Get down!" Then, Quinn ducked, rolled, and jumped. Bladed weapon out, Quinn sliced up and he cut and severed Priest's hand right off from his damn and dirty and crooked arm!

"Ah!" Priest writhed in agony as the hand once holding his precious remote dropped to the floor.

Then, with an open hand, Quinn snatched the detached limb and held it tight. With one problem solved, Quinn was up again. And, still relying on the power of his tonfa, Quinn cut Priest several times across the chest and slashed him up like chop suey. Each cut was more lethal than the last, and soon, Priest had no choice but to let go of his weapon completely. After, Quinn snagged the madman by his throat and stared into his soulless, blood-shot eyes.

"You're too late," Priest said. "Ship's going down. There's nothing you can do to stop it."

"Yeah, well, sometimes you can't stop a crash," Quinn replied. "Sometimes, you just have to suffer the wreck and pick up the pieces after."

Quinn tossed Priest aside like he was trash. Then, torquing his lips, Quinn raised his legs. Rage converting into raw, uncontainable power, all Quinn's malice had been transformed into superhuman strength. He had everything he needed to end this fight. Then, with a quick push, Quinn booted Priest into the window like a spartan.

He watched Priest fall to his death in a pathetic ending to a pathetic life.

"Gah!" Out the window, Priest plummeted like a disgraced king.

Grabbing the hand cut off, Quinn sprinted at Ally, who was hunkered by a pillar outside the pit. "Hold onto something." Quinn said this as he peeled Priest's dead fingers from the remote and examined the device.

"Is there any way to stop it from going down?" Ally asked Quinn.

"No," Quinn said. "I don't think so. Just...just hold on."

He wrapped his arms around Ally and clicked the remote. Quinn pressed whatever he could to try and slow down the Bull, but doing anything and everything, still... the ship continued its fall. Next to Ally, still together, she and Quinn waited and they hoped.

For a time, Quinn prayed or did what he thought was praying.

"I want you to know, Kyle," Ally said. "I want to tell you..."

"Whatever you're going to tell me, wait," Quinn said. "I have a plan."

Now up, Quinn raced to a broken window and stared down below.

"What?" asked Ally. "What do you see? A place to land?"

"No," Quinn said, head poking out. "A place to... *jump*."

"Jump?" exclaimed Ally. "Jump where?"

"*Water*," Quinn said, just barely.

"Water?" Ally glanced as Quinn began to back away.

"If we jump down while this thing's still falling, we might be able to land in that pool down below!"

"And the ship? It's still going to crash."

"Exactly, which is why we can't be on it when it does."

"But...the people...the houses...*it's*..."

"No time to explain! We can't stop! We have to jump...*now*!"

"Where?" Ally's lip quivered and she was descending into full-on panic. "Jump where?"

It was a good question, one not even Quinn knew how to answer. Ally was pregnant. Asking her to jump was insanity but then there was no other option when heading for a crash.

"*Lake*," Quinn said. "I see one, yeah?" Quinn pointed down to the land below. There was a black pool isolated from the rest of the suburb separate from Kayla's property. It was there, and it was low, and it was also...*their only chance*.

"But..." Overcome by uncertainty, Quinn was burdened by the fact that the Bull was going to land on the homes of many innocent, unsuspecting people.

"Come on!" Snatching Ally's hand, in one last explosion of pure exertion, both charged at the window. Storming after this gap, both began the near one-hundred-and-fifty-foot descent from sky to land.

"Ah!" Screaming all the way down, Quinn looked up at the Bull.

Still falling, oddly, the vehicle had changed course. In the distance, Quinn caught sight of two F-22s that had come to halt the impending destruction. Although this was supposed to be good news, the jets fired their missiles into the falling vessel and incinerated the Bull into a fiery cloud.

Seeing this, Ally's screams were louder, if that was even possible

"Ah!" The searing heat singed the back of Quinn's neck.

Though the ship was destroyed, the fallout was immense, and judging by the incoming fighter jets, this also indicated to Quinn a possible evacuation for the citizens below.

Quinn's focus was on the water—the small lake—which was still their only chance.

Going down, Quinn was freefalling—parachuting—like he did back in Special Forces. In this case, Quinn didn't have a parachute. He also didn't have someone with him who could help.

He knew how to dive, but Ally, however...did not.

Quinn held onto her as best he could. Falling far and fast, Quinn and Ally cratered the murky surface as stems of dank black liquid spread in broken tendrils. Together, both Quinn and Ally landed in a crash that shook them almost to the point of being unconscious and Ally could barely hold onto Quinn after making contact. This fall, combined with the impact, didn't concuss Quinn, it only left him in horrendous shock.

"Ally!" Quinn was the first to emerge.

He cut the body while screaming Ally's name. "Ally!"

Quinn approached Ally as she bobbed along. He picked up her head and ran his hands through her drenched hair. Rubbing her cheeks, Quinn exclaimed again into Ally's ear like this was his last chance to be heard.

"Can you hear me? Ally, can you hear me?"

Quinn, who tried shaking her awake, Ally gawped as she puked out more water. Knowing he did all he could, jumping was the only way for them to survive. If they stayed onboard, they'd both be dead, no doubt.

As Quinn looked at Ally, her lashes fluttered and her throat constricted. Then, just as her eyes began to peel back, she gasped for more precious air.

But still...she did not move.

"Come on." Quinn swam with Ally's arm slung over his burly shoulders. He kicked and headed to the shore-line. In this "reservoir", more exploding noises echoed from inside the Bull, which was half on land, half on water. Quinn could hear more screams coming from more random citizens and watched them as they all ran.

"I got you," Quinn said to Ally. He pulled her closer.

"Oh, no," Ally said, "this is bad. This is *real* bad."

Quinn was gentle as he eased Ally to the shore as the sirens blasted the setting. Quinn carried Ally to the marshes on the other side of whatever he was in. He thought he was in a pond.

Maybe it was that or maybe it wasn't.

"Hold on," Quinn said. "Lay down. Don't talk."

"I..." Ally quaked.

Quinn scanned her top to bottom. The entire time, her hand stayed pressed to her stomach. She was holding this as well as the wounds she suffered during the course of the invasion. "Jesus."

"I'll be all right," Ally assured Quinn. "Just need to rest, just need to..." Ally, blacking out, all the energy and emotion once present on her face melted away. Now, she was empty, stripped to bare, and barely awake.

Ally's hand slid to Quinn's arm. He shuddered. "Ally!" Quinn screamed as he nudged Ally's head. Heart rate jacked, he found himself shaking while continuing to try and wake the love of his life as she lay still in his arms. Ally's body had gone cold. Quinn stood, experiencing so much emotional peril he didn't know what feeling to start with.

"Ally!" A new voice came and Quinn looked to see who it was.

On the scene, somehow, Kayla was there and she was wheeling after her brother, following by several paramedics and police. Quinn watched this while cradling Ally's limp body. Quinn noticed his sister, though his sight was mostly obscured. Although Quinn was pleased to see his sister survived, amid the cluster of uniformed men, the Custodian did see another shape, another man.

"Dad?"

———

Surviving a crash landing, what Quinn recalled afterward was only a haze.

Seeing little, after everything happened so fast, Quinn was back in yet another hospital, only larger, with bigger hallways and higher ceilings. In a tent comprised of beds and filled to the brim with many patients, all injured and in urgent need of care, Quinn sat in this room with Kayla and...with his father.

"What the hell..."

Before being taken to the emergency wing inside this great big tent, Quinn caressed Ally and refused to let her go. The paramedics had pulled her off Quinn and she was loaded into an ambulance and rushed away. In this hospital, Quinn sat up in the cot and there, he was greeted by a surprisingly familiar face. Standing in scrubs was William, a doctor called in because of the catastrophe, this explicably united Kayla with her daughter and her husband.

Quinn watched Bethany fall into her mother's arms and kiss her on the cheek.

She was enthused to see Kayla return. This hospital

was an emergency ward set up on the crash site. After the Bull's destruction, debris rained down on the people below and some suffered burns while others were burdened by other kinds of terrible injuries. None of this boded well for the only person Quinn wanted to save. Pacing back and forth, there was so much Quinn wanted to say to so many people, including the police.

All of them wanted to ask the most basic questions, but Quinn didn't know what to say or where to begin. He was one of the most wanted men in the country. It would be no surprise to see him in handcuffs and forbidden from seeing Ally at all.

Folding his hands as if in prayer, Quinn was a monk in desperate need of spiritual guidance. "Please, save her," he begged. "Please make sure she's okay."

Quinn, not much of a praying man, God didn't answer people like him, he thought. He was what some would call irredeemable. And, though he might be on a better path now, still, Quinn had a long way to go. This was something Quinn had already accepted. Redemption and good graces were reserved only for people like Ally, and that's why Quinn was praying for her.

He was praying only for her.

Quinn understood why he didn't deserve much, but she did. Ally deserved the whole world.

"She'll make it, Kyle. She will."

Quinn looked at his father. Stripped of his gear, Broder stood there in raggedy garbs, appearing like a house painter on the job. Quinn often wished his old man was dead. Having wanted to kill him for so long, when Quinn saw him now, he felt different.

"And now you're going to pretend like you care. Last time I checked," Quinn said to his dad, "you were standing alongside him."

"I was," admitted Broder Quinn. He didn't deny this,

nor did he refuse to take any responsibility. "But last time I checked, he also wanted to kill me too, and I am here because I want to stand...someplace else."

Quinn's father struggled to admit this next part.

"I wasn't standing with him at the end. Man was going to offer me what I wanted more than anything in my life, and that anything was purpose, maybe even the chance to go back and start again. And well, when you're someone who's done the things that I've done, you go to the people who give you something other than more guilt and pain. Even if it's what you deserve, still...you go."

"Well," Quinn said, "I guess none of that matters now. Priest is dead, and so is KEYS, and his plan for a new Custodian program is over and done. I guess this leaves you without your precious purpose. No job and no future, same as me."

"No," said Broder, "you have a purpose, and I do too."

"Oh yeah?" Quinn, justifiably skeptical, didn't buy what his father was selling.

Quinn was harboring less anger toward his old man and the reason for doing this?

For Quinn, it was Kayla. Not long ago, she forgave Quinn for all the horrors he committed. It was not the same as his father, which Quinn knew, but the act of granting peace was similar.

"I got a lot of apologies to make," admitted Broder. "It's going to take a long time to fix the things I've broken, if they even can be fixed. I thought maybe I could help with what Priest was doing. But now, I gotta ask myself, why start again when what I built first...*still needs work?*"

Quinn's dad—the man he hated more than anything or anyone—now stood before his only surviving son, broken and ashamed. As he did this, Quinn saw himself as he was now. He and his old man were almost exactly the same. This could be where Quinn ends up in the next ten to twenty years. Vowing to make different choices, Quinn did also seek to live a different life.

He wanted to break the cycle, and his dad was part of that cycle.

And he could change it. He could end it right here, right now.

"Thanks," Quinn said. "Thanks for being here. Thanks...for coming back."

Quinn meant what he said in more ways than one.

Broder Quinn nodded. Being a man with heavy baggage, his eyes were glassy but not hollow. As Quinn was the only son he had left, a fondness was now there that wasn't before and, two seconds later, Kayla herself rolled across the room when still in her chair.

William followed.

Quinn sprang to attention. "What's happening? Where is she? Is she going to be all right?"

William removed his mask, bowed, and paused for a moment too long for Quinn to handle. "I got to her as quickly as I could, but..." William looked away from Quinn. Biting his lip, Quinn knew a clear sign of a struggle when he saw one. Instantly, Quinn's intestines felt knotted, his whole body strained.

"But *what*?" This question was Broder's. He stood with Quinn, just as concerned.

"But...she's *pregnant*," William said.

"She is," Quinn confirmed.

"Do you know how far along?" William asked.

Quinn thought about the question. It was one Quinn *should* know. Given that he had only just received word of Ally's pregnancy, he couldn't calculate or recall when the baby was actually conceived.

"No," Quinn said. "I don't."

"Why?" Kayla asked. She was next to Quinn and

looking at William with doleful eyes. "Why does that matter?"

"She's about *five months along*," William said. "Barely showing, or did you not notice?"

Quinn nodded. Was Ally heavier? *Maybe*. She always looked the same to Quinn.

Did she have a tummy, was she noticeable?

To Quinn, all of this was possible, but given his priorities, where he was mentally, he couldn't see how he could have made note of Ally's physical changes, not that he would have even if he did notice.

"The baby was hurt," William said. "But the injuries Ally suffered were substantial, and I had no choice but to operate. It was tight and difficult, but..."

"But?" Quinn demanded. "*But what?*"

William declined to answer. Looking at Quinn like he was trying to say something, William was doing it only with his eyes. "The baby...it survived *somehow*," William said, "but Ally she..."

Quinn wasn't told how his unborn child had managed to survive.

He assumed it was a result of Hyper-X, the synthetic that altered Quinn's DNA and had been a part of him since before he could remember. Evidently, it altered his child's life too. Now Quinn's unborn child was a warrior, and warriors survive. This explained the baby's miraculous ability to continue to breathe despite having almost died. It explained this but it did not explain Ally. She was a warrior too.

"What?" said Quinn. "What happened to her?"

"The bleeding...I couldn't get it to stop," William said. "That, and the impact to her brain, her body, she suffered a severe traumatic cerebral injury, and she..." William said no more. He frowned. Quinn knew what this was. Quinn was already standing there for too long. He was needed somewhere else.

"Can I see her?" Quinn asked William.

"Yes."

Quinn stepped out of the waiting room, but before he did leave, Kayla rolled next to him. "I can go with you," she said.

"No," Quinn said. "Stay."

Kayla, in her chair, Quinn's father was standing behind her, and neither one said anything, yet Quinn did.

"This is something I need to do on my own."

"Of course," Kayla said.

Quinn nodded.

And then he followed William through the crowded hallway, which was only just a narrow passage, and to one room located six paces in front of him.

Into this new space, there Quinn saw Ally in the bed, alone and asleep.

————

When he first entered this room, Quinn was experiencing an illness that rivaled any of his past afflictions. Ally's lips moved but her voice was a gaggle of misplaced vowels. Like a toddler trying to pronounce their first words, amid the struggle, Ally fought to finish. When she did, she was barely heard.

"Ally." Quinn rushed to Ally's bedside. William's voice spiked as Quinn ran.

"Careful."

Quinn slowed and heeded the advice of his brother-in-law.

"I'm okay," Ally assured, struggling to sit straight. Pushing herself up with her hands, Ally stared at Quinn with sunken cheeks and a pronounced frown.

"Stay," Quinn said. "Don't move."

"I want to," Ally said. "I need to."

"Are you..." Quinn wanted to ask Ally if she was okay. Before he could, he saw what a silly question that was. Far from okay, he didn't finish his query. Instead, he looked at Ally's hand, cupped it gently, and then brought it to his lap.

"I'm still breathing, that's something, but the baby... it's..."

"*Alive*," Quinn said.

"What?" Ally's voice went high and a twinkle glinted in her eyes.

These signs of joy were not only infectious for Quinn, they were also necessary and desired.

"You..."

"Not me," Quinn said. "It wasn't me. It was..."

Quinn pointed at William. Quinn's brother-in-law stood in the doorway and he waved.

"Oh my god...it's...a..." Ally's words were present but barely formed. It was only Quinn's proximity that allowed him to hear.

"Miracle," Quinn said. "*It is*."

"Thank you," Kayla said to William. "Is the..." Ally's throat tightened. She fought to speak, and fortunately, William already knew what she was going to say.

"*The baby's safe.*"

"How?" asked Ally, puzzled. "It should be..."

Ally didn't say dead. Quinn thought the same thing. Then he knew what to say too.

"Let's just say our child is a rare blood type. For the time being, he's safe. He's going to be okay."

"I want to see our baby." When Ally said this, she tried turning in her bed. She scooched toward the edge of the mattress. The second she moved, William stepped in.

"No," he said, alert. "You need to stay...*you need*..."

Ally fell hard into her pillow and Quinn helped to guide her down gently. Quinn quivered. He noticed Ally's hand starting to shift and she wrapped one hand around the other to stop it from shaking. Yet, it continued even as Ally held.

"*Shh*," Quinn said. "Just rest, okay? Just rest."

"Tried," Ally said. "Been resting for too long, but..."

Ally wearily looked at Quinn. Jaw dropped, he was prepared to speak, but the aches previously experienced had now returned. Still, the Custodian stayed tall and kept still despite the struggle.

"What did he say?" whispered Ally.

"You mean William?" said Quinn. He didn't expect this to be Ally's question.

"Yeah," Ally said. "What did he say about me?"

Quinn knew well what William said. Ally was hurt. Her organs were impacted to the point where they were inoperable and there was just nothing Quinn could do to change what was now...an absolute certainty.

"He said..." Quinn gulped his next words down. There was truth and then there were Ally's last moments. Quinn remembered both. "He said you're going to be just fine..."

An outright lie, Ally stared at Quinn with a forced smirk. She could see right through her man's obvious fib, and though Quinn's intention was to provide Ally with comfort during her final moments, still...even he could not accept them.

"*Liar.*" Tears spilled from Ally's pallid face, and Quinn's agony flowed through him water exploding as a result of a collapsed dam. No way to contain this sadness, in a second, Quinn crumbled. He sobbed. Filled with more water than a house during a flood, once this happened, there was nothing for Quinn to do except let on and let go.

"I should have protected you," Quinn beckoned. "I should have. I..."

"Kyle," Ally said. She held Quinn's hand. Bawling now, Quinn shivered as more tears washed away the blood that once stained his face. He couldn't hold back, but he tried to. He fought to.

"I shouldn't have brought you into this, but I did. I should have tried harder, fought better..."

"Kyle, you won," Ally said. "You're alive. You made it, and you did what you thought was right. You did what you thought you never would. You made the right choice."

"But I couldn't save you!" Quinn's shouts echoed, his booming voice trailing out from the small room. "I couldn't save you! I should have and I didn't! I didn't because I was—"

"You think you're weak?" Ally said. She squeezed Quinn's hand. "Don't say you are. It's the one thing you're not."

Hand over his face, the woman Quinn loved was going to die and there was nothing he could do to stop it.

"But you have to be strong," Ally said, "as strong as you can be."

Strong as Ally was, Quinn was now weaker.

"I need you to not spend the rest of your life plagued by regret," she said. "I need you, because they will need you, do you understand?"

Ally was right about everything. Quinn couldn't argue with anything.

"And I need you to do something else for me too, okay?"

Quinn nodded.

While he had accepted Ally's fate, whatever she wanted, Quinn didn't care because he was prepared to accept it. He waited for Ally to finish so he could fulfill her last request, held her hand, and gazed sullenly into her now fading eyes.

"Okay."

"Promise me you will protect them, our child...protect them no matter what."

"I will." Quinn, who was never more serious about anything in his entire life, was a man who honored his word, and, for Ally, he would die defending it. At the end, this was all Quinn could give.

"Promise me you will leave this life and you will not pursue a life of vengeance or retribution, that you will let it go and never bring it back. Please, Kyle...you have to." Ally blinked. Tears erupted from her face the same as Quinn.

"I know. I promise."

"And please, don't ever accept the idea that some people are too broken to be fixed," Ally said. Initially, Quinn wasn't sure what this meant. He chose to listen. What came after, Quinn understood. It was beautiful. "Never think that, Kyle. *People can amaze you.*" Ally's head came to a static slump, and she exhaled. "People...are *good.*"

"Ally!" Quinn's exclaims echoed through the entire hospital room, once silent but now thrashed by rancor and rage. Holding nothing back, he watched Ally slip away.

Her heart monitor altered its pitch and now flatlining, Ally was entering the unholy jigs of death and moving into that great black void of unknown and unclear.

"Ally!" Quinn reached for her while the blinking monitor punctured every fiber of his being. "Ally!"

"Kyle!" William shouted from the door.

Time ended with Ally, and so much of it would end with Quinn too.

What remained now was only his word, his oath, and his promise.

"Kyle," William said, reaching for Quinn's arm.

"Ally, no!" Quinn knocked William's hand off his shoulder.

"Kyle, you have to..." William pleaded with Quinn, who knew what his brother-in-law wanted to say.

Let go.

William tried to keep Quinn calm, but the Custodian was immersed in a cloud of deep sorrow and crippling grief. Two nurses stood alongside William and they also tried to pull Quinn from Ally's bed. Although Quinn could have easily knocked them all down, now was not the time for violence, for selfish disruption. Quinn continued to shout and became further absorbed in the beauty of his breakdown. Hysterical, Quinn repeated Ally's name as his body trembled. He did whatever he could to continue to see her, whether in his mind or here as she slept.

Ally Shepherd, the love of Kyle Quinn's life, his everything, the greatest person he'd ever known, was now... gone.

"Ally, I love you! I..."

Fallen to his knees, with Kayla and with William, and near his father too, all Quinn wanted was to hold Ally in his arms for as long as he could. He would do anything to have just another second of time with her, even if she wasn't here, even if she was gone.

But that time was no more, and so Quinn cried more.

"I love you, Ally, I love you! I've always loved you!"

Quinn liked to think Ally could still hear him. And so, as he said the same words again, he hoped she did. She had to. She was still with him, still with Quinn.

———

Once taken away from Ally's bedside, Quinn was sitting on a bench distant from where he was before. Thinking of Ally and only of her, the very last thing Quinn wanted was to be disrupted, least of all by someone in a suit who addressed him by his full name.

"Kyle Quinn."

Glaring at the people approaching, no doubt they were government and, if they were here to arrest the Custodian or not, Quinn didn't care. Jail sounded like a good place to be right about now.

"Who wants to know?" The one Quinn spoke to him was a tall, black woman.

She was the same person Quinn remembered back when the Bull crashed and Ally was lying in his arms. Stepping toward Quinn, his guess was CIA, but this woman could also be FBI or NSA. Whatever she was, it didn't matter. Few things did now.

"Tashawna Wallace, Staff Operations for Langley, I..."

"You work for the CIA," Quinn cut the woman off before she could continue.

"What gave it away?" asked this woman, Tashawna.

A cross between Tyra Banks and Jennifer Lopez, Tashawna had implied she knew Ally. Quinn assumed they were friends. Here to offer a little context and personality, Tashawna Wallace's presence made Quinn blurt out the first thought that entered his mind.

"I'm sorry, by the way. I know it's a little late for apologies, but..."

"It's a little late for lots of things," Quinn added, "but I still appreciate it, no less."

Quinn saw two men in suits walking alongside Tashawna. They siphoned the space so no one could pass by or see Quinn with the female agent.

"Yes, well, Ally Shepherd was one of our best," Tashawna said. "When she left us, it was clear she would go on to do other things. Certainly, we didn't expect this to be it."

"So...you did know her?" When Quinn asked this, Tashawna's leg slipped over her left and she sat next to Quinn cross-legged. Quinn found her friendly and kind. Then again, Tashawna was government—cut from the same cloth as Priest. Perhaps, it was Quinn's sadness making Ms. Wallace seem so affable but he trusted his instincts. They assured him she was different. She was better.

"I did," Tashawna said. "I knew her well."

"You two were friends?"

Tashawna nodded, biting her lip and displaying a clear sign of a struggle. It seemed hard for Tashawna to make more comments than those made so far. From what Quinn could see, she and Ally might be what he thought they were.

"Yes, as a matter of fact," Tashawna said, "we were. She wasn't the only one who notified me. I was close with Paul too."

"Paul?" said Quinn. Initially, he didn't know who Tashawna was speaking about. Then, it became obvious.

"Paul Heinreich," Tashawna said. "He told us everything. Actually, he was one of the reasons we arrived as quickly as we did. You have more friends than you think, Kyle."

"Had," Quinn corrected. "*Had* friends."

"Right," answered Tashawna, disheartened by Quinn's need to clarify. "Sorry."

"Why are you here? To mourn?" Quinn's tone cut right through his words. He wanted to get on with the reason why Tashawna was here and he refused to wait.

"I am here to talk about the future, *your future*, Mr. Quinn."

Quinn continued to examine the appearance and

manner of this mysterious woman. His hands felt heavy, like his palms were stacked with weights. Quinn's future was not set. What would become of him now was based only on a promise and a dream. Nothing else.

"Oh?" said Quinn. "*My* future."

"Yes," replied Tashawna. "See, we all knew about Priest, about the kind of man he was. We also knew that his Custodian program, while somewhat effective and some might even say necessary, wouldn't pan out the way he thought it would. And, the one whom we relied on for intel about it, all of it, well, that person was Ally."

"Ally?" said Quinn. "You relied on Ally?"

"Yes. See, she was our mole inside the mole, so to speak. She worked with Priest in some capacity, as you know, but given the secrecy of his program, the trajectory he wanted this country to follow, we couldn't get very far, so we dropped one of our informers in to help see what we could see."

"Then you should know...the buck doesn't stop with him. There will be others too, others who were involved," Quinn said. "Some very powerful and also very dangerous."

"I would assume so," Tashawna said, "but now that Priest is gone and his experiment over, I imagine the people you're speaking of will all scatter. They'll go back to their little hiding places where they will remain, for now, at least."

"Well, if you're looking for someone to go and find them, you're asking the wrong guy."

"Oh, I'm not asking," Tashawna said. "That's not why I'm here." Tashawna paused, took a beat, and then continued to speak. "No, I'm here because it would seem that Ms. Shepherd cared enough about you to reach out to her friends and carve out a nice insurance policy for herself should anything happen, and now that something has—"

"You've come to collect?" interrupted Quinn, abrasive, almost to the point of losing his cool.

"Not exactly," Tashawna said. "Let's just say I'm a woman of my word."

Quinn glimpsed at a folder tucked under Ms. Wallace's left arm. Until now, Quinn hadn't noticed. This was the same gesture Priest would perform when presenting the Custodians with all of their missions.

Quinn couldn't take his eyes off the folder.

Tashawna slipped it to Quinn. He snatched it. "I see."

"Ally spoke about you often. She discussed your situation and she told me that, should Priest go too far, which he clearly was going to do, then there was only one person who would be able to stop him. You."

Quinn examined the contents of this folder. From what he could gather, it was nothing more than a bunch of blacked-out documents, with some photographs, a few detailed ones pertaining to the other Custodians, all now dead, but it also described KEYS, Hyper-X, TAURUS, Priest's past, as well as Quinn's.

All of it was here, in the palm of Quinn's hand.

"What is this?"

"That," Tashawna said, "that's all that's left of it, of everything."

"Of what exactly?" Quinn asked.

"Of everything Priest wanted to create," Tashawna said. "The Custodians. Kinetic Youth...whatever the hell it's called. TAURUS, NX-17, and..."

Quinn knew NX-17 only as Hyper-X. But what Tashawna said and mentioned all seemed so present and outlined.

"And whatever else he was trying to control or create, all of it's there, right in front of you."

"Interesting," Quinn said.

"Yeah, well, I want you to get a good look at it," Tashawna said, "because all of it is going away, forever. I'm going to see to it that all evidence of this program is terminated and anyone else connected to it is found and sent away for a very long time."

When Tashawna informed Quinn of this plan, if that's what it was, he wanted to offer his hands so he could be handcuffed and taken away. Anyone connected meant him too. And so, now Quinn understood why Tashawna Wallace was here and exactly what it is she wanted.

"Everyone," Tashawna said. "Everyone except *you*."

"Me?" Quinn asked. "Why...*me*?"

"Don't know," Tashawna replied. "But...let's just say given what you've done, what you are, maybe Kyle Quinn doesn't belong in a cell. Maybe Kyle Quinn deserves what the woman who loved him thought he should get."

Quinn turned so he could face Tashawna. The love mentioned was a secret. Quinn assumed no one else knew this except him, but he was wrong.

"She told me that too," Tashawna said. "And because Ally loved you, she provided an alternative solution to your life's plan, one whereby she gave me her word that you'd fulfill better expectations, the expectations that she has left for you."

"What are they?"

"Keep reading," Tashawna advised Quinn to stay on the file. He flipped through the pages and soon came across a new sheet, one that showed a picture of Quinn himself. Below, however, was a different name, address, and an entirely different past: all a part of Quinn's new identity, a path that Ally had created for him and her to follow.

"She wanted you to have a new life," Tashawna said,

"and should you make it through all this, then it was going to be a life she wanted the two of you to have together."

Quinn moved on to the next picture and his once trembling hands stilled. "Quinn Shepherd," he said. "*Her name.*"

"That's the one she selected for you, yes," Tashawna confirmed.

"I see," Quinn said.

"She wanted you to be happy, Kyle. She wanted you to be better, and she brought lots of things to our attention along the way. We should have known better but we didn't. Without Ally, we wouldn't know what to do now. Without her, we would have known absolutely nothing."

"She brought a lot of things to light," Quinn said, "things no one would ever find on their own, including me."

"Of course," Tashawna said. "I'm sorry it didn't work out, but this deal is something you can still have, Mr. Quinn, if you're willing to uphold your end of it."

"Deal?" Quinn asked.

"Yes. Disappear. Go someplace far away. Live your life as a man, and not as a killer. If you do that, you will have your freedom."

"And that's it?" Quinn replied. "I get to just...walk away?"

"The way I see it," Tashawna answered, "you've been walking away for a long time now. You've lost a lot. What more can life take from you? Besides, it's much easier to keep all of this buried once you're out of the picture. I mean, what good would it do to arrest you now? At the end of the day, Kyle Quinn, and I know this is hard for someone like yourself to believe, but—"

"But what?" Quinn interceded. With a sly grin, Tashawna was content. She was not in the company of a mass murderer; like Ally, Tashawna was one of the first people to see Quinn as more.

"We're the good guys, and that means we do what we can to make sure the bad ones pay and the good are rewarded, given a break, and if necessary, *a way out*. Sometimes, we just have to make adjustments so we can help good people too."

"I'm not good," Quinn said.

"Maybe," Tashawna said. "But then again, a woman like Ally Shepherd wouldn't have chosen you if you weren't. She believed in you. The question is, do you believe in yourself?"

Quinn gripped the folder, ensconced by silence. Tashawna uncrossed her legs and adjusted the collar of her posh business suit. Now prepared to make her way down the hall, Quinn stayed. "Thank you."

"Don't mention it," Tashawna said. "And I mean that literally," she said. "This meeting here..." Tashawna moved her hand up and down, pointed at herself, and then back at Quinn. "It didn't happen."

Quinn nodded. Understood.

"Stay out of trouble, and try to be happy, Quinn. Remember, you're getting a second chance here. Don't let it go to waste."

Tashawna stepped aside and the men in suits followed her on her way out. Quinn, still holding the folder, everything inside was all he would ever need: new passport, driver's license, a new social security number or social insurance number, and the address to his new home. And so, Quinn would go to the place that Ally had selected. In this case, it was Quinn's first home. It was Saskatchewan.

"Home," Quinn said before closing the folder.

With Tashawna gone, Quinn was left alone and was now recalling the life he had once back in Canada. He imagined Ally thought it would be the best location for their newest start. Quinn could raise his family better than how he was raised and this was what he wanted; all he would ever want.

"Excuse me." Quinn addressed a nurse with red hair and freckled skin. She was about to pass Quinn when he spoke to her.

"Yes?"

Quinn's formerly numb expression blossomed to show new life. He leaned in and made his best and last request. "Can you take me to see my child, please?"

———

In a separate section of the makeshift hospital, there was only one baby being taken care of.

In its "cradle," Quinn knew the key to his son's survival was his DNA. Hyper-X had altered Quinn's DNA, so consequently, it made his own child stronger, more resilient, and it's what made him capable of surviving these next few months.

Quinn didn't blink once as he stared.

Kyle was with Kayla and she was with Broder, their dad. They were all together while looking at the emaciated, slender body of the newborn baby boy. All watched with every ounce of focus just to be sure Quinn's son kept breathing.

"He'll be okay." Quinn was assured of this by his own sibling. Quinn trusted Kayla more than anyone. Being a mother, Kayla knew more than Quinn.

"He's strong," Kayla said, "like his dad, like his mom. He'll fight."

"Yes, he will," Broder Quinn said, standing farther away.

"What's his name?" Kayla asked.

Quinn's eyelashes fluttered and he was mystified by

the thought. Until now, he hadn't considered what to name his son. He didn't, and then a name struck him as he stared. Eyes wet, Quinn was almost in tears when he thought of what name to use. *Almost*. "Cane. His name is...*Cane*."

Since Cane, Kyle Quinn's and Kayla Quinn's brother, was no more, to honor his memory was a solid step in a long series of steps needed to repair their broken family. And so, Quinn felt here was a good place to start.

"That's..." Kayla said, now struggling to find the right words.

Touched by the decision, Kayla's twinkling eyes indicated she was enamored by the bittersweetness that came after hearing her dead brother's name. "Perfect."

Quinn's father eased closer to his children.

"Do you..." Quinn watched his dad look at his grandson.

Cane Quinn II was now in a container the size of a laundry basket. With tubes sticking out of his mouth, his tiny chest moving in and out, Quinn looked at his sister and then at his dad. "Want to stay with me? Just a little longer?"

"Only if...we're *allowed* to," Broder added.

Together for the first time in a long time, the Quinns were united by a common purpose. Quinn supposed he always thought this was impossible. Actually, he thought a lot of things were impossible. Often, he associated this concept with physical achievement. He equated it to winning impossible fights and defeating impossible enemies, but Quinn had come a long way since. He'd grown beyond the spectacle of fearsome acts and, along the way, had learned newer, more incredible ones. As Quinn stared at the cherubic face that belonged to his son, he was so close he felt like he could reach out and touch him. And right now, Quinn was only where he needed to be. He envisioned the future that succeeded his old one. Having reflected on his past, he recalled the faces of all those he had killed over the years, over too much time. But now, all of these faces eluded him. Quinn supposed he was ready to call himself a new man, *maybe a better man?*

He had accepted his new destiny and was inspired by the bright possibilities tomorrow might bring. He could see Ally. She was standing with Quinn like she always did, but as he closed his eyes, he believed he could still hear her, wherever she was.

"Ally."

The pain subsided, if only for a time, and Quinn could now say her name without breaking and he knew why. She wasn't gone, not as long as Quinn could keep her in his heart for all time, always and forever...a *Custodian.*

"I swear."

ACKNOWLEDGMENTS

I would like to extend my warmest gratitude to everyone at Wolfpack Publishing and Rough Edges Press for allowing me to share stories of my beautiful tragedy, Kyle Quinn.

I will be forever grateful for this.

Thank you, John McManus, Douglas Martin, Jan Clausen, Melodie Campbell, David Bergen, Brian Drake, Mark Allen, and Michael Black. Thank you, Brent Van Staalduinen, who gave time and thanks to my great friend and confidant, Mark Jordan Manner. I would also like to thank a man who is more than a friend but a mentor, Mr. John Corr. I thank Naben Ruthnum, Lucy S. Snyder, and Andrew F. Sullivan and I offer my gratitude to all my family and friends, including my fellow teachers, good and decent colleagues. Thank you to my guardian angel, Sharmaine Gobind, my best friend and brother, Cody, and my sister, Jenna, a relentless voice of concern always and forever. I thank my father, a good and decent man, my Bentley bully, and above all else, my mother, Sheila. Still my first and best fan, you are an amalgamation of encouragement, power, strength, and truth, which is often inconvenient, but most importantly...*of love.*

Thank you for following me on my many journeys.

I always know where I'm going, and because of you, I am never lost.

A LOOK AT:

DAWN OF THE TRADE (DOORMEN BOOK 1)

After years of serving his country overseas, former Marine Jon Haze returns to the familiar streets of Queens, New York, with hopes of reconnecting with his roots and finding peace in the aftermath of war. Yet, peace remains elusive for the 24-year-old veteran, who feels more lost than ever in the civilian world.

His quest for direction takes an unexpected turn when a night out with an old friend introduces him to the pulsating heart of Manhattan's nightlife at the exclusive nightclub, The Conquistador, where Jon, recognized for his resolve in a chaotic brawl, is drawn into the complex world of bouncing by the club's charismatic head bouncer, Addison Krowe. With no experience but a soldier's instincts, Jon enters the ranks of the legendary Doormen, discovering a realm defined by wealth, decadence, and the lurking dangers of organized crime and greed.

As Jon adapts to his new life, he uncovers the dualities of his role —protector and enforcer—within the opulent yet perilous empire of Manhattan's elite. The challenges are immense, but the rewards are intoxicating, offering him a sense of purpose he's desperately craved. However, the glittering lights mask a darker truth, one that threatens to erupt in a conflict as unpredictable and dangerous as any he's faced in combat.

With a storm brewing in the world of nightclubs, Dawn of the Trade sets the stage for an ultimate showdown where loyalty, survival, and identity are tested. Can Jon Haze emerge victorious in a war fought in the shadows of society? Uncover the truth in Dawn of the Trade, now.

AVAILABLE NOW

ABOUT THE AUTHOR

Jarrett Mazza is a graduate of Goddard College's MFA in Creative Writing Program in Plainfield, Vermont as well as The Humber School For Writers.

Before completing his terminal degree, he studied writing at the University of Toronto School of Continuing Studies and comic book writing under Ty Templeton and Andy Schmidt. He has had stories published online in the GNU Journal, Bewildering Stories, Trembling With Fear, Aphelion, The Scarlet Leaf Review, and Toronto Prose Mill, The Fictional Cafe. His work is featured in anthologies by Silver Empire Publishing, a best seller, Zimbell House Publishing,NBH Publishing, MuseWrite Press, twice by Dragon Soul Press, Gypsum Sound Tales, Hellbound Books and The Ginosko Literary Journal. All are available on Amazon for purchase. He was also an Honorable Mention for the Freda Waldon Award for Fiction, nominated for an Indie Book award, and was featured as a visiting author for the nationwide We Read Canadian event in 2020. His mystery short story was published in an anthology under the editorial supervision of Michael Bracken and was published by Down and Out Books. He is currently a pulp fiction writer for the companies Airship 27 and Stormgate Press and Rough Edges Press.

He lives in Hamilton, Ontario.

You can follow him on Twitter @JarrettMazza